LOVE'S FIRST LIGHT

The Women of Black Hawk Canyon Book One

By

Linda Broday

EPITAPH PRESS

<u>LOVE'S FIRST LIGHT</u>

ALSO BY LINDA BRODAY

The Hangman's Daughters

WINNING MAURA'S HEART

COURTING MISS EMMA

Lone Star Legends:

A COWBOY OF LEGEND

A COWBOY CHRISTMAS LEGEND

A MAN OF LEGEND

Outlaw Mail Order Brides:

THE OUTLAW'S MAIL ORDER BRIDE

SAVING THE MAIL ORDER BRIDE

THE MAIL ORDER BRIDE'S SECRET

ONCE UPON A MAIL ORDER BRIDE

Men of Legend Series:

TO LOVE A TEXAS RANGER

HEART OF A TEXAS COWBOY

TO MARRY A TEXAS OUTLAW

The Bachelors of Battle Creek Series:

TEXAS MAIL ORDER BRIDE

TWICE A TEXAS BRIDE

FOREVER HIS TEXAS BRIDE

Texas Heroes:

KNIGHT ON THE TEXAS PLAINS

THE COWBOY WHO CAME CALLING

TO CATCH A TEXAS STAR

Single Title:

ONE SHOT AT LOVE – April 2023

HOPE'S ANGEL – October 2022

FANCY (Love Train Series) August 2022

TEXAS REDEMPTION

Anthologies:

THE COWBOY WHO SAVED CHRISTMAS

LONGING FOR A COWBOY CHRISTMAS

GUNSMOKE AND LACE

CHRISTMAS IN A COWBOY'S ARMS

GIVE ME A TEXAN

GIVE ME A COWBOY

GIVE ME A TEXAS RANGER

GIVE ME A TEXAS OUTLAW

A TEXAS CHRISTMAS

BE MY TEXAS VALENTINE

HEARTS AND SPURS

Watch for WILDWOOD HEALER – release date TBA

And a novella, LOVE COMES DOWN AT CHRISTMAS, in November

FOR ALL MY BOOKS, VISIT MY AMAZON AUTHOR PAGE

https://www.amazon.com/stores/Linda-Broday/author/B001JRXWB2

CHAPTER ONE

Black Hawk Canyon, West Texas
Summer 1882

Time marched slowly as though mired in mud and grief. If only she could roll back the days, weeks, and months, this wouldn't be necessary. She stared wearily at the hole.

The grave wasn't large enough.

Rachel Malloy's vision blurred with unshed tears. She jabbed the shovel into the rocky ground and struggled with all her might to lift another shovelful of dirt from what would be her little sister's final resting place.

The spring rains hadn't come so now in late August, right on fall's doorstep, the ground had hardened to granite.

At the next plunge of the shovel her booted foot slipped off and her knee slammed into the metal scoop. Instant, paralyzing pain took her breath.

Everything inside her wanted to slide into the grave and not climb out.

Never far from her side, her dog Jax of questionable heritage huffed and lay down in the sun, his brown gaze seeming to say he knew her pain and would take it away if only he could.

For the past four months caring for her sick family, digging graves, and burying loved ones had consumed all of her energy. Alice's grave today would make seven. They lined up like a row of mute broken soldiers.

Rachel choked back the tears clogging her throat, making it impossible to swallow.

She was the last remaining Malloy to walk the earth. Why were they taken leaving her behind? Was she too bad? Too good? Too vain? Why?

The loneliness, the eerie silence created hopeless despair inside unlike any she'd known.

Seeming to give voice to her overwhelming grief, the wind swept down the sides of the scarred rocky cliffs into the canyon with a wild shriek, blotting out the sunlight.

Her hands trembled as she pulled herself from her knees and again lifted the shovel. She bent once more to the task, sparing the small, blanket-wrapped form of her little sister a glance. Despite working hard to keep sweet Alice apart from the sick, the four-year-old had contracted the same fever.

Rachel's heart shattered anew, and she lost sight of the shovel through the flood of tears. Why? Alice had never gotten to know much about life. Had she lived, Rachel would've loved and raised her, sacrificing whatever she must to give her sister the best life possible.

At least they'd have had each other and Rachel wouldn't be alone and forgotten with no one, nothing, to banish this deafening disquiet inside her head so deep she wanted to scream.

"Go on with your life, Rachel," her stepmother Jane had whispered in a weak voice five days ago. "Do not give up. I'll be with you always. When you hear the chirp of a sparrow or the wind sighing through the tall prairie grass, I'll be near."

Rachel vowed to care for little Alice, to love and protect the child. That broken vow now sat like a wagonload of sharp spears on her chest.

Harsh sobs burst from her throat. She hadn't known how to keep death from stealing Alice. Maybe she hadn't tried hard enough or long enough. Or done things right.

While she contemplated her deep failing, the sky turned a dull reddish brown before she noticed. Wind-whipped sand stung her skin. Rachel struggled to remain on her feet. She'd lost sight of the house two hundred feet away. Everything familiar had disappeared. She dug faster. She had no choice. She had to get her baby sister safely in the ground.

Particles of grit embedded in her skin, coating the inside of her mouth. After what seemed like hours, she straightened. Though the grave wasn't deep enough by half, she gave up. Yet another failure. Grabbing one end of the blanketed form, she gently lowered her sister into the narrow space.

If only it wasn't so hard to believe and to trust that the giver of life had a better plan.

If she had some small hope to cling to.

And if only she had something left to live for.

Jax raced around, barking as though anxious to be indoors out of the sandstorm.

Rachel impatiently pushed disheveled tendrils of hair from

her eyes and glared up at the angry sky. Had she strength to spare, she'd have shaken her fist at God. Why hadn't he kept the storm back until she finished? That was little enough to ask.

In all her twenty years she'd tried to live the best she knew how. To never say a cross word even when her ten-year-old brother had dragged her clean wash in the dirt. Or when her fourteen-year-old brother had teased her unmercifully about being an old maid.

What had it gotten her?

The deaths of every last member of her family.

But maybe Alice's death *had* been her fault. Maybe she'd brought this on herself.

Maybe it had to do with her shameful secret, a secret that lodged in her chest like a clump of spikey thistle and clung to her tongue.

For a moment she didn't know if the raging storm was real or if it was only inside *her* where everything was bruised and raw. As though angry that she doubted the reality of the storm, the wind increased, becoming like a crazed beast, knocking her off her feet. She clawed at the brambles that grew close to the rocky West Texas ground and rose, bracing herself.

In the murky haze she could barely see her hand in front of her face.

Fear set in. She'd known of others who'd lost their bearings in such a storm and never reached safety. She didn't mind meeting her Maker, in fact would dearly welcome it. She just didn't want to be injured and lie in pain for days before anyone found her.

Rachel struck out blindly with Jax barking and racing in circles around her. Bending into the wind, she stumbled on. If only she could see.

Something struck her between her shoulder blades and the ground gave way underfoot. She tumbled head over heels, sprawling, her head striking something hard.

At last her prayers were answered and she'd get to join her family. Peace washed over her as she plunged into blackness.

Was that a scream? Heath Lassiter reined in his horse and listened for other noises.

But when the sound didn't come again, he dismissed it as the shriek of the wind. The foul weather could play tricks on a man, make him hear things that weren't there.

He strained to see through the air so thick with dirt it clogged his throat and stung his eyes. Where was that sick heifer he'd set out to find? Despite the bandana he'd tied around his nose and mouth, particles of sand clawed at the tender lining of his throat and chest like marauding little beasts. His eyes probably had half the dirt in the county in them.

What he wouldn't give to be safe inside the sod house in which he and his sister lived on the canyon rim.

He leaped across a big root on top of the ground and spotted a dark form lying face down. He rushed toward the figure and upon drawing closer saw the dress.

Whether the woman was alive or dead he couldn't tell.

A dog of varying shades of brown and gray lay beside her with his head resting on the woman's body. A low growl rumbled from the large animal's throat as it sprang to its feet.

"It's okay," Heath tried to soothe the animal. "I'm here to help. Let me see to your mistress."

After a moment, the dog seemed to understand and lay down, watching him with wary eyes.

It appeared the woman had fallen striking her head on a huge rock. He knelt and gently rolled her over, praying she was still alive.

Relief came when a moan sprang from between her pale lips.

Heath thought he recognized her as one of Isaac Malloy's offspring. He'd heard that the fever had swept through the family and some hadn't made it.

Maybe this girl was ill with the fever.

Didn't much matter though. Most people who lived a good ways from town on the desolate West Texas plains depended on their neighbors for help. Isolation tended to make them a close-knit bunch. But the Malloys were different. They'd always kept to themselves. Heath had respected their privacy and not forced himself on them.

Whether or not this girl had come down with the fever, he wouldn't turn a blind eye. He'd take her home and his sister Sally could see to her.

If Sally deemed the woman's injury in need of more medical attention than she could provide, he'd ride to the nearest town of Estacado. The Quaker town some twenty-five miles northeast had just sprung up, only he hadn't heard if they had a doctor.

Heath carefully lifted the thin young woman in his arms. A sack of potatoes probably weighed more than she did. She snuggled against him as if unconsciously seeking respite from the wind. A protective urge wound through him.

Propping her with one hand, he used the other to pull himself into the saddle behind her.

"Come along, dog. Let's get to the soddy."

The canine gave a sharp bark and fell into step with Heath's horse. Surrounded by the screech of the wild Texas wind they began the climb to the rim.

A short time later, Heath pulled up in front of the half soddy and half dugout, built back into the hill. Along the front, he'd placed a row of mesquite branches to provide added strength.

His older sister Sally flung the door open before he got to it with the unconscious woman.

"I was worried sick about you," Sally scolded. "This storm is fierce. I told you I had a feeling in my bones something was coming but you insisted on going out. No more stubborn man was ever born. You never listen to a word I say."

"Found an unconscious woman near the Malloy place. Seems she hit her head on a rock."

"Get her inside." Sally held the door for him then ran ahead and swept back a curtain to the alcove where she slept. "Put her on my bed for now. I'll tend to her."

Heath eased his load onto the stuffed feather mattress and stood looking down, wondering who she was and how she came to be out in this weather.

"Do you recognize her?" Heath asked. "Don't think she'd been out there long. I heard a scream before I discovered her."

"I don't like it that she's unconscious. Could be serious. We'll know soon I reckon." As usual Sally's voice was an octave shy of a foghorn. If Heath didn't know better, he'd think she'd raised it to be heard above the storm. The bad thing was he did know better. This was her normal way of speaking to him. Years ago, he'd gotten his fill of her bossing him and decided to ignore her. Now, she thought he was deaf.

The dog, a male now that Heath could see, leaped upon the

bed and bared his teeth, taking his protective nature a bit far. Still, he admired his loyalty.

"Good heavens, get that animal out of here," Sally hollered, putting her hands on her ample hips. "I can't doctor my patient if he keeps threatening to tear into me."

Heath cautiously reached for the mottled dog only to draw back when he leaped, snapping at him. "I'll offer him some food. Just a moment."

When he returned with a bowl of water and a small portion of last night's chicken, the dog looked at it longingly but made no move to get off the bed.

"Come on. Aren't you hungry?" Heath asked softly.

Though loath to leave his mistress, the animal finally leaped down.

"There you go. See?" Heath crooned then glanced at Sally. "I don't think he's going anywhere. He just wants to make sure we don't harm his lady. Appears we have little choice but to let him guard her."

Sally sighed and smoothed back the woman's tendrils of blonde hair so light they had a silvery cast. "She looks like a beautiful angel. You say you found her near the Malloy place?"

"If I was a betting man, I'd say she's one of the Malloys. I can't imagine what she was doing out alone in the storm."

"Well, it blew up in an all-fired hurry. She probably got caught in it." Sally turned. "Don't just stand there like a big galoot. I need some water. I'll see about finding a nightgown. Get along now. Shoo."

Heath knew when it was best to give in and do as his sister asked. Sally had a heart of gold and he loved her dearly but sometimes she was a tad overbearing. Six years older than he, she took her bossing to a higher level as though it was some righteous calling. After their parents were killed in a wagon accident, Sally had assumed her place at the head of the family and refused to relinquish the reins now despite the fact that Heath had made the cattle ranch profitable through enough blood, sweat, and tears.

Yep, he figured when Judgment Day came Sally would stand with her hands on her hips and demand to know why the Good Lord had taken so long. Muttering, he shook his head and left to fetch water for the patient from the kitchen. He could refill their supply later.

By the time he got back, Sally had a nightgown laid out at the end of the bed.

"Thank you, brother," she bellowed as usual, taking the pail and towels.

"Shoo!" She held them with one hand and pushed him out of the alcove with the other. "Make yourself scarce. Got work to do."

"Let me know if you need anything else. When this wind stops, I'm going to mosey over to the Malloys."

But, by the time he got the first three words out, the curtain separating the alcove from the rest of the house snapped shut in his face and left him talking to himself. Muttering, he shook his head and went to add some mesquite limbs to the fire in the stove.

A rabbit stew simmered on the top, filling the dwelling with a delicious aroma. He lifted the lid and glanced at the thick brown bubbling gravy that caressed the vegetables and meat. He couldn't wait for supper.

By his estimation, he had about two more hours of sunlight. Tying the bandana again around his nose and mouth, he trudged back out to tend to his horse. But the black gelding had already found his way to a barn made of limestone that offered respite from the biting wind.

"Smart boy," Heath murmured as he removed the saddle and rubbed down the animal.

Once Hondo was comfortable and fed, he drew a second pail of water from the well and returned to the soddy to wash the grime from his face.

His thoughts turned to the mysterious woman. There wasn't room to pace in the small soddy to calm his nervous energy so he stood at the only window, staring out. A niggling feeling told him something bad had happened over at the Malloys' place and he chafed at marking time until the wind eased.

Sally emerged from the alcove with an armful of the woman's clothing.

"How is she?" Heath asked. "Does she have the fever?"

"No, just a big goose egg on her head."

"Not surprised."

His sister folded the dress and petticoat and stacked them neatly on a low stool. Then she filled a teapot and set it on the stove. "That girl's lucky you came along. She could've died."

"It was meant to be I reckon." He rose and went to the door to look out. "The wind's finally starting to die down just a hair."

An hour later, he looked out again and trudged to the alcove. "If you don't need my help, I'm going to ride out to look around. See about the damage."

"Good idea," Sally blared. "If that girl in there does belong to them, they must be worried sick. Watch the sky and be careful going down into the canyon. I can't come looking for you. And don't be late for supper. And if she does belong there, tell the Malloys I'm right sorry."

Heath wagged his head, mentally comparing his sister to a snapping turtle. Get your hand too close and you'd regret it. He frowned, grabbed his hat, and saddled up the mule, letting his gelding rest. The Malloy place lay about three miles from his property.

The standoffish family had settled in Black Hawk Canyon where the Comancheros met the Comanche Indian tribes to swap rifles and stolen horses in exchange for white captives. The Comancheros would then ransom them back to grief-stricken families. If the families couldn't or wouldn't pay the ransom, the ruthless traders sold their prisoners to the highest bidder.

Three other families—the Malloys, Gregorys, and Quinlans —along with the Lassiters had fought to settle the rocky land that covered thousands of square miles. It hadn't been easy, and blood stained every inch of ground.

Yet, the floor of Black Hawk Canyon was a beautiful place with an abundance of water, trees, and wildlife, unlike his spread up on the rim. His father had chosen up there for the ability to spy trouble before it reached them. There were always Indian and outlaw raids and they stood a better chance of surviving than those down in the valley.

The storm had slowed to a low roar, but occasional big gusts almost knocked Heath off the mule. With the slow pace, it took some time to reach the trail leading down.

The hair on the back of his neck stood as he neared the Malloy homestead.

Everything was eerily quiet, and the smell of death permeated the land.

He rode past a big cottonwood tree that hadn't begun to turn yellow for fall and the fresh mounds of dirt. His breath caught painfully in his throat. He counted seven graves. Two were within days of each other.

To the best of his recollection, that would account for the

entire Malloy family except for the woman he'd rescued. A shovel lay beside the last one that appeared hastily dug. This had been the reason she'd been out in the windstorm. She'd buried the last of her family.

A big black crow sat perched on one of the graves. Its angry caw seemed to mock, daring Heath to approach.

He didn't have any answers, only dozens of questions. Stopping to pick up the shovel by the half-filled grave, he finished spreading dirt on top then continued on to the weathered barn. After he checked and fed the livestock, he'd take the animals to his place. Only that would require several trips.

A glance at the timepiece he took from his pocket and flipped open revealed he only had about an hour. Moving the animals would have to wait until morning.

From the looks of things, it appeared the Malloys had precious little. About a dozen goats, a strange looking black Angus bull, a handful of chickens, and a broken-down swayback horse were about all he saw.

Heath's heart ached for the injured woman in his sister's bed. So much loss.

He only knew one thing—she needed a friend.

And as long as Heath drew breath he'd sign on for the job. Because that's what one soul did for another.

CHAPTER TWO

A bright August sun shone the next morning, leaving few signs of the horrible storm other than the fence posts and the side of the soddy where sand had drifted. It seemed a bit odd that Heath Lassiter could take deep breaths of the clear air but he was most thankful.

Their patient was drifting in and out of consciousness, never lucid long enough for questions. The dog refused to leave her. Heath sat by her bedside while Sally made breakfast.

She looked vulnerable lying there still and lifeless.

Discounting the swath of white bandage circling the top of her head, she put him in mind of a beautiful China doll he'd once seen in a store window in the bustling town of San Antonio. Long dark lashes rested on this woman's high cheekbones. Her lips were perfectly formed and softly parted as though she might speak at any moment.

As far as her age, she appeared young, twenty at best if even that. Her eyes fluttered open briefly several times only to close in sleep. He'd give ten of his prized herd to see more than brief glances of the startling green orbs with dark gold centers that added depth.

The slight woman weighed less than a sack of feed. Too thin. If she'd been tending her family for a length of time, maybe she hadn't had time to eat. He didn't want to consider that she'd been over there without food.

Heath reached for her hand and the dog rose from beside her, growling. "Hush. I'm not going to hurt her. It's all right."

The dog gave him a baleful stare, chuffed, and lay back down. Heath turned the woman's hand over. Calluses and ugly blisters, some cracked and bleeding, attested to the hard work of digging graves. An unfamiliar feeling ricocheted around inside him. He wished she'd have asked for help. He'd have dropped everything.

For sure, he had plenty of burning questions to ask when she could talk.

Heath reached out to finger a tendril of silky pale hair between his thumb and forefinger. Who knew if she had anyone other than him and Sally. He again searched his mind for a name to put to her, but Isaac Malloy had kept those children, especially the girls, away from folks and Heath had never heard any mention of names.

The woman suddenly moaned in pain and tried to reach for her head.

"Sally," he called. "She needs more of that willow bark tea you made."

"Be there in two shakes."

While he waited for Sally, he murmured comforting words and the woman quieted.

When Sally entered, Heath rose from his chair to give her room. He whistled to the dog that had glued itself to his mistress's side. The animal had eaten very little since being there. Except for hurried outings to take care of business, the canine parked himself next to the patient, often laying his head on the pillow next to hers and whimpering. Heath had to admire the pooch. The animal's persistent loyalty touched something deep inside him. Perhaps the faithful companion sensed that his mistress needed to know he wasn't going to leave her like the rest of her family evidently had.

Despite the rocky beginning, Heath and the animal had called a truce. The dog no longer tried to bite him or Sally when they came close, but Heath couldn't rightly say it had developed a liking for them either. The animal merely tolerated them, sounding a warning growl at sudden movement.

Now, at Heath's whistle, the dog cocked his head from side to side.

"Let's get something to eat, boy." The canine whined, and Heath recognized the plea. "You can come right back. I promise."

Seeming to understand, the short-haired pooch leaped off the bed and padded after Heath. Cutting off a generous piece of salt pork, Heath watched the dog gobble it up, then turned to his own breakfast.

His plate of eggs and ham sat on the table in his usual place with a platter of hot biscuits. He ate quickly then rose, told Sally he was leaving, then grabbed his hat.

An hour later, he rode onto the Malloy property. Smoke hung in the light breeze. He urged Hondo into a gallop.

When he rounded a dense growth of scrub oak, his heart froze.

The Malloy home lay in smoldering ruins. Everything was mangled and charred. The house had once stood tall and proud on the banks of a crystal blue lake on the canyon floor, a lake that had provided water for many a weary traveler and their animals.

What? How? Had someone set it to possibly stop the spread of disease? Or had a spark caught in the windstorm. Or—?

Heath stared in disbelief, not wanting to consider the third scenario—that someone had deliberately set fire to the structure.

To consider that would mean Miss Malloy had enemies and he didn't want to think that anyone harbored ill will against the pretty lady.

No, the fire had to be an accident.

What would she do? Where would she go?

He gave Hondo a gentle nudge. "Let's see what we can find."

RACHEL'S HEAD THROBBED and she raised a weak arm, trying to touch it. How strange that she'd feel pain in heaven.

She sniffed and the smell of moist earth swam up her nose. She sensed she was underground. Was she in a grave? If she was dead, how come she could still smell? Panic washed over her. The only conclusion she could draw was that she'd possibly been buried alive.

Someone had given her a shove then put her in a grave. But why?

It was a struggle to open her eyes, but she finally succeeded. As they adjusted, the dim figure of a man took shape. He looked nothing like how she'd pictured her Heavenly Father. This one was just a plain ordinary man. No, she took that back. Nothing about this man was plain or ordinary. What she meant to say was that he was earthly. No white robe and no halo.

He sure had a nice smile though.

"Hey there." The man rose from a chair and leaned over her. "About time you woke up, ma'am. I'm Heath Lassiter."

"I'm alive?"

"Yes, praise God."

Bitter disappointment coated her throat like a thick dose of castor oil. Why couldn't she get some relief from her misery?

Her mouth was as dry as parchment but she managed a whisper, "Where am I?"

"The Lassiter homestead. I found you during the sandstorm unconscious on the ground. You weren't far from the Malloy place, so we assume you belonged to them."

Rachel winced. She remembered digging her sister's grave, the horrible wind, and falling. She nodded. "I'm Rachel, their eldest daughter." She winced. "Or at least I was."

"Nice to know you, Rachel. You're welcome here."

"How long have I been like...this?" she whispered.

"Two days."

Panic rifled through her as she looked around for her clothes. "I have to be going."

Just then an older woman entered the alcove. She was a tall, big boned woman but the no-nonsense way about her was what struck Rachel most. "Good, you're awake. I'm sure you must be hungry enough to eat a horse. I'm Sally, Heath's sister."

Something moved on the bed beside her and licked her face.

"Jax." Her arm felt as though it weighed a ton when she lifted it to grasp a handful of fur.

Heath's deep voice filled the small space. "He hasn't left your side."

"I suppose I should thank you for rescuing me, but you should've left me where you found me. You should've let me die and join my family." She couldn't keep the brittleness from her tone.

"Evidently the Good Lord isn't ready for you yet." Sally Lassiter moved her brother aside to plump Rachel's pillow.

"Could you please bring my clothes?"

"You're not up to leaving yet." Heath's deep voice was like an old familiar friend she didn't know she had. "I've been taking care of your animals so don't worry your head about them. The only thing you need to concentrate on is getting well."

"I'm going to get you some nice hot stew." Sally bustled into the next room. The woman yelled everything at the top of her voice, making Rachel's head hurt even worse.

Heath shifted his weight from one foot to the other. "When you're up to it, Rachel, I have something to talk to you about. No rush though. You just get well."

"Will you tell me something? Why does your sister talk at the top of her voice?"

A crooked grin tilted the corner of his mouth. "She thinks I'm deaf."

"And you keep letting her think you are?"

"Saves having to talk when I prefer not to. She likes to chew on my backside something fierce. This way I can pretend I can't hear her when my ears get sore."

Right then she knew Heath Lassiter was a scamp.

"I saw the graves," he said quietly. "I heard you had the fever going around over there. I just didn't know it was so bad. Why didn't you come to us for help?"

"Not our way. My father hammered into us that it was a sign of weakness to ask for help. He said we could take care of ourselves. No need bothering other folks with our problems. That's just the way we did things." Rachel felt as though her skin had opened up and all her insides leaked out. She was so tired. Weak. Heartsick.

"The Good Book teaches us to help one another. There's no shame in leaning on a brother." He stood. "But, you're too ill to listen to me harp. You need your rest."

Rachel watched until he vanished from sight then her gaze scanned the portion of the house she could see. The earthen walls told her she was in a sod house. Though the floors were dirt, everything had a tidy appearance.

She closed her eyes and tried to remember what she'd heard her father say about the Lassiters. Oh yes, their parents had both died in a wagon accident. They went off a steep cliff. Heath had spent an entire day climbing down to where their broken bodies lay. Then he'd dug the graves where his mother and father were instead of trying to get them to the top. Folks said he was just a boy of eleven when he went down and a man by the time he finished and made it back home.

Heath Lassiter would know what it was like to lose people he loved. But at least he had his sister, even if he did let her think he was deaf.

Rachel had no one. Not one single person to laugh with, to eat with, to care whether she lived or died.

God had forgotten her.

Unshed tears swam in her eyes. She blinked hard and tightened her jaw. It was fine with her if He had. She'd do all right without Him. If God didn't want her, she didn't want Him either.

HEATH SADDLED HIS gelding, Hondo, and rode to the escarpment overlooking Yellowhouse Draw. He needed to do some thinking.

True, he didn't know her very well. But he felt her anguish and it tore a big hole in his heart. He felt he owed it to her to help find a way out of her problem.

What could he have said when she'd told him she wanted to die? He couldn't imagine being in a place that dark. Even on his worst day, he'd never felt like giving up. As long as there was breath there was hope for a better tomorrow. If only he could convince her of that.

How would she take the news when he told her she had no house left? If she was in deep despair now, what more would that do to her?

To lose her entire family then her home would deliver a major blow.

One thing for sure, he'd have to wait until she got a little stronger.

Thank you for rescuing me, but you should've left me where you found me. You should've let me die and join my family.

He'd known despair and heartbreak when his parents died and left him and Sally orphans, but he'd clung to his faith. To lose everything including faith would do anyone in.

How in the world could he help her see that she still had things to live for?

An idea had begun to roughly take shape. He just didn't know if marriage was the answer or not.

God always had a plan though. Heath just had to be patient.

But just in case, he needed to practice up on a marriage proposal.

He wasn't exactly sure how to go about it. He'd always been tongue-tied around women. Females were a mystery to him. Even Sally. Sometimes his sister could sorely test his sanity. She often said no when she meant yes and go yonder when she meant come here.

A man could get in a heap of trouble without half trying where she and the rest of her gender were concerned.

But Rachel needed to know she had options and one being he'd like to take care of her.

She would ease some of the powerful loneliness of the wild Texas plains where a man could ride for days without seeing another human.

Seemed to him that marriage could benefit them both.

There was a reason he found Rachel and saved her from the storm. Excitement rippled along his veins.

If she were to say yes, Rachel could be the wife he'd never had.

Heath thought about how best to propose.

Maybe begin by laying out all his worldly possessions and listing all the reasons why she should tie her lot to his. After all, he'd acquired ten thousand acres on which five hundred head of the best longhorn in Texas grazed. Pretty impressive if he said so himself.

But he didn't want this union to be about monetary gain. He wanted her to marry him because they shared a fondness. And because they needed one another.

Over time, maybe she could even come to love him.

Maybe it was possible, for both of them.

He wiped a layer of sweat from his brow. This proposing business was hard work.

Heath decided the best way was to just be honest and direct. No beating around the bush. Just open his mouth and let the words pour out. He'd simply tell her what was in his heart and that he'd be proud to take care of her. His sacred duty would lie in keeping her safe.

No need to tell her he needed a wife. After being around Sally she must've pretty much seen that for herself anyway.

He thought of the load of lumber he'd hauled all the way from Colorado City a few months ago. He needed to get started rebuilding Rachel's house. After all, he didn't expect her to be all that thrilled to live in a soddy. Besides, he and Rachel would need their privacy.

Sally probably would want to remain in the sod house which was the only home she'd ever known or wanted.

And who knew? Maybe Sally would get married herself. She might be lucky enough to find a man who didn't mind that she'd died on the vine while waiting for West Texas to become more settled. More folks arrived every day, some of whom weren't too particular.

Heath shook his head to clear it and got back to this proposing.

The next thing he had to decide was finding the best time to broach the subject.

Not today. She'd just woken up and was not feeling up to snuff yet.

One thing for sure, he didn't want to hammer her over the head with the notion. Give her time to get her bearings slow-like.

But it'd have to be before she left to go back to the smell of death on the Malloy land. She should know she had another option and didn't have to face her problems alone.

CHAPTER THREE

The following day, Rachel asked Sally to help her outside into the warm sunshine to a willow chair cushioned with blankets. Rachel dropped onto the soft perch and Jax settled at her feet. The spectacular golden rays thawed some of the icy coldness that had frozen everything inside her.

Rachel rested her head against the back of the chair and let the delicious warmth seep into her bones. Sally made a roaring fire in front of the dwelling and set about scrubbing dirty clothes.

She watched the strange woman attack the task like it was a sworn enemy. The dimness of the soddy had disguised the woman's age. Now that Sally was in the bright sunshine Rachel could tell she was a seasoned woman who had probably withstood many storms and life's disappointments. This was a woman who would bend but not break. Rachel wished for more of Sally's fortitude.

The creak of the windmill at the corner of the soddy lulled Rachel into a tranquil peace. She dearly loved the sound of a windmill. To her the structure powered by the breeze seemed to echo the heartbeat of the land.

In the distance came the comforting coo of a mourning dove and the call of a mockingbird, interspersed with the cattle's mooing.

Although most of the dizziness had left, Rachel was as weak as a day-old colt. Each time she stood her legs wobbled and buckled.

Jax's ears perked up and Rachel's attention was drawn to Heath Lassiter on horseback. He trotted to the corral and dismounted. Tall and lean, his shirt stretched tight across his broad shoulders as he undid the saddle and lifted it off as though it weighed a little of nothing.

She didn't know exactly what to make of Heath and his sister. The way they'd taken her in and doctored her revealed genuine care. But her papa had never allowed his children to know the Lassiters or any of the other two families occupying Black Hawk Canyon.

They'd never had any friends or been normal.

Isaac Malloy had drilled into their heads that they had to protect themselves by living apart from everyone. Folks didn't cotton to people like them he'd said.

When baby Alice had come along four years ago, her papa had grown even fiercer in his demands.

Even though her stepmother Jane hadn't given birth to Rachel and her three brothers, she'd seen their desperate need and wrapped her love around them. Jane more than filled the void left by Ruth Malloy's passing nine years earlier and made not only Rachel, but all her siblings, feel special.

From what Rachel had seen firsthand of Heath and Sally Lassiter, they were honest, hardworking people. Even so, they probably wouldn't understand the ways of her father.

Neither had she. Rachel had harbored deep resentment.

Heath's boots struck the hard rocky ground as he strode toward her with a wide smile and his tall shadow fell over her. "It's something to see you outdoors, Rachel. Must mean you're getting well."

He upturned an empty barrel and sat on it.

"You'll get rid of me soon enough."

Awkwardly he cleared his throat. "I have something to tell you but been waiting until you're up to it."

"Sounds serious."

"I just rode over to your place." He paused. "There's no easy way to say this."

Rachel's breath hitched painfully in her chest. "What is it? Tell me."

He inhaled sharply. "Your house is gone."

"My house...gone? What do you mean?"

"It caught fire and burned. It's still smoldering."

"Why? How?" Her hand flew to cover the sob that rose. Not only was she alone, she had no home left. Nothing. Everything was gone.

Not one shred of her familiar life left.

For several heartbeats, she sat there in shock, unable to speak. Blow upon blow of life's unending catastrophes had knocked her flat. God had stripped her of everything. What had she done? She'd assumed everything was fine and she'd go home as soon as she recovered. But it was a long way from fine.

Heath clenched his hat tightly. "I'm sorry."

Still reeling from news that she was homeless, other thoughts flew into her head. Had the locket Jane had given her survived? The family Bible where they'd recorded births and deaths?

What about her father's hidden metal box with its iron lock?

Quite possibly the fire had uncovered many secrets. Her hand trembled.

Had the fire been her fault? She searched her memory. Had she left a pan on the stove when she'd gone out to bury Alice? She couldn't believe she'd been that careless. But then she had other things on her mind at the time and was exhausted. But no, she remembered she hadn't cooked that day. She'd been too grief stricken to even eat. She knew she was losing baby Alice and there hadn't been anything in her power to stop the hand of death from reaching down and snatching her little sister up.

What now would be her fate? Rachel buried her face in her hands.

"Do you have other family somewhere?" Heath asked. "An aunt or uncle perhaps?"

Her eyes met his. "None that I know about."

She knew next to nothing about her heritage. Her papa hadn't encouraged questions.

All she really knew was that her papa had once made a living as a buffalo hunter and that her grandfather had settled the land in Black Hawk Canyon. But she hadn't a clue about her first mother Ruth's past.

"I wish I could help you." She met his anguished gaze. "I'm not your problem. I'll be gone as soon—" her voice broke. And go where exactly? She had nothing to tether her. The world had suddenly become a scary place.

Heath picked up a stick and threw it, watching Jax race to retrieve it. "You're welcome to stay here as long as you need to. Sally will be grateful for the companionship of another female. She doesn't say anything, but I suspect she's awfully lonely with only me to talk to."

His gentle voice was comforting and he was so good with her dog. Strangely, he began laying sticks in neat rows and throwing them for Jax to fetch. If Jax in his enthusiasm got them out of alignment, Heath straightened them. He liked things in order apparently. So had her oldest brother. He, too, had an orderly nature.

Rachel blinked back gathering tears. The life she'd known was gone. Snatched from her as swiftly as it had taken her family. It would've been a blessing if she could've joined Alice. But God had evidently deemed her unworthy of even that.

She didn't share her thoughts. Heath already pitied her.

Pity was something she could never tolerate. Let him scorn, mistrust, or ignore her. Anything but pity her.

She couldn't still her trembling hands or melt the ice that had formed inside. Rachel straightened and pulled the shawl tighter around her shoulders. "I'll only stay until I can make other arrangements."

"When you feel stronger, Sally and I will help you sort through the rubble. Though it doesn't appear so on the surface, there'll be things the fire didn't destroy under the ashes. No hurry on that though." Heath took the stick from Jax and patted the dog's head.

Relief flooded over her. Maybe the cherished item she and her family had guarded had survived the flames.

"I'm sure I'll manage," she answered with a heap more confidence than she felt. She needed to make plans but was simply too weary to think.

"I've been doing a lot of pondering." Heath's honest gray gaze met hers and a hint of a smile flirted with the corners of his mouth. "Marry me. Let me take care of you. It would solve everything."

The notion robbed Rachel of breath. She struggled with a

reply. Marrying the handsome rancher had certain appeal. If only things were different. But they weren't. She'd made mistakes that couldn't be undone.

It was too late. Way too late.

"Marriage?" She shook her head. "No, I couldn't."

"Are you already spoken for?"

She wished that were the case. Heath Lassiter didn't know just how unworthy a wife she'd make.

Rachel picked at a loose thread on the blanket. Her voice was barely louder than a whisper when she answered. "No, there's no one else."

"Then maybe if it's because of the soddy, I've already bought enough lumber for a real house with wooden floors that you can sweep and mop. Just tell me how you want it built and that's what you'll have."

His sincerity touched her. She didn't wish to hurt this man offering to share all his worldly possessions and his life with her. She didn't see any way around it though.

"Mr. Lassiter—" she began gently only to be interrupted.

"Heath. Please call me Heath."

"Very well. Heath, you're a wonderful man who deserves all the happiness you can get. You have so much to offer." A dark frown formed but she hurried on before she lost her courage. "Any woman would be thrilled to have you for a husband."

He scowled. "Go ahead and get to the 'but' part. I know it's coming." He lifted his hat and ran his hand through his hair. Rising, he stood with his legs apart as if braced for a blow. "You don't have to spare my feelings."

"I'm not the kind of woman you need." There. She'd said it. Let the chips fall where they may. In the silence that stretched, the sound of the wind ruffling the tall grasses on the gently rolling plain reached her. The sky was so crystal blue it took her breath.

Better to disappoint him now rather than later.

He stubbornly crossed his arms. "I see. And just what kind of woman do you think I need? I'd love to hear it."

Rachel cringed at the hurt that overlaid his words. She licked her dry lips. "You need a woman who can throw herself wholeheartedly into marriage. A helpmate. Not someone like me."

If he ever found out what she'd done he'd run far and fast in the other direction. She wouldn't be able to bear the disappointment, and possibly loathing, in his eyes, hear the coldness in his voice.

HEATH DROPPED BACK onto the barrel. His voice was quiet as he took her icy hand. "You're hurting now and grieving for the people you love. But you'll get over it. Trust me. Time heals all things."

"Not this." She gave him a weary smile.

"You can find joy again if you let yourself," he insisted. "We aren't allotted a certain number of people to love and care about. Love is like a flowing stream. It's never-ending. Just give yourself a chance."

"Right now, I'm consumed with anger," she answered, her voice shaking. Tears began to fall. "Anger at God for taking my family and leaving me alone. Anger at my family for dying on me. Anger at myself for not knowing enough to keep them alive. Why couldn't I make them well? Why couldn't they recover? I did everything I knew."

Her pain and anguish broke Heath's heart. "It didn't have

anything to do with what you did or didn't do. I wish I had the answers, wish I could help you see you did nothing wrong. I only know that it was time for God to call them to Glory."

"Why did He leave me behind?"

"It wasn't your time. The Good Book says, 'To everything there is a season and a time to every purpose under the heavens.' " He squeezed her hand and stared at the distant horizon, praying that his words would help make a difference. "For now, let's just focus on getting you back on your feet."

"I don't care what happens to me."

The anguished whisper jolted Heath. "It's too soon. You're not well enough. Give yourself a few more days. In the meantime, our home is open to you. Stay as long as you want."

Rachel pulled her hands away and folded them in her lap. "You're a kind generous man, Heath Lassiter. But I guarantee I won't change my mind."

"Begging your pardon, Rachel, but I doubt that. Life doesn't stand still. It's always moving and changing. And we change in the process."

One thing he was sure of. He'd not give up on marriage. Rachel Malloy was the one for him despite all her protests. Maybe when she got to know him better.

One thing he knew. If he was supposed to marry her, God would send him a sign.

Maybe not a burning bush or a horde of locusts, but something.

Heath had always been a planner. He thought things out and calculated his life right down to what color shirt to wear on which days. For as far back as he could remember he'd worn a blue shirt on Mondays and Fridays and brown on Tuesdays and Wednesdays. He reserved his black and gray for Thursdays and Saturdays. White was his color of choice on the Lord's Day.

He'd determined a long while back that he wouldn't marry until he'd gotten his herd where he could turn a good profit and give a wife the kind of life she deserved. He now had everything in place. Even the lumber to start on a new house.

He'd prayed, begging God to send him a wife, and then here came Rachel.

Didn't that make her a divine gift from heaven?

Besides, his father, grandfather, and great-grandfather hadn't lived past the age of forty. Heath was two years shy of thirty. If he only had about ten good years left, he'd have to get started on bringing some children into the world. He wanted a son as badly as he wanted a family, a son to carry on the Lassiter name, a son to take over the ranch.

In time maybe Rachel would let him provide for her. After all, they just met.

Meanwhile, he'd get started on the house. When she saw how serious he was about taking care of and protecting her, she'd be more receptive.

Also, he'd court her while he built the new house. He'd pick her some flowers that grew wild in the pastures and along the creeks and streams.

A few years ago at a barn raising, he'd heard some bachelors talking about their courting. They said women liked being sung to. Heath didn't know any courting songs but he did know a lot of hymns. And Sally told him he had a real nice singing voice.

Flowers and singing would surely bring Rachel around.

THE NEXT DAY at her insistence, she rode with Heath and Sally to the only home she'd ever known. The smell of death swirled around Rachel like a buzzard circling its prey. The house was nothing but a shell that had been reduced to ashes. The big stone hearth that stood like a proud but battered soldier was all that was standing.

"There's nothing left. It's all gone," Rachel whispered.

She wanted to run. But run to where? She had nowhere to go and no way to provide for herself.

There had to be another option other than taking Heath up on his marriage offer.

And would he even want her after he found out what she'd done? Her gaze swept to the seven mounds of dirt and a feral cry sprang from her throat. She urged her horse toward the burial site. Tears streamed down her face as she slid from the saddle and ran unsteadily to Alice's grave, collapsing to the ground.

"No! I can't. I can't. Come back," she cried.

Footsteps sounded and Heath took her upper arm, helping her up. "I know this seems like the end of the world, but it really isn't. We'll help you get through this. Come."

Swallowing around the thickness in her throat, Rachel managed, "The scope of it just hit me."

Her stepmother's last words telling her she had to go on and make a new life for herself crossed her thoughts. Except Jane hadn't known the enormity of the task.

With Heath on one side and Sally on the other they put her back on the horse and she rode on to where the house once sat. Then they helped her around piles of debris to a stone ledge at the base of the hearth. He swept it off and Rachel collapsed on it. Sheer panic rose.

She had no clothes, no place to lay her head that belonged to her.

"I knew you were trying to rush things," Sally blustered,

throwing a worn shawl around Rachel's shoulders. "You needed a few more days rest before you tackled this."

What was that horrible smell? She covered her nose.

Heath removed his worn Stetson. Holding it tightly, he shifted his weight from one foot to another. "This is all a bit too soon. I propose we get you back home and into bed."

"I need to find my papa's tin money can. It probably doesn't have much in it, but I can sure use what's there," she murmured.

"Where did he keep it?" Heath asked.

Rachel looked up, blinking hard to hold back tears. "In a cabinet in the kitchen."

"I'll find it. You sit right here."

She was weary to the bone but doubted he'd find it. "I'll have to show you."

With her clutching his arm, they made their way through the blackened mess to the kitchen area which she recognized only by the cast iron stove that sat like a beacon amongst the charred remains. It reeked of kerosene. A large blackened can lay in the charred ruins.

Chills crawled up her neck when she saw footprints in the ash where no one had yet walked. Heath stooped to examine them, a dark frown on his face.

Someone had been there. Someone who had no right to be. The person who started the fire?

CHAPTER FOUR

Rachel clutched the blackened money tin they retrieved from the burned kitchen. It only held a few measly coins but she needed every cent. Heath was helping her onto Blackie when Jax commenced to bark. Keeping a firm grip on the horse's bridle, she turned to see Chantilly Gregory or Tillie as she preferred. The neighbor was Rachel's age.

Tillie's pink sunbonnet didn't hide curling tendrils of hair as dark as midnight around her face and a long braid down her back. Rachel had never seen the pretty girl's hair down. It was always tied back or in braids.

A friendship had developed during berry-picking outings, times Rachel's papa had known nothing about. She'd known the risk of keeping things from him but had yearned for a friend so badly she'd have done anything. Life on the Llano Estacado was dreary enough. And without even a friend her own age to talk to it had been downright unbearable at times.

"Whoa, Beulah," Tillie said softly. She slid from her mule and ran to throw her arms around Rachel. "I just returned from visiting my parents in Tucson and learned about the loss of your family and now your home. I'm so sorry. Although I've only seen your house from a distance, I always loved it. I can't imagine what you're going through. What will you do? Where will you go?"

Heath moved next to Rachel. She knew Tillie had lots of questions, but how could she answer them when she hadn't a clue how to respond?

Rachel motioned to her companions. "This is Heath Lassiter and his sister. If it hadn't been for their kindness, I don't know what I'd have done."

"Miss Rachel is staying with us for now." Heath's smile crinkled the corners of his gray eyes as he stuck out his hand. "You must be either Miss Grant or Miss Quinlan."

A good deduction, seeing as how only two other families besides hers lived in Black Hawk Canyon. Heat rose to Rachel's face. How embarrassing that she'd forgotten to introduce her visitor. "Where are my manners? This is Tillie Gregory, my nearest neighbor."

Sally pushed her way forward. "I'm Sally. It's a pleasure to meet you at last, Miss Gregory."

"Likewise." Tillie smiled. "But call me Tillie."

Rachel clutched her friend's arm as a sudden bout of dizziness came over her. She swayed, willing the ground to stay beneath her feet.

"Are you okay?" Concern colored Tillie's question.

Putting a hand to her forehead, Rachel answered, "I was injured in a storm a few days ago and only now felt like coming to view the damage for myself."

"She needs to get back in bed before she faints dead away." Sally's brusque statement seemed to take Tillie aback.

"I didn't mean to keep you." Tillie gave Rachel a warm hug.

"Come see me when you feel up to it. I can fix some tea and we can talk."

"Sounds wonderful."

Now that her papa and stepmother were gone there was no reason to avoid contact with people. And she could sure use a friend.

With a big smile, Tillie squeezed her hand. "Let me know if I can do anything. You have only to ask."

Genuine concern filled Tillie's dark eyes and touched Rachel. The girl had trials of her own. Her mother had taken consumption and was away in Arizona with her father for medical treatments. Tillie, along with a man named Yancy Tucker, was struggling to take care of the farm but Rachel had heard it was falling into disrepair despite their best efforts. Yancy did the best he could, but his advanced years worked against him.

Tillie climbed onto her mule and Rachel waved as she rode back the way she came. An inexplicable sense of loss washed over her.

Heath touched her arm. "Are you ready to go?"

"Yes. I'm very tired."

He created a make-do step by cupping his hands for her. She put her booted foot into them and mounted Blackie.

"Get some rest, Rachel." Turning to his sister, he said, "Take her back to the house. I'll be along directly. I'm going to look around here a bit."

"Don't be too long, brother," Sally said in her customary bellow. "I'll have supper on the table shortly."

Rachel smothered a laugh as Heath glanced down, apparently to make sure he was the one wearing pants. The pair provided entertainment.

Questions filled her mind. Why did he stay behind? Heath

did nothing without a reason. But her energy was gone and the Lassiter soddy was a welcome sight.

Rachel slid from Blackie and stood clinging to the animal's mane for support. Her papa's money tin slipped from her grasp and landed at her feet. She took deep breaths and tried to will her buckling legs to stiffen.

Sally retrieved the tin and placed an arm around Rachel's waist. "Let me get you inside. Then I'll take care of the horses."

"I hate this feeling of helplessness. I thought I was made of sterner stuff and need to be pulling my own weight."

"There's time for that later on." Sally moved her toward the door and into the house. Rachel had a feeling if she hadn't been able to walk, Sally would've picked her up and carried her. The stout woman appeared as strong as an ox.

Rachel collapsed on the bed and let Sally remove her shoes. Tomorrow she would have none of this coddling she lectured herself. Tomorrow she would set about taking care of her livestock and easing the Lassiters' load.

Tears welled up and clouded her vision. She hadn't even felt like seeing if the metal box containing her father's secrets had survived the fire. She needed to find out soon and put it in a safe place. Otherwise, everything would come out and she'd suffer for it.

Isaac Malloy had talked out of his head in his last hours and she'd roughly put together what his mysterious absences, secret trips to the padlocked box in the root cellar, and their forced isolation meant. "Have to hide the loot where no one'll find it. Can't hang."

Then the last time, he'd yelled, "I'm the leader of this gang and what I say goes, got that?"

So many secrets. But the bottom line was her father was an outlaw. Sadly, she was an outlaw's daughter.

Not only that, her brothers, Anthony and Jim had started going with him. Anthony had been eighteen, but Jim only sixteen. No doubt to teach them the family business.

Weary down into her bones, she closed her eyes to rest them. Just for a minute.

When she awoke, she felt much better. Rising, she put on her shoes. She found Sally making bread. A pot of chicken and dumplings was bubbling on the fire and the fragrance filled the soddy.

Busy kneading the dough, Sally glanced up. "Do you feel better, dear?"

"Like a new woman. I'm sorry I collapsed on you like that."

"No need to apologize. The trip to Black Hawk Canyon took the starch out of you. I fear it was too soon."

"I can't lie in bed all day. I have far too much to do." Her gaze lit on a bowl of apples on the table. "Do you need help?"

A smile curved Sally's mouth and softened the hard lines. She was still a pretty woman with hair the color of deep chocolate and honest eyes that spoke of endurance. If only she smiled more. But then, she probably didn't have much reason to. No, she seemed to view living as a chore and only to be endured. Seemed Sally and she had that in common.

"I thought I'd make an apple cobbler for dessert. Heath does love them." Sally rolled the dough into a ball and sprinkled more flour on the bread bowl so the soft dough wouldn't stick. "You can pare them if you want while I make strips of dough."

Grateful for something to do, Rachel slid into a chair at the table, lifted the knife, and selected an apple. "I don't suppose Heath's returned."

"Not yet. You know men. They know how to take their blessed sweet time, especially that brother of mine." Sally's tone relayed that if he knew what was good for him he'd not dawdle.

Glancing around the room that served as a kitchen and parlor, Rachel spied some bedding neatly folded in a corner. Since she had Sally's bed, Sally must sleep out here. But what about Heath?

"Can I ask a question?"

Sally carefully put the dough into a pan and dusted her floury hands. "Ask away."

"I'm just curious. Where does Heath sleep?"

"In the beginning he was sleeping in a lean-to, but once he got the barn finished, he sleeps out there. He built a small room separate from the animals. This way he can snore to his heart's content and I don't have to listen to it. Suits me just fine."

Putting the pared apple into a bowl, Rachel got another. "Now that I've recovered, I want you to take your bed back. I've put you out long enough. Tonight, I'll start sleeping out here."

"You'll do it over my dead body!"

Sally's gruff voice took Rachel aback. "I apologize if I offended you."

"Don't mind me." Sally patted Rachel's shoulder. "I forget myself sometimes."

SOMETHING WAS AFOOT on the Malloy land and Heath needed to find out what. His conscience berated that he should've stressed the danger Rachel might face living alone but she had enough on her mind without adding more. Best to just watch over her silently as best he could no matter what she said.

He turned his attention to trying to figure out who had been poking around the blackened ruins.

It didn't take long to find dozens of boot impressions and the tracks of many horses. He knelt to get a better look.

That's when he saw the hole that someone had dug beneath the wide leafy canopy of a cottonwood tree behind the barn. He moved for a closer inspection. Telltale marks indicated a shovel had dug it which ruled out that wild animals had been responsible. A scrap of wadded paper caught his eye.

He picked it up, straightening it out, and stared at the words.

HaHa! Gotcha! You'll never find the money.

Who? What money? It was unsigned but he guessed Isaac Malloy wrote it.

Maybe this note made someone mad enough to burn the house.

Looking across the shimmering blue water of the canyon lake that had provided an oasis for generations of untold Indians, buffalo hunters, soldiers, and the like, Heath set his jaw. This was far worse than he'd guessed. Malloy hadn't been overprotective of the family at all. Some criminal activity had been afoot.

And if whoever burned the house meant to harm Rachel, they'd best think again.

His gaze swept the landscape and his breath stilled at the flash of something white. He moved cautiously, not making a sound. There it was sitting in a cedar tree.

A white dove.

The sign he'd asked God for if he was supposed to marry Rachel. A white dove was very rare, a symbol of hope and love. Never in all his years of living had he seen one in the canyon.

The bird sensed him and stirred.

"Please don't fly," Heath murmured.

Even as he begged, the bird lifted its wings and took to the air. Heath shaded his eyes against the sun and watched. As the dove disappeared, peace settled in his soul.

Now with the confirmation from God, he had things to do and didn't want to waste a moment.

At the whinny of a horse outside, Sally went to look out the soddy's only window. She whirled, jerked the door open, and yelled, "Don't you dare think you're coming in here before you've washed up. You look like you've wallowed around in those ashes."

Rachel didn't hear the mumbled reply. Did Sally realize she acted more like Heath's mother instead of his sister?

They had the apples in the Dutch oven by the time the door opened. Heath stepped inside, took off his hat, and propped his rifle against the wall.

Her pulse quickened at the sight of him.

His damp hair curled around his neck. With his broad shoulders back, his hands behind him, he carried himself with an aura of confidence. She doubted there was anything he couldn't do.

Except get her to marry him. That she could never agree to.

Not that it would be that unpleasant. She'd give anything if she could say yes. He didn't know how many nights she'd lain awake and wished someone would come along and sweep her off her feet and a new chapter of her life would begin.

The problem was she harbored too many secrets she would never be able to speak of. She wished she was the virtuous woman Heath evidently thought her to be. But she wasn't.

Heath came closer and brought his hands from behind his

back. He held a handful of wild yellow sunflowers and purple asters. "Some pretty posies for a pretty lady."

Rachel's face heated as a blush rose. She reached for the unexpected gift. "No one's ever brought me flowers before. They're lovely. Thank you."

She met the warmth of his smoke-colored eyes. There was much about this man to admire. But mostly his strong jaw that said he'd face whatever life brought head-on. Heath Lassiter wouldn't run and hide. Were he to do something he was ashamed of, she imagined he'd own up to it and take the consequences.

Unlike her.

She mentally pictured a wagon train and the practice to park the wagons in a circle at night for protection. Heath Lassiter would be someone to circle the wagons with.

He pulled out a chair. "My pleasure. More's the pity that these are your first."

Flowers were just one of many things she'd missed out on, she suspected. When you lived in such isolation, the less your chances to experience the niceties. However, with the Quakers establishing Estacado more people were beginning to settle in this area. She'd never had occasion to visit the town, but Papa had told her they had a hotel, a church, and two general stores. Someday she'd like to see it for herself.

Sally handed her a Mason jar for the flowers, then checked on the bread and stirred the chicken and dumplings. The woman had her head oddly cocked toward them so she wouldn't miss any of the conversation. The fact that she listened to something private that passed between Heath and herself made her uncomfortable.

"Can we talk outside for a moment?" Rachel asked.

"Lead the way."

Dusk had settled over the land, bathing everything in shadowed hues.

"Thank you for the flowers, Heath."

"I'm glad you wanted some privacy." Heath pulled a scrap of paper from his pocket and handed it to her. "I found this today where someone had dug a hole back of your house."

She smoothed the wrinkles and read her father's handwriting. Color drained from her face. A glance into his eyes revealed questions. "I wish I knew what to say. I don't have a clue what he was doing. He often left for a while but we never knew why."

"He didn't tell anyone?"

"My brothers maybe, but not me and my stepmother. I'm sorry you found this."

"Rachel, I think something bad is going on and you might be in danger."

"Don't you think with my father dead they'd leave me alone?"

"Rachel, they're back and they're looking for whatever your father buried. Understand?"

"I had nothing to do with any of that. Nothing."

"I believe you. Let's drop it for now. I worked on your place today, clearing a spot to build you a new house." Heath glanced up at the sky. "Will you insist on staying there, despite all we know?"

"Yes. That's the only thing left of mine. But—" The whole conversation jolted Rachel but when she spoke, her tone was firm and brooked no further discussion. "I won't let you build me a house. You've already done more than enough."

He shrugged. "I already have the lumber set aside. Why not use it?"

"That's for a house of your own," she insisted. "I absolutely will not take it."

"This soddy has served us well and will do so a while longer. I can always buy more lumber."

Heath's plan bothered her. If she let him build her a house, it would make her more obligated and owing him made her uncomfortable. "No, thank you."

"Then pray tell me. Will you live in the ashes?" he asked.

"I'll figure it out. You've done more than enough." She could be mulish about this.

"The new house will be small and enough for you, but I figure we can get it built and have you in it in two months." Heath's voice was low and deep and seemed to vibrate the air as he continued. It was as though he'd never heard a word she said.

Maybe he really was deaf. No matter how many houses he built for her she wouldn't change her mind.

Marrying Heath was out of the question. He had to understand that.

CHAPTER FIVE

Rachel collapsed onto her borrowed bed as soon as she washed the supper dishes. She couldn't rightly say what the problem was; she felt so faint and everything she looked at was double.

It was difficult to think straight, and she had a list of things the length of her arm to sort out.

Tomorrow. She closed her eyes. Everything would be better tomorrow.

But morning dawned with no improvement. In fact, she seemed worse. Oh, her splitting head. She wanted to stick it in a bucket of icy water to cool off.

Holding to the wall then chairs, she finally made it to the breakfast table.

Sally looked up from her task of cracking eggs into a skillet. "Oh, my blessed Lord! Your face is whiter than a peeled turnip. What's the matter, child?"

Rachel tried to force a smile. She hadn't been a child in a long time. "I don't know," she whispered.

Bustling around the small table, Sally felt Rachel's forehead. "You're burning flat up."

Heath opened the door and came inside. "What's wrong?"

"Infection would be my guess, brother." Sally glanced from Rachel to her skillet of eggs. "Can you help her back to bed? I don't want our breakfast to burn."

"I can manage," Rachel weakly protested.

"You're about to fall over." He helped her to her feet and put an arm around her waist. "Just lean on me, pretty lady. I'll help you."

"The room is spinning like a top," she murmured.

His voice was low, his breath ruffling the tendrils of hair at her ear. "It's all right. You need more rest and you'll feel right as rain as my mother was fond of saying."

Rachel laid her head against his broad chest. The sound of his beating heart was strong and sure. The fragrance of wild desert sage and fresh rain enveloped her. Even if she could've objected to his nearness she wouldn't have been able. His strength and gentleness wrapping around her made her feel safe and secure—and most treasured.

The emotions it stirred left her shaken.

This connection between her and Heath was something indescribable and brought a delicious warmth.

Whatever it was she wanted to close her eyes and savor it.

She let her eyes drift shut for just a moment. Someone softly kissed her cheek. She smiled and lifted a hand to caress his whiskered jaw. Then she snuggled into the down of the feather mattress. She wasn't alone.

When Rachel opened her eyes, she found Tillie Gregory perched by the bed.

Tillie rose and touched Rachel's forehead. "How are you?"

"The room isn't spinning and I don't seem as feverish. What time is it?"

"Eight o'clock. The Lassiters left and I'm in charge." Tillie reached for a glass on the small bedside table. "I'm supposed to make you drink lots of water."

Rachel sat up and took a sip from the glass.

"You're probably wondering what I'm doing here," Tillie said.

At Rachel's nod, Tillie explained. "Heath Lassiter appeared at my door about an hour ago and asked me to sit with you while he and his sister worked at your burned-out house. They're clearing away the charred timbers and getting ready to rebuild."

"I told them I didn't want them to do that." Guilt lay heavy on her heart. She didn't want to be even more obligated to the Lassiters. Lord knows they'd already done more than enough.

And here she was lying in bed while they toiled to give her a place to live. If they insisted on carrying through with their plans, the least she could do was help them. Or take care of her animals and not leave that chore for Heath.

"I need to get out of this bed."

"Sally threatened me within an inch of my life if I let you. Would you like some breakfast?" Tillie took the glass from Rachel and returned it to the little table. "You're probably hungry."

"Not right now."

A smile curved Tillie's lips. "Heath wanted to go alone and leave Sally here with you but she wouldn't hear of it. You should've heard the ruckus. In the end, Heath threw up his hands. I get the feeling he doesn't win many arguments."

"Sally's a force to reckon with all right."

Suddenly Rachel's breath stilled.

Oh, sweet Lord! In clearing off the debris from the fire, they'd find the trapdoor to the root cellar beneath the house.

Once inside, it'd only be a matter of time before they found the strong box and knew her father's secret life. Why hadn't she remembered it before now? Rachel threw aside the bedcovers and swung her legs to the floor.

"What do you think you're doing, missy?"

"I have to get up. I have things to do."

"Sally gave me strict instructions and I'd hate to have her ire turned on me." Tillie gently lifted Rachel's legs back onto the bed. "Whatever it is you think you need to do can wait until tomorrow. I won't fall down on my duty."

With a long sigh, Rachel did as Tillie requested. "Sally put the fear of God in you then?"

Tillie chuckled. "You might say that. She reminds me of an aunt I once had. Lord, how that woman made me toe the line."

It was comforting to hear her friend talk of family.

"How is your mother? I do hope the treatments in Tucson are going well."

"Mama is a little better. The dry Arizona climate is exactly what she needed and the doctor there is very encouraged."

Rachel's thoughts turned to beloved Jane who rested beneath the soil in Black Hawk Canyon. Her father was another matter however with his surly disposition and harsh treatment. At the time when she'd needed him most, he turned his back and called her horrible names.

"Will Mrs. Gregory ever be able to come back one day?" Rachel asked.

Pain filled Tillie's dark eyes. "I don't know. I miss her very much."

"Keeping the farm going with only Mr. Yancy to help must be a terrible burden."

"Sometimes I don't know how much longer I can hold on." Tillie's anguished whisper filled the small alcove. "With each passing day the house and barn...I'm afraid I'll wake up one morning to discover it's fallen in on me during the night. Yancy does what he can but he's getting old and many things he once did he simply can't do anymore. I don't want to let my papa down but I don't know what more I can do."

Rachel covered Tillie's hand with hers. "Let's have some tea. I promise to do nothing more than walk to the kitchen table. Then I'll come right back to bed. I promise."

A few minutes later they sat, sipping a cup of fragrant tea and enjoying each other's company.

"This is nice. I always yearned for a friend, Tillie. I wanted to get to know you."

"And I you."

"In the past, my father forbade any friendship. You probably wondered about that."

Tillie ran her finger along the edge of the square table. "I assumed you had your reasons. It wasn't my place to pry."

"I treasured berry-picking because I looked forward to seeing you."

"Do you ever lie in bed at night and wonder when your life will start? Or even if it will?" Tillie's voice had turned soft and wistful. "I yearn for a husband and children to love."

Rachel bumped her tea and sloshed it then hurried to wipe it up. She'd wanted far more but had been grateful for Alice and being able to pour her love on her baby sister. Painful memories surfaced along with a desperate need to make sure Alice knew she mattered and not suffer the coldness of their father.

"I dreamed more than once of a different life." Rachel had seemed stuck, mired down, unable to move forward for so long.

All she'd been able to do was look back and think of what could've been had circumstances not thrust her into an impossible situation.

"I fear I shall never get married or have a family of my own." Tillie rose to refill their cups.

Rachel turned. "With women severely outnumbering men, I don't hold much hope either. And our isolation in the canyon only adds to that."

Except, she had an offer, her conscience berated. Heath Lassiter wanted to make her his wife and would tomorrow if she'd only say yes. But how could she when so much stood like a barrier between them? Far too long she'd fought like a dammed-up river being kept from its natural course, getting nowhere.

Rachel reached for the wildflowers Heath had picked for her that made a beautiful centerpiece on the table. She removed a yellow sunflower and absently fingered the petals.

Could she have a normal life with Heath? The ticking of the clock was the only answer she got.

Needing a place to live and someone to take care of her was a poor reason to get married. Putting aside the biggest reason of all, her secret shame, maybe she and Heath could come to love each other over time.

And maybe not. It seemed a foolish risk to take.

Tillie rose to look out the window. "Let's make a pact. We'll help each other through these dark times."

"I'd like that."

"We'll start with you first," Tillie said turning. "We need to make a list of everything of value you have. We'll find you a way to survive and make a living."

It didn't take long and to Rachel the list was pretty pitiful.

"Of course, the goats provide me with milk and butter. And the chickens lay eggs."

"What if you take some butter and eggs to the trading post? George Singer might buy them. What with the post being located where four military routes cross, he gets lots of business from soldiers."

Rachel brightened. "That's a good idea, Tillie. Except it's dangerous going there. Lots of bad men hang out in front." Fear raced through her.

"Not anymore. Soldiers and ranchers keep an eye on that store now. It seems safe enough when I go." Tillie rose. "Want more tea?"

"No, thanks."

A few seconds later, Tillie returned and stared at the short list. "What else? A bull won't do you much good. Maybe you could sell it. At least you wouldn't have to feed it."

"Who on earth would want my bull? He's ugly and mean." Rachel's papa had always been in his element when he was trading something. It didn't matter what the offer. Five months ago Isaac Malloy had brought the worthless bull home after one of his long absences. Never said where he got it.

Tillie pursed her lips. "Maybe some of the ranchers around here would take the bull off your hands. It's worth a shot to see."

"You're right. I have nothing to lose." Rachel tapped the pencil on the table. "I just wish I'd start feeling better. I have so many things to do. I'll bet the garden looks a tangled mess."

Tillie's eyes lit up. "What did you plant?"

"Lots of squash, beans, carrots, cabbage, and potatoes. We also planted a few pumpkins but those won't be ready yet." She thought of Jane who'd brought lots of different seeds. "Let's exchange seeds. My stepmother was of Comanche blood and brought some seeds with her when she came. I don't know how you feel about Indians." She wouldn't apologize for that.

"I think that's wonderful. What different seeds did she bring, and can I have a few?"

"Absolutely. I'll be happy to share. She brought different squashes, corn, pumpkins, mesquite beans, and things like that. I meant to can a lot of it but then the fever came."

"I've got just the thing. You can make pumpkin bread and sell it out of the trading post. Prickly pear jelly. Mesquite jelly. Those along with the goat milk and butter might provide some much-needed income. I'll help you."

Rachel rose and hugged Tillie. "You're a godsend. I'm so glad you came to stay with me today. I can't wait to get started."

Tillie shook her finger. "Slow down. You have strict orders not to lift a finger today."

"Oh posh!" She'd do as she wanted yet she lacked a little bravery. "Okay, let's talk. You've had the freedom to get around so tell me what you know of your neighbor on the other side of you."

"Cora Quinlan?"

Rachel nodded. "One time when I was picking berries, I paid no attention to how far I'd gone and found myself at her farm. She came out the door wearing a thick black veil. What's her story? Did someone die?"

"She's very mysterious but she's always worn that veil. Of course, we hear all kinds of stories, but it has nothing to do with anyone dying. Maybe she has a scarred face."

"Or she could be pockmarked and ugly," Rachel threw in.

Tillie grinned. "What if she worked as a soiled dove and bought her land with her earnings?"

A soiled dove? Was that similar to a whore? Her father had

thrown that word at her but she hadn't known what it meant. She must've had a strange look on her face.

"You know. A woman of ill-repute who works in one of those bawdy houses that men go to," Tillie explained.

Unable to ever go to town, how would she know? But it must be bad. Rachel pretended to understand. "Oh. Maybe so."

"I overheard Yancy and his son Noble talking one day and Yancy said Cora mourns a lost love, but I don't know where he got that from. Maybe he made it up." Tillie rose. "I'm going to make you an egg and a piece of toast. You don't have to eat it all. Just a few bites."

"I guess." Rachel watched her friend, so competent and sure. "Don't you think it's strange that all three farms here in the canyon are now run by women?"

"A little I guess but we can do it. Women are smart and capable. Sometimes we need a bit of muscles and then have to let men help. I'm just happy that I could get you pointed in a new direction. I can't imagine what I'd do in your situation."

"You do what you have to and get through each day as best you can." Rachel bit her quivering lip. Often that wasn't enough to stave off the deluge of memories.

"I'm sure you miss them something fierce."

Rachel's hand trembled and her whispered voice thickened with tears. "Waking up each day to this emptiness is unbearable. I've lost a sense of place and my purpose for being on this earth. I don't belong to anyone anymore. And no one belongs to me."

CHAPTER SIX

That evening Heath entered the little sod house singing a rousing rendition of *I Shall Not Be Moved*. His deep baritone reverberated, bouncing off the earthen walls. The music made Rachel smile. For someone who'd worked all day clearing away the blackened timbers of what had once been her home he seemed extraordinarily happy.

At Sally's insistence that left no room for discussion, Rachel had gotten back into her borrowed bed. She lay fully dressed on top of the covers, listening to the sounds of life that filled this home.

Pans rattled in the kitchen, doors opened and closed. And Heath sang to beat all. Living, real living, was noisy. Not like the deathly quiet that filled her head.

Despite the loss that sat on her chest and strangled the breath out of her, she had a tiny glimmer of hope.

Soon she could do as she wanted without someone bossing her to death.

Jax padded softly into the little alcove and stuck his cold

nose to Rachel's hand, begging to be loved. One pat on the bed was all the invitation he needed. With one bound, Jax leaped onto the bed and settled beside her. She'd thought it a little odd, and frankly it had hurt her feelings, when Jax left that morning with Heath and Sally. Footsteps sounded.

"I might've known," Heath remarked, entering the small room. "I do think he missed his mistress today."

She glanced up. "I heard you singing. You have a beautiful voice."

"Thank you." His tall muscular frame used up all the space in the small alcove. "How are you feeling?"

"Like I'm ready to get on with living."

He took the chair beside the bed. "I'm real glad to hear it. I've been worried about you. If you don't mind me asking, what happened to make you change your mind?"

Rachel met his smoky gaze. "Tillie's visit. We made a pact that we'll help each other get through these trying times. At her suggestion we made a list of the things I have and thought of what might bring in enough income for me to survive on. Tillie had some wonderful ideas and I can't wait to start on them. I'm an independent woman, Heath. I was raised to take care of myself. I'm no good at accepting charity."

"Everyone has to rely on the kindness of others occasionally." His deep voice filled the small room. "Learning to accept help that is freely given with grace and dignity is as important as giving it."

"Still, it doesn't sit well."

Heath gave her a crooked grin that deepened the lines at the corners of his eyes. "Then I should tell you some news while you're not up to raising too much fuss."

Her breath caught in her throat. "What is it?"

"Some of the ranchers up on the rim like me got wind of

what I was doing and they came in droves to help rebuild your house."

Would they be so quick to help if they knew about Jane and her Comanche father, a proud chief? And her father's lawless activities?

She stiffened. "So you're saying I not only owe you and Sally, but a whole passel of other people?"

"Afraid so."

Rachel threw her legs over the side of the bed and sat up. "I appreciate all you've done but please let me take care of my own affairs. I can't sneeze without someone telling me what to do and when. Or how to feel."

"That's not it at all. We just want to help. You've suffered an enormous blow."

"There's a difference in helping and taking over." She regretted the sharp tone that crept into her voice and it seemed unfair, but she had to make Heath listen to her. "I'm getting up from this bed before I sprout roots and grow to it so don't try to stop me."

HEATH GRINNED AND raised both hands. "I wouldn't think of interfering with so determined a woman."

The steam coming out of Rachel's ears told him she had a bee in her bonnet and wasn't about to let anyone swat at it but her, even if it stung.

She was sure a pretty thing, especially when she was mad enough to melt lead and make bullets.

And she'd remarked on his singing.

That must mean his plan was working.

It was only a matter of time—if she didn't kill him after he told her of the latest developments.

He'd been relieved to discover a logical explanation for most of the holes on the Malloy land. Some had been made by coyotes. And those footprints in the ash? Maybe they had been made by a curious cowboy from one of the ranches up on the rim. They must've seen the smoke.

Except the crumpled note didn't fit that theory.

Still, Heath believed in his heart Rachel would be safe or he'd never have decided to build her another house where the old one had stood.

Things were going to work out. He felt that in his bones. He was contemplating the goodness and mercy of the Almighty God when Rachel stood. She grabbed his arm to keep from falling. The room must be spinning again. Her continuing dizziness worried him.

"Here, let me help you."

"I am not getting back to bed," she said firmly. "That's the problem now. I've been in bed so long I've forgotten how to balance myself."

Heath slipped an arm around her slim waist. "Far be it from me to say different."

"I can do it. Please."

He quickly stifled a frustrated groan. Anything he did or said at the present was going to be wrong.

"Tell me what you want, Rachel," he asked quietly, arms crossed. Waiting.

"I want…I want…" A sob escaped her.

His heart broke. He didn't have to be a mind reader to know she ached for things to return to normal, to the way they were before even if they weren't ideal.

He folded his arms around her and drew her close. "I've got

you, Rachel. Go ahead and cry," he murmured into her silky hair. "It'll do you good."

Jax whined and then threw back his head and let out one of the most mournful howls Heath had ever heard.

Sally came running. "Good heavens! What's all this racket?" She sent him a glare. "What did you do, Heath?"

"Why do you always assume I'm to blame for whatever goes wrong?"

Sally threw up her hands. "Well, bring her in here."

Sweeping Rachel up into his arms, he carried her into the next room and gently placed her in the rocker.

Pressing a handkerchief in Rachel's hand, Sally murmured, "There now. Everything's going to be all right."

"I'm sorry to be such a blubbering mess." Rachel blew her nose. "Sometimes the enormity of it all comes flooding over me and I can't stop it."

Heath patted her arm. "You have nothing to apologize for. I'm sure it's more difficult than anyone knows. It'll get better. Each day that passes will get a little easier."

"And don't forget you're feeling poorly," Sally reminded. "You've got to get your strength back."

Huffing and giving Heath a look that said he'd better mind his p's and q's, Sally went back to her cooking.

Heath sank into the chair beside Rachel. His gaze tangled with her glistening pale green eyes. Something soft and gentle wound around his heart. He yearned to take care of her.

"I don't know how you both put up with me," she murmured.

The barely spoken words were colored with thick emotion and sadness.

"Well, the good thing is that you'll soon have a place of your own." He leaned back and stretched his long legs out in front of him. "With all the extra hands we'll finish the house a lot sooner than we planned. I figure we'll have it livable in three weeks. Of course, furnishings will be a little sparse until I can get to Colorado City for some."

Rachel straightened her spine. "Until *we* get to Colorado City you mean."

Good grief, he was going to have to watch what he said and remember her blessed independence that she set such store by.

"Yes, of course. I meant to include you," he said with a grin.

"I don't have any money so I may have to wait awhile," she said stiffly.

"I didn't tell you the best part." Heath leaned forward until his knees almost touched hers. "Several of the ranchers in the area are aware of you single ladies down here in the canyon alone and are falling all over themselves to help. They're donating some of their extras. One has a bed, another a cook stove, and one is offering a table and some chairs. I figure that's enough to get you started." She hadn't hit him yet, so he went on. "Of course, I think a few are looking for wives."

The sight of a fresh batch of tears filling her eyes was almost more than he could stand. He wanted to take her in his arms again, smooth back her silvery blonde hair, and assure her everything was going to be all right.

But she surprised him this time and gave him a watery smile.

"I don't know what to say. This is all so overwhelming."

"A thank you will suffice. These ranchers don't want anything in return. Some things are more important than money, especially out here in the canyon."

"And you, Mr. Lassiter. What do you want?" Her words were wrapped in soft velvet.

"What's with this Mr. Lassiter business? What happened to Heath?" he growled.

"I just needed to remind myself not to take advantage of your generosity."

"As though you could. And I'll tell you what I want. It's simple. I only want you to smile and be happy again." And to be his wife, but he didn't add that part.

It was better to go slow where that was concerned.

"I don't think I can do that right now."

"Then just grant me one request. Don't call me anything but Heath."

"I don't feel comfortable doing that, but if that's your desire."

"It is. You'll get used to it."

"Then, Heath, I need to ask something."

From the way she chewed on her bottom lip, it wasn't easy to get out. Curiosity filled him.

"Ask away."

"When you were clearing away the debris from my house, did you find a trapdoor by chance?"

"Yes. And I'll build it back just like it was before."

"Did you remove anything?"

"I only glanced into it but debris blocked the stairs. Why?"

"Just curious."

He took her hand. "Rachel, I won't bother your things or let anyone else."

Relief flooded her gaze and she squeezed his fingers.

Though curiosity rose, he'd keep his nose out of her affairs.

CHAPTER SEVEN

The next three weeks spent waiting for a house to be built passed in a whirlwind of activity. Rachel and Tillie had ridden to the trading post and talked it over with George Singer. The man agreed that their plan was an excellent idea and looked forward to selling her goods. They'd come back and set about implementing the plan they'd drawn up. They made potato bread, churned butter, made prickly pear jelly, and carrot cakes. Rachel had delivered the first batch to the trading post several days ago.

It made her feel good to be doing something. She wanted, no needed, to be in control of her life. Not that she wasn't grateful for what Heath and Sally had done. Truth was, she owed them far more than she could ever repay. But for the first time in her life, she was truly independent and free to make her own way.

While she still grieved for her precious Alice and Jane, she was getting stronger and feeling more capable with each sunrise. It had only been a month since she'd buried Alice and at times she could barely breathe for the pain.

True to Heath's promise, he and his small army finished Rachel's house in three weeks. She moved in on Saturday, September 16, 1882, amid a hotbed of activity with men and women unloading furnishings from their wagons.

She stepped aside to let Sally by with kitchen chairs. Men carried in the table, a rocker, and a kitchen cookstove. Her heart swelled as tears filled her eyes.

Despite her constant heartache, she loved the feeling of being home. She was at last back on the land where she'd grown into a woman and where she'd laid her family to rest.

It wasn't much but it was hers and she counted each blessing.

The house consisted of two rooms. The combined kitchen and sitting area was small but big enough and a door led to the bedroom. The rough, planked floor was far better than dirt. In short order, a rocker and two cane-bottomed chairs stood in front of the stone fireplace she'd always loved.

Memories flooded of holding Alice, rocking her to sleep. She remembered how the girl's small fingers curled in her hair. She blinked hard and swallowed. It didn't matter that smoke now stained the rock. How she'd loved those times and those old stones brought comfort now.

Maybe in time the grief would ease.

A table and black iron cook stove made up the kitchen part. The structure had two windows, one by the front door and one in the bedroom. Friends and neighbors had even slapped a coat of whitewash on the exterior.

"It's perfect. I'm…" She looked at Heath through her tears. "Thank you."

He shifted the iron bed frame he carried. "You're welcome. If there's anything you need to add let me know."

"It's perfect, Heath. What more could I need?"

Her gaze landed on the braided rag rug that covered the trap door leading to the room underneath.

Despite Heath reassuring her things were safe, she couldn't wait until she was alone so she could check for herself to see if the padlocked strong box was still there.

He gave her a crooked grin and continued into the small bedroom.

She hugged herself. Tonight, she would sleep in her own bed and hopefully dream of better times to come.

Except for the crumpled note Heath had found in her father's handwriting and the deep suspicion that Isaac Malloy was a criminal. Her gut told her he'd done some bad things. Strange disappearances and the note along with his mumbling talk on his deathbed pretty much confirmed that he robbed stagecoaches. And if he'd done that, maybe he'd also killed.

She released a deep, troubled sigh.

Worry churned. If others found out about him, they'd turn on her. That's just the way it worked. They'd say she had to have known and she could lose everything she'd gained.

Something else troubled her. Could she cope with the dreadful silence once everyone left and returned home?

How odd that silence was the one thing she'd most yearned for when her brothers and sister were alive. Now that she had it, she'd give anything for the noise and bustle that had been part of her life as long as she could remember.

Tillie entered with an armful of quilts and bedding. "We had more than enough of these. They need to be used."

Rachel took a deep breath and blinked back sudden tears. "I

don't know how or why I ended up with so many friends. I'm truly grateful."

"You'll find that people around here have some mighty big hearts." Tillie blew a tendril of hair off her face. "I'm sure it's difficult for you to believe right now. Weeping may endure for a night, but joy comes in the morning. You'll see."

The heaviness that still sat on Rachel's chest didn't feel temporary in the least. But maybe Tillie was right. Maybe life could hold some joy again. And maybe she could find a measure of happiness in the coming days and months.

Since she didn't have much choice in the matter, she'd try to find peace.

Tillie shifted her load. "Are you ready to resume baking bread and making butter tomorrow?"

"Sure am."

"There you are, Miss Malloy," said Susan Slaughter, wife of rancher Skeet Slaughter whose ranch was on the rim next to Heath's. "We have everything from our wagon. I suppose we'll head home." The woman with strands of silver in her dark hair put her arms around Rachel and hugged her. "Again, I'm sorry about your folks. If you need anything or if I can do anything to help you, you have but to say the word. Out here we all have to stick together to get by. If you ever get lonely come see me."

"Thank you, Mrs. Slaughter. I'll keep that in mind." Rachel had the urge to snuggle deep in the woman's generous arms. It would feel almost as good as hugging her stepmother Jane.

"Please call me Susan."

"Only if you'll use my given name of Rachel."

"It's a deal. I'm really glad we could help. I never got a chance to know your parents, but I sure want to change that with you."

"Then we'll plan on having tea sometime, Susan."

One by one, everyone left until it was down to Heath and Sally.

Heath stood with his hat in his hands. "I was going to bring your animals back today but it's getting too late in the afternoon. I'll do it first thing tomorrow."

"That'll be fine," she said quietly.

"I have a feeling you're too tired to worry with them now anyway. You've had a long day and you're still puny."

A wry smile formed. "I am a little worse for wear."

Without a word, Sally Lassiter marched to the stove and began to sling pots and pans around as though she was slaying a herd of fire-breathing dragons.

Curious, Rachel covered the steps to the small kitchen area. "Sally, can I help you do something?"

"No, you go sit down. I'll have a meal fixed in two shakes."

"You don't have to do this. Really."

Putting her hands on her hips, Sally faced her. "It's my duty to put some meat on your bones. You're too thin by half. Besides, I'm spending the night. Can't leave you by yourself on the first night in your new house."

Rachel smothered a groan and cast a glance at the trapdoor in the floor. She chafed at interruptions that kept her unable to satisfy her curiosity.

HEATH STUDIED RACHEL and the different emotions playing across her face. Something was bothering her. Her knuckles were white, relaying the tightness of her grip on her apron. And why had she been worried that he'd removed something from the room beneath the trapdoor?

Rachel Malloy harbored a secret.

Wishing he had some answers, he crossed the room and gently took her elbow. "It's best to get out of her way when she's on a mission to save the world against sinners and sorrow." He led her to a rocking chair the Slaughters had brought then took a seat on the hearth in front of the fireplace. Jax gave a huff and stretched out at Rachel's feet.

"Now, tell me what's troubling you. Don't deny it I see it in your face."

It took a long moment for her to answer. "I'm tired and need some time alone except that's very difficult to find."

"I think you'll be safe enough during the day, but I'm afraid you're stuck with Sally at night." He happened to think the arrangement was necessary. Though he hadn't seen any other signs of a trespasser, he didn't want to risk being wrong. He'd do what he must to keep her safe. "What else?"

"I am grateful for this house and able to live here again, I truly am, but what if I lose what little I have again?" Her bottom lip quivered. "I don't think I can start over."

The anguish in her quiet tone tore through him. It was all he could do not to take her in his arms, protect her from everything that created insurmountable barriers for her.

"It's futile to worry about something that hasn't happened yet." He laid a light hand on her shoulder. "I've learned we're not tested during the good times. It's during the dark night of our soul's despair that we discover what we're truly made of and find the strength we need. Every person on this earth has trials and tribulations. It's not just you."

"I know but it seems like it."

He took her hand in his. "You have amazing strength. And you have me and Sally and your friends to help you. We're not going to let you give up. Now, what else?"

Her green eyes became guarded. "I may have lost something. Something that…"

"Tell me what it is, and I'll help you find it."

Indecision flickered in her face. Something told him she'd been betrayed before.

"Rachel, you can trust me with your secrets. They won't go any further."

Finally, she said, "You remember that crumpled note you found?"

He nodded.

She lowered her voice. "I don't know for sure, but I suspect my father was an outlaw and robbed stagecoaches. He kept something very important in a strong box in the root cellar. If someone took it or discovered it during the construction, things could get bad. Real bad."

"I understand. I think we should go look and put your mind at ease." He glanced toward Sally. "After supper. Okay?"

Rachel nodded, looking relieved. It had been hard for her to confide in him. What a sad life she must've had and from what he could gather, her father had not treated her well.

"Time to eat," Sally bellowed as though her voice needed to carry across several miles to reach them.

An idea brewed in Heath's head as he watched Rachel throughout the meal. If she accepted his plan, he had it in his power to make her life a bit easier. But he had to put it to her in such a way that it kept her pride intact. Easier said than done.

After Rachel washed and dried the supper dishes, she turned to Sally, "Heath and I are going to see what remains in the root cellar under the trapdoor."

"Good idea. I'll just go rest my bones for a minute," Sally answered and moved to sit in front of the fireplace.

Health reached for the kerosene lamp and took Rachel's

hand. Carefully, they made their way down into the cool storage space. At the bottom, he held the light high.

The little space was empty. Someone had cleaned everything out.

"It's gone! Oh no." Rachel wrung her hands.

"Now, don't panic. We'll find it. I'll go to every worker and see what they know. It'll turn up," he assured her.

They made their way up the short stairs to the kitchen. Sally was waiting. "I just remembered that the men took everything out to the barn to be sorted."

"See, Rachel? It's probably safe in the barn."

She brightened. "Oh, thank goodness. Let's go."

Heath grabbed her arm. "Hold on. We can't see anything in the dark and that's a big barn. Best to wait until daylight. Besides, you're dead on your feet."

"I guess you're right," she conceded.

"I'll return early. I promise." He tried to read Sally's hand signals from behind Rachel's back. Finally, he understood. "Would some fresh air interest you?"

She allowed a wan smile. "As you pointed out, I'm a little tired. But maybe for just a moment."

"We won't be long."

"Take your shawl," Sally ordered. "The night air is cool."

Heath caught Rachel's low murmur. He knew Sally grated on Rachel's nerves for his sister seemed to have assumed the role of mother. That she bossed around someone else for a change was a welcome relief for him. But he knew Rachel found it more than a tad unbearable.

At least Rachel waited until they'd shut the door behind them before she spewed. "I know Sally has a big heart and I love her dearly. She cared for me when I had no one. But does her bossiness ever end?" Rachel jerked the shawl around her shoulders and slipped her hand in the crook of his arm. Jax padded along beside them happy to be outdoors.

"Best to just accept it. She does care about you even if it's a bit too much."

The chirps of crickets amid the croaking of frogs blended in a song of the night. And off in the distance he heard the howl of a lone coyote. Each sound affirmed how very alive not only he was but everything around him.

Rachel tilted her face to take a long look at the brilliant full moon. "It's beautiful," she breathed softly.

His throat tightened. He certainly could agree, and he wasn't talking entirely about the moon.

"That it is. I love how the shimmering lake reflects its light. The night air smells so clean and fresh. This is the most favorite part of my day." They strolled down to the water's edge. "Rachel, I have something I'd like to talk to you about."

"Am I going to like it?"

"I hope so." However, he wouldn't bet good money on it. "Would you loan me your bull for a little while?"

"Whatever for? I was planning to sell it so I won't have to feed the ugly thing."

"I want to breed it with my heifers. I've talked to Skeet Slaughter and he tells me your bull is a black Angus and very valuable. It'll improve the quality of my herd." He let that sink in before he continued. "And, in exchange, I'll give you ten calves when they're weaned. It'll be nice start to a herd of your own."

She released his arm and knelt to drag her fingers in the tranquil water. She seemed pensive. He rested against the bark of a cottonwood to wait.

Finally, she spoke. "If you're just doing this because you feel sorry for me, forget it."

He should've known his offer wouldn't come out right.

"No, Rachel," he said quietly. "That's not the way of it. I'd purely take it as a favor if you let me breed the bull with my heifers. I'd have one of the best herds you ever saw here in Texas."

"In that case, keep the bull as long as you like."

The breath he'd been holding came out in a rush. "You should know that Slaughter and some of the other ranchers will ask for the same deal. Before this thing is through, no telling what size herd you'll end up with and give you some long-term independence."

She rose and faced him. Silvery moonlight bathed her pretty features and created a glorious halo around her. "I don't know what to say."

An angel sent from heaven couldn't have looked lovelier.

Heath couldn't say a word if his life depended on it. His tongue got stuck to the roof of his mouth. She seemed to have put him in a spell of some kind.

Before he could stop himself, he lowered his head and covered her soft lips with his.

CHAPTER EIGHT

Under the moon's silvery rays, Rachel closed her eyes and leaned into Heath's strong arms. She savored the kiss that rocked her and the feel of his gentle hands.

The soft lapping of the waves on the lake faded away.

It would be so easy to love this man. Already he invaded her thoughts. In fact, her very dreams.

Heath Lassiter made her feel beautiful. Wanted. Every inch a lady.

She was hard-pressed to remember all those years when he wasn't in her life. Oh, he made her mad enough to chew nails sometimes with his penchant for taking over and ordering her about. But he had the biggest heart she'd seen.

When he broke the kiss, he continued to hold her as he might've a delicate china teacup. "I won't apologize for kissing you, but I do for not asking you first. The moonlight, the lake behind us, the fragrant air is all so magical. I'm afraid I lost my head. I hope I didn't frighten you."

"No, I wasn't afraid. I trust you." She touched her lips that were still tingling.

His breath ruffled the hair at her temple. "I'm glad although I expected you to slug me for taking liberties."

He must think her an emotional wreck. These last four weeks when she hadn't been crying at every turn, she'd been so angry she couldn't see straight. He probably thought her unhinged and maybe he was right.

"I still want to marry you," he said quietly. "Maybe in time you'll see that it wouldn't be so bad."

Rachel took a step back, breaking his hold on her. "I never said it would be bad. I only said that it was wrong to marry someone I don't know. To marry simply because I have no one left is the wrong reason to enter into a union and I won't do it."

"Well, just so you know I plan on changing your mind."

The challenge in his voice made her issue one of her own. "And just so you know you're welcome to try. I'm awfully stubborn though."

"I noticed that." He fingered a strand of hair beween his thumb and forefinger.

His touch was so gentle, tender. Unlike the rough, dirty hands that had held her down five years ago when she'd been taken and used as leverage against her father after he'd cheated his partners. A dark shiver raced through her. They'd done such horrible things.

We're gonna get our share one way or another, a voice in her ear repeated.

Sometimes she woke from a dead sleep, hearing that grating tone, thinking she was still in their clutches.

A noise brought her back to the present. Sally opened the door and stepped out, glancing their way.

Rachel turned to Heath. "I should get inside. As we all agreed, I'm very tired."

"Wait." Heath put a hand on her arm. "Thank you for the walk. I enjoy your company."

Rachel cast one last look at the brilliant moon beaming down on the man who almost made her feel whole again. "We'll do it again sometime."

His voice was as soft as the night. "Count on it. See you in the morning."

By the time Rachel got inside, Sally had made a bed for herself on the floor in the main room. The smothering woman was bound and determined to have the final word on everything. Though Rachel loved her dearly, she'd let Sally know come morning she could care for herself. When she wasn't so weary.

She went to sleep with warmth in her heart and the memory of Heath's kiss.

Wonder of wonders, she beat Sally up at daylight. She'd awakened with the urge to watch the sun rise over the lake. Quickly dressing, she tiptoed to the door. Silently pulling it open, she almost fell headlong over Heath.

He looked up from the bed he'd made on the wooden porch. Jax had curled up beside him. Heath blinked, rubbing his eyes. "You're up mighty early, Miss Rachel."

"What are you doing? Did you sleep here last night?"

His crooked grin disarmed her. "You weren't supposed to catch me. I meant to be up and have the evidence put away by the time you awoke."

"Why on earth are you sleeping in front of my door?"

A sheepish grin gave him a boyish air. "Wanted to make sure you were safe," he growled. "I don't want anything to happen to you."

"For pity's sake. I'm able to care for myself now, Heath Lassiter."

"Yes, so you keep saying."

"And I've got to learn to handle my own affairs. You've got to let me make my own mistakes and take my lumps. I mean it. I'm tired of you wrapping me in layers upon layers of downy goose feathers, afraid I'll stub a toe or get a hangnail."

Just then Sally joined them on the porch. "What are you doing here, Heath? Did you think I couldn't watch after Rachel?"

Good grief. It was doubly bad when they both got it in their heads she wouldn't survive without their watchful eyes. Rachel turned on her heel and marched back into the house. Enjoying the sunrise would most definitely have to wait until her two wardens left.

Her thoughts turned to going to the barn for her father's metal box. At last, she'd look inside and find out if her hunches were right.

After breakfast was out of the way, Heath rose. "Are you ready, Rachel?"

"Yes, please. I have to find it."

With Jax at her side, she matched her stride with Heath's and went inside the barn. She glanced around. "Do you see the things from the root cellar?"

"There's something stacked against the wall. Maybe that's them," he answered.

Only it wasn't. They tried two more stacks, and she was losing hope.

"Maybe in the loft?" she asked.

"I doubt it. They wouldn't have wanted to tote something so heavy up the ladder."

Finally, she spotted them inside one of the horse stalls.

"There!" She hurried to them weak with relief. But now that she'd found them, she hesitated. Truth was, she didn't want to confirm what she suspected. Maybe best to not know. She chewed her lip.

"Get it over with," Heath murmured, rubbing her back.

"I know." She took a deep breath then took the key she'd found in her father's pocket after he passed and slid it into the padlock. Rachel's gaze met Heath's. "Will you open it?"

When he did, they found four burlap bags emblazoned with Wells Fargo in big letters.

Rachel's fingers shook so badly she couldn't remove the twine securing the top of one. Heath undid it for her, and she stared at paper money plus gold and silver coins galore.

Even more surprising was the big array of jewelry—rings, necklaces, hair ornaments. All manner of men's and women's timepieces her father had stolen.

"Oh no!" Her heart plummeted to her stomach like a rock as the truth sank in. She pulled a wanted poster from under one of the bags and stared at the crude drawing of her father with his name in a bold headline and a ten-thousand-dollar reward offered. She whispered, "I really am an outlaw's daughter."

"Appears that way."

"Part of me always knew. Whoever burned the house was looking for this. Put it back and lock the lid. I don't want to look at it. This isn't mine and I want no part of it. Stick it back in the root cellar. It's as dirty and ugly as my father."

"Think about that a minute. Someone burned your house before while looking for it. Do you want them to burn it again?"

Rachel wrung her hands. This was worse than she'd imagined. "You're right. Okay, load it up and take it to your barn. I have to return it though as soon as I can."

"I understand and would share those feelings if it were me."

"Don't say a word of this to Sally," she begged. "Keep it between us."

He brushed her cheek with a knuckle. "You don't have to ask." Heath shut the lid and locked it then hid it beneath a mound of hay. "I'll be back for it with a wagon later."

As they turned to go back to the house, Rachel spied one of Alice's ragdolls, lying on a low shelf. A sob caught in her throat. Alice always had a doll in her arms. A sob escaped as she clutched it to her and kept walking.

"That your sister's?" Heath asked.

The big lump made it hard to talk so Rachel nodded and they moved on.

With luck, Sally was outside. Once the padlocked box was safely out of sight, Rachel threw herself into mindless chores so she wouldn't have to think. Sally went with Heath to fetch her goats and chickens back home. The bull would stay with Heath for a while as per their agreement.

They returned with a wagon around noon and Rachel kept Sally busy while Heath loaded the strongbox. She breathed a sigh of relief that it would soon be gone.

She was relaxing under a big cottonwood tree with Heath and Sally when Tillie came.

"Join us for some fresh lemonade," Rachel said. "Sally bought some lemons from the trading post. It's rare to get some."

Jax raised to look and yawn then lay back down.

"I can't resist." Tillie climbed from her horse and looped the reins around a branch. "How are things? The house looks great. Very welcoming."

"I'm trying to give it that feel. We just finished bringing my animals back home."

Tillie accepted a glass of lemonade. "I figured as much."

"What brings you out our way, Miss Gregory?" Heath rose to offer her the empty nail keg he'd been sitting on. Rachel liked how he always tried to see to another's comfort. That was the mark of a good man.

In fact, if not for his annoying habit of taking over her life, he'd be awfully close to perfect. Everyone, it seemed, had flaws and maybe that was a rule of some kind.

Thanking Heath, Tillie perched on the nail keg. "When my problems start to strangle me, I like to get on my mule and ride. I just happened to end up here."

"I'm glad you did," Rachel said quietly. "Is there anything I can help you with?"

"My problems are just more of the same, I'm afraid. Nothing worth bothering you over."

Rachel wished she could be more like her ebony-haired friend whose pretty dark eyes belied the fact that her life wasn't the easy one she let on. Tillie never let her troubles get her down. She seemed to take what came and persevered as best she could.

"How's Yancy today?"

Tillie's light laugh was nice. "He's a little down in his get-along as he's fond of saying. I guess it's to be expected. After all, he's about to celebrate his sixtieth birthday."

"You don't say?" Heath chuckled. "Yancy can still work circles around me. I think I need to pay him a visit. It's been far too long."

"I didn't know you and Yancy are friends." Tillie took a sip of her lemonade. "He's never said anything."

"Yancy taught me a lot about ranching after my parents were killed. I doubt we'd have survived without his help. He treated me like a son until one day it all changed and I never knew why." A pained look filled Heath's gray eyes. Rachel wondered what he'd been about to say. He handed his lemonade glass to her. "It's time I headed home to do chores. You coming, Sally?"

"I'll be along directly," Sally said in her booming voice.

"Now, I'm sure Miss Rachel and Miss Tillie would probably like to visit. And we have things to take care of at the ranch."

Sally eased her bulk up. "We do for a fact. I'll be back later, Rachel."

"No, please. I'll be fine. I need—" Rachel paused, hoping to escape this current arrangement without hard feelings. Her gaze flickered to Heath waiting. "Lord knows, I'd hate to sound ungrateful, but I have to have some time to myself."

"Now, that's the last thing you need. I'll be back by suppertime," Sally said forcefully.

"Thank you, but no. Please." Rachel hadn't meant to sound so rude, but she'd had quite enough smothering.

Sally wore a puzzled expression. It was probably the first time anyone had stood up to her. "Well, if you insist."

"I do." Rachel hugged the hefty woman.

Heath looked from one to the other. "We have to respect and give Rachel her privacy."

"Thank you both for all you've done and are still doing." Rachel released a breath she'd been holding.

"We couldn't let you go through this alone," Sally said. "We care about you."

"If you need anything, anything at all, you know where I am," Heath said softly, taking Rachel's hand. "Just promise you'll lock your door. I don't want anything to happen to you."

For a moment, she thought he'd kiss her and her heart fluttered. To her disappointment, the moment quickly passed.

"I'll be fine. Please don't worry about me."

Sally went into the house and came back with the makings

of her pallet. Rachel watched Heath help his sister up onto the wagon seat. He tied his horse to the back and they slowly headed up the canyon trail.

"They're really nice people," Tillie remarked.

"There's no disputing that." Rachel just wished she knew how to convince them she wasn't as helpless as she seemed. "I hope I didn't sound ungrateful for all they've done."

"It didn't sound that way to me. Wasn't Heath's statement about knowing Yancy a bit odd though?" Tillie gathered up the lemonade while Rachel collected the glasses. "It's not like Yancy to have overlooked mentioning him all these years."

Rachel walked toward the house with Tillie. "I just wonder what could've happened between them?"

"I don't know but you can bet I'll ask Yancy about it."

They ate lunch and made plans for the following day. They'd bake more bread for Mr. Singer and start churning the butter.

It was late afternoon by the time Tillie left for home.

With no sign yet of Sally returning, Rachel breathed a sigh of relief. It appeared the woman just may have listened for once.

The clock's loud ticking now filled the house. This was the first time she'd been truly alone since the day she laid Alice to rest beneath the soil. How she ached for the child. She sat down in the rocker, holding the rag doll.

Alice's tiny voice flew from her memory of the day she died. "Love you, Chel."

She never could say Rachel, but it didn't matter. Fear had clouded the girl's eyes as she'd clutched Rachel's hand. "Don't leave me. I scared."

"I won't, honey. I'll be right here." But Rachel had closed

her eyes to rest them and went to sleep. When she woke up, it was too late. Alice was gone.

Who does that? Rachel wiped the tears from her face and hugged the rag doll. She finally rose and set about busying herself in the kitchen, preparing something for supper.

Life had to go on whether she liked it or not.

CHAPTER NINE

The strongbox occupied Rachel's thoughts as she made herself an unappetizing meal of cold egg between a dry biscuit. What a relief to have it gone from her land. If only she'd never seen it.

The contents of that box had bound her to things she wanted no part of.

Her mind drifted back to earlier days and how her father had become obsessed with keeping everyone away. He'd been as cold and mean as his first wife, Rachel's real mother. She'd never really known a mother's love until Jane came into her life. There had been none quite like stoic gentle Jane, forced into a marriage she didn't want. Still, she had a mother's touch when fever raged or in the dead of night when nightmares haunted.

She didn't know how long she sat at the kitchen table, motionless and morose. The food she'd fixed still untouched.

When she first heard the cries, the shadows had begun to

lengthen, and the first purple rays of twilight drifted over the canyon.

At first, the sounds were very faint, gradually becoming more insistent.

A whippoorwill called as it probably settled down for the night and an owl hooted nearby.

But the cries persisted. Curious, she rose and walked to the door. Seeing nothing, she decided she must have imagined it.

Jax whimpered and pressed his cold nose to her hand.

Maybe it was Jane crying for her from beyond the grave.

But the cries were young. Alice?

Everything stilled inside her. Her palms grew moist and her heart pounded.

Alice had good reason to haunt her. Rachel's throat constricted and her mouth got as dry as cotton. She'd never told Alice the truth. She should've told her.

Rachel dabbed at her forehead with the hem of her apron and stepped outside.

Maybe she'd been a bit hasty in practically ordering the Lassiters from her land. What would it have hurt if they'd stayed a few more nights with her? After all, she'd have nothing but a burned-out hulk of a house if not for them. Or much of anything else for that matter.

With Jax by her side, Rachel took a few tentative steps away from the house. The cries came again and definitely from the direction of the row of graves.

The dog left her side and darted ahead.

With trembling legs, she crept toward the new mounds of dirt. As she drew closer, she could make out a woven basket sitting on top of Alice's grave.

Barking, Jax raced ahead, sniffing all around.

Reaching the mysterious object, she stared down at the tightly wrapped bundle that was nestled inside.

She sucked in a quick breath.

A tiny baby.

A note lay on top of the squirming, crying form. It consisted of only four words written in neat penmanship.

Her name is Eden.

As Rachel looked around, hoping to see who had left the child, she spied a beautiful white dove on a juniper branch. Her skin prickled. She'd never seen one in the canyon before. Was it a sign? The bird lifted its wings and took flight. Though too dark to see well, Rachel scanned the area for the person who left the infant. There was nothing but shadows.

Lifting the basket, she hurried into the house. Setting it on the table, she carefully removed the baby, cradling the small form to her.

Eden, the note had said.

"Hello, baby Eden," she crooned. "Where did you come from? Who is your mother?"

And why had the infant been left by the graves? And what did the white dove have to do with it?

What if she hadn't heard the cries? What if some wild animal had come along and carried the infant off? And why leave the infant here? A million questions raced through her mind. Jax too it seemed. The dog didn't quite know what to do. He started to lie down then stood, sniffed the baby, and whined.

A piece of old quilt wrapped the tiny form. The square section was tattered in places but clean. Baby Eden stared up with round blue eyes. She had stopped crying when Rachel picked her up. The smattering of hair on top of the baby's head looked to be quite fair by lamplight.

Laying the babe on the table, Rachel removed the quilted covering. The child wore a crudely made gown fashioned from an old flour sack. Lifting the hem, she glanced at the cord that hadn't even started to dry up, telling her Eden was only a day or two old. A quick glance discovered a wet diaper. Jax watched her every move with dark, soulful eyes.

With the infant secure in one arm, she searched for something to make a dry diaper from. Moments later she located a clean dishtowel that would have to do for now.

Putting Eden on the only bed, Rachel removed the wet clothing. She lifted the crudely tied cord out of the way. Quickly changing the diaper, she wrapped Eden in a soft towel. It'd do for the moment.

Holding the infant girl to her chest, a powerful love came over her. They were two people alone in the world, but they had each other.

What had happened to the mother? Was she unable to care for her child? Sick?

Eden let out a soft mewling cry and sucked a fist.

"You must be hungry, my darling. Thank God for the goats."

Rachel carefully laid the tiny girl in the middle of the bed and hurried to the spring house for the crock of milk from the day's milking. Next, she put her mind to thinking of how best to get the fresh milk into the child. If only she had a bottle.

Then she suddenly remembered that Jane had fashioned a bottle to feed the baby goat kids that had lost their mothers— stretching a rubber nipple over a blue Hostetter's Stomach Bitters bottle. It had worked wonderfully well with the goats. Hopefully it would for Eden.

She put the goat's milk on the table and sprinted to the barn with Jax right beside her. Lighting a lantern, she held it up high as she tried to think of where the bottle might be. Jax sniffed at everything and barked at the cat at home with the hay and horses.

Scanning the area where the tack was stored, she spied the blue bottle on a shelf. It was dusty and covered in cobwebs, but a good washing would fix that.

A scant half hour later, she sat in the rocker with Eden in her arms. The baby sucked greedily on the nipple making little contented sounds as the warm milk filled her belly. Rachel's heart went out to the tiny babe that someone had apparently dumped with no more regard than a shoe that had grown too small.

Eden was a throwback. A child no one wanted.

Whoever had left her had discarded her as though she meant nothing at all. But then—maybe desperation had driven the person to leave Eden. She knew a little about that. She would stop judging the mother until she found out more.

Why had the mother left Eden here of all places? They were so isolated.

Tears suddenly filled Rachel's eyes. Right then and there she made a vow that the child would never know the way she came into her care.

Kissing the tiny forehead, Rachel found a joy she hadn't had since Alice died.

In each person's life there were moments that are meant for them to remember forever, in the tiniest detail, smell, and shade. Finding Eden had been such a moment. She remembered the deepening purple sky, the sound of the water lapping gently against the bank of the lake, the lonely whippoorwill's call, and the fragrant patch of wildflowers that grew near the house.

She put Eden on her shoulder to burp her. A peace drifted over her like soft, warm fleece. Her heart swelled and the wish to die that had been with her since she buried little Alice suddenly left. She had a purpose. Someone needed her and that felt good.

The next morning Rachel woke early and dressed. She had much to do. Her gaze found the sleeping babe lying next to her. The infant had awakened several times during the night but had gone back to sleep after getting milk into her small stomach. She was a good baby, never crying unless she needed something.

Today Rachel would look for the trunk of baby things of Alice's. There were gowns, blankets, and diapers. Everything Eden needed. The last time she'd seen the trunk had been when Papa had moved it from the house to the barn. And he'd also stored Alice's cradle out there. Seemed as though everything wound up in the barn when it outgrew its usefulness. One thing about it, Isaac Malloy hadn't thrown anything away. He'd been too busy.

How fortunate the barn hadn't burned. Rachel rose and dressed. She could probably milk the goats before Eden awakened.

She opened the front door and again nearly stumbled over Heath Lassiter. Busy folding a blanket, he had the grace to blush. It was clear he'd spent another night sleeping in front of her door.

"Good morning, Rachel."

His quick grin that showed the whiteness of his teeth sent flutters through her chest. And for a moment it felt as though she was hurtling off a high cliff.

"It's a beautiful day," he said.

"Good morning, Heath."

"You're not mad?"

"That you spent the night here against my wishes? I'm

quite perturbed, but not angry."

He raised a dark eyebrow. "You feeling all right?"

"Never better."

"Something has changed. Would it have something to do with the cries I heard coming from inside the house last night?" He tried to peer past her.

"It would. I have something to show you. Follow me."

She led him into her bedroom and pointed to the bed. "Someone left her out on the graves late yesterday."

"You don't know who did it?"

"No." She told him about the note lying on top of the babe's blanket. "That's all I know. The babe isn't more than two or three days old."

Eden opened her eyes and yawned. Heath picked her up as if she might break. "Hey there. You're a mighty pretty little thing. You're going to have so much love you won't care how you came to be here."

Rachel's throat burned seeing the gentle care he took of the baby girl and his crooning words. There was something in the way Heath's big hands wrapped around the tiny form so protectively that deeply touched her.

He lifted his gaze. "I'm constantly amazed at the working of God. Remember me telling you there's a season and a time to every purpose under the heavens?'"

"I recall. What are you trying to say?"

"I think maybe this sweet babe is the reason God left you behind when he took the rest of your family." He kissed the baby's cheek.

Rachel stiffened. "How do you figure that?"

"Eden would need you, so He left you here to care for her."

She let Heath's words sink in. Could he possibly be right?

"Maybe. But if he cared so much, why let this happen to such an innocent babe? Why punish her?"

"When a high wind knocks baby birds from their nest and dashes them to the ground, do you think God is punishing them?"

"Of course not."

"All living things have a season. A time to live and time to die. This is Eden's time to live and there's a purpose for her being here in your house. In your care."

"It's nothing but a coincidence," she insisted.

"I don't believe that. Sometimes when things happen, we don't know why. It's often long after the fact that we can see the intricate workings in our lives. Like now. It's very plain that you're needed here on this earth. I don't know why you refuse to see that."

Could it be true she was needed? "When I found Eden, I saw a white dove sitting on a juniper branch. I don't know what that meant but I think it was important for some reason."

A look of wonder came over him. "It was a sign, an old symbol of hope."

His words shook her, but she wasn't about to let him know. She wasn't sure she wanted to let her anger go yet. If she did, she'd be forced to change her opinions. Her father had been despicable, treating her and Jane so badly.

She still felt the sting of his words. "You asked for this," he'd said following her abduction and return. "You're nothing to me. You are just something men use. I should've let them kill you."

Ice knotted in her stomach. She waved an arm. "We could stand here swapping beliefs until we turn blue in the face, and it won't change a thing. I don't know about all this, but I do know I need to milk my goats. Eden will be hungry soon."

"Here, you take her, and I'll milk the goats in exchange for some hot coffee."

"You have a deal, Heath Lassiter."

She took the child and followed him to the door. He stopped to pick up his battered hat lying on top of his bedroll and adjusted it on his head.

With long strides he covered the ground to the goat pen.

The man who had such strength in his convictions sure cut a nice figure with his long legs and broad shoulders.

He loved babies. And he was a good secret-keeper.

If she could only bring herself to reveal her shame and the fact she was too damaged for a good, kind, decent man.

CHAPTER TEN

"I'll take the little one off your hands." Sally's blustery statement sent alarm rushing through Rachel that afternoon. "You're in no shape to tend to her."

"No thanks," Rachel announced firmly. "She was put in my care, and I'll see to her." She prayed she didn't sound rude. She hadn't meant it that way. Sally Lassiter was like a bull that charged at anything that fluttered in the wind. Yet, Rachel knew deep down underneath all those rough, jagged edges lay a sensitive caring woman.

Sally sniffed and finished folding the last of the baby clothes that Rachel had found in the old trunk and washed. "Well, I just thought you might want me since I'm older and more experienced. I didn't mean to offend you."

"You didn't." Rachel put her arms around the stout woman. "I think of you as an older sister. You and Heath have become very special to me."

Concern replaced Sally's hurt. "Thank you, dear. I feel the same about you."

Glad she handled that well, Rachel stepped around Sally and picked up the stack of clean laundry. "I appreciate your help. Had I been doing it by myself it would've taken all day." Rachel lovingly smoothed each wrinkle from a tiny gown that Alice had once worn.

Dear, precious Alice. She'd never done a single bad thing in her short life. But the more Rachel thought about Heath's comparison to the baby birds that the wind blew out of their nest the more it made sense. Surely God didn't punish innocent animals and babies.

Still, she was another story.

Blackness and evil had touched her life through no fault of her own. She couldn't choose her father but was stuck with his legacy. Whatever punishment lay in store for her she well deserved since she now knew full well she had to pay for the sins of her father and would be followed by the reputation he'd left. He'd taken every opportunity to tell her she was no good. Nothing but a whore.

The abduction and rape hadn't been her fault. She'd fought her attackers until they'd overpowered her and fighting back only made them meaner.

Rachel shook herself from the nightmare. "Sally, who do you suppose left Eden here?"

"Don't rightly know. She might belong to one of the ranchers' daughters. Or one of the Quaker women over in Estacado. It's surely a puzzle."

Just then Eden let out a cry to let Rachel know she'd awakened from her nap and was starving.

Sally took a step toward the bedroom then stopped and turned around. "You'd best go see to her. You're the only mother the poor little thing has now."

Rachel fed and changed the infant. Each time she held the precious bundle her love grew.

All of sudden she froze. What if whoever left her came back for her? It would kill Rachel to have to give up the baby. In fact, she wouldn't. She'd hide the child first.

She laid Eden back in the wooden cradle she'd found in the barn and tiptoed to the door. Heath and Sally sat at the kitchen table talking.

Rachel didn't know why, but she kept out of sight, listening.

"Sally, you've got to stop being so headstrong," Heath said. "Just leave Rachel be. She needs this baby to care for right now. It's the best thing in the world."

"I'm just saying she may not be in the right frame of mind to tackle a child. She's fragile and I still think Eden would be better off with us."

"God knows what Rachel needs and he sent this baby to her. Are you saying you know more than our Heavenly Father?"

Sally released a huff. "Don't be silly."

"Then that's the end of it." Heath rose to pour himself a cup of coffee.

Rachel eased the bedroom door open and closed it again to make some noise before she entered the room and just in time to see Tillie ride into the yard. Excited, she opened the door to greet her friend. She had much to tell.

Upon Tillie's arrival Sally and Heath said their goodbyes.

Heath held her hand for a long moment beside the wagon. "Since my sleeping in front of your door bothers you, I won't do it again. But if you need anything, no matter how small, you come for me."

He kissed the baby. Then before he said a final goodbye, he

ran the back of knuckle gently across Rachel's cheek. "I care for you, beautiful angel."

For a moment Rachel thought he would kiss her despite Sally and Tillie watching. But the moment passed. As he helped Sally into the wagon then climbed up himself, an unexpected disappointment swept through her.

When she could breathe again, she turned to her friend. "Come into the house, Tillie. I'll tell you all about Eden."

Rachel and Tillie spent the afternoon talking, baking bread, and acting like fools over the baby.

"You've got even more reason now to get some money coming in," Tillie pointed out.

"That's true. I no longer have just myself to consider." She was going to do the very best she knew how to raise Eden and find redemption somehow. Someway.

RACHEL OCCUPIED HEATH'S thoughts all the way home and into the night as he lay in his bed. It was the first time he'd slept in his room in the barn since Rachel moved into her new house.

But sleep refused to come. He was worried about Rachel's safety. Even though he hadn't seen any more evidence of digging, he couldn't shake the feeling that something troubling loomed on the horizon.

It frustrated him to see trouble coming like a blinding twisting sandstorm that cared not what lay in its path and being unable to prevent it from destroying everything.

The simple fact was he loved Rachel and baby Eden. Loved them with all of his being.

"And she saw the white dove too," he whispered to himself. God had a plan.

Would she but say the word he'd take them both in his arms and protect them to his very last breath.

But how did a man protect someone he loved when she refused to let him?

The way he felt about Rachel Malloy could most likely be seen as irrational by some people. Truth was, she made him crazy. The pretty woman was mulish by half, but she was also nurturing, understanding, and drove him to distraction.

A deep sigh escaped him. He punched his pillow and turned over.

For two cents he'd saddle up and ride over to her place just to make sure everything was all right. But he'd given his word, and the word of a Lassiter was his bond.

Unless breaking it was in Rachel's best interests. Of course, then it was different. He reached for his trousers.

RACHEL HAD JUST doused the lamp when a knock came at the door. Jax, curled up beside Eden's cradle, growled low in his throat and leaped to his feet. Terror gripped her and thoughts of her abduction sprang into mind. She grabbed her shawl and threw it over her gown. Striking a match, she re-lit the lamp. Jax sprang to the door. She was grateful for the dog's presence. His fierce barking deafened her.

"Who is it?" she yelled through the locked wooden door. "What do you want?"

Jax leaped onto the door, baring his teeth.

"Beggin' your pardon, ma'am. Don't mean to frighten you. Is this the Malloy house?" The voice belonged to a man.

"Yes. May I help you?"

"Might you be Rachel Malloy?"

Surprise flittered along her spine. Who would come calling in the dead of night? She prayed that whoever it was hadn't come for Eden. She couldn't give her up. She just couldn't.

Not without a fight.

She tried to stop her trembling. "My dog will tear into you, mister."

"Can you hold him? I don't wanna get bitten."

Throwing the bolt on the door, she took a firm hold on Jax and opened it a crack, shining the lamp on the caller. The shaft of light illuminated a man of middling age, well past his prime on her stoop. His grizzled features sported several days of beard growth and streaks of silver created paths through hair that was the color of worn saddle leather.

"I'm Rachel. State your name and your business, please."

"Zeb Thacker, ma'am. I'm your uncle." He ran his hand through his thick shock of hair. "I apologize for the late hour. I've traveled a far piece."

The hackles on Jax's back rose. She wondered what the dog was sensing. Leery, she considered slamming and bolting the door. "I don't know who you are, mister, but you're mistaken. I have no kin. Now, be on your way or I'll turn my dog loose."

"Wait a minute, ma'am."

It occurred to her that quite possibly she was again hasty in insisting that she could take care of herself. If only she hadn't sent Heath and Sally home.

"Now, ma'am, I understand. I really do. But, truth of the matter is I'm too tired to go another step. If I could—"

"The lady said no," interrupted a firm, male voice that could only belong to Heath. She opened the crack wider and sure enough Heath stepped from the shadows. He pointed a rifle at the stranger. She could've hugged him. "Now, if you've got good sense you'll get on your horse and ride on, late hour or not."

The stranger's eyes widened, and he held up both hands. "I didn't mean the lady no harm."

"Then you should've come in the daylight," Heath snapped.

"I can sleep in the barn and clear up everything tomorrow," the stranger suggested, a hopeful tone in his voice. "I won't be any trouble."

Rachel opened the door wide. "Heath, may I have a word with you?"

"Sure." He turned to the stranger. "Stay right where you are." Heath lowered the rifle and joined Rachel inside the door. "Are you having second thoughts?"

She chewed her bottom lip. "I can't turn him away. What if he really is my uncle? I'd give anything to have a family again. Maybe he really is who he says."

He gently touched her cheek. "I reckon it won't hurt if he sleeps in the barn and we can sort things out in the morning. But I'm staying to make sure you and Eden are safe. Just so we're clear on the matter."

Relief swept through her. She patted his chest. "Thank you, Heath. I wouldn't have it any other way."

"Good. Now, close this door and bolt it. I'll see to your guest."

"Goodnight, Heath. I'll have coffee ready at daybreak."

"I'll need it. Get some rest now. You're safe."

And that's what she did. Her head barely touched the pillow before she was sound asleep. It was as if unseen arms had slid around her and protected them from harm.

The next morning the stranger who'd called himself Zeb Thacker sat with Heath at her breakfast table. Rachel tried not to stare, but she found herself desperately searching his face for any sign of recognition.

She wanted, needed to believe.

"Mr. Thacker, I don't believe I've ever seen you before."

"Well, I should hope not. You weren't even born when my sister, your mother, left Tennessee and came to Texas."

Rachel handed him the plate of biscuits. "Pardon my asking, but why are you here?"

"Word reached me that your father died. I didn't know that all the rest had died too until I got here. You're all alone and in need of kith and kin. I can help you."

Heath frowned and pushed back his plate. "I've been taking care of Rachel. I hate that you've come so far for nothing."

"That's right neighborly of you, Lassiter, but friends can't take the place of family."

The two men glared at each other over their plate of eggs and flapjacks. For a moment she was afraid they'd come to blows.

"I never knew my mother's maiden name," she murmured.

"Stranger, what proof can you give her that Thacker is indeed her mother's family name?" Heath asked.

Zeb's eyes shifted to a spot on the floor. It took him a long minute to answer. "Well, sir, I have a Bible that Rachel's grandmother wrote everything down in. It's in my saddlebags."

"I think Rachel would like to see that if you don't mind," Heath said, a measure of steel in his words.

"Sure thing. As soon as I'm done here."

"Thank you, Mr. Thacker." Rachel offered him another biscuit. She'd breathe much easier once she saw proof of his wild claims. For all she knew he could be making up the whole thing. And she could tell that had occurred to Heath as well. "Tell me, what was my mother like as a girl growing up? How did she occupy herself? What did she like? Do you know her favorite color?"

"Hold on there, missy. That's a lot of questions."

"Can't you satisfy my curiosity?"

The footprints in the ash in her burned kitchen swept into her mind. She had to move slowly on this sudden turn of events.

"Well, yeah. But give me time to get my bearings." Zeb made a move to rise.

Jax got to his feet and growled low.

The color left Zeb's face and he eased back onto the chair. Thank goodness for Heath and his watchful eye. She'd stop complaining and keep her eyes open for that white dove, hoping it would hang around.

Heath was convinced it was a sign. Rachel not so much. The man carried his convictions deep inside and couldn't be dissuaded by anything.

And he could kiss the daylights out of a girl.

So why was she refusing to marry him? It was getting harder to remember.

CHAPTER ELEVEN

*D*awn broke over the canyon, lifting the gloom of night. Heath sat at the table eating breakfast and watching Rachel. She had to be tired since Eden had awakened every three hours. But she didn't seem to mind. A glorious smile never left her face.

"I reckon I'll go get that Bible now." Zeb Thacker gave Heath a nod and pushed back from the table.

A growl rumbled in Jax's throat. The dog plain didn't like the man. And more than once this morning Jax had bared his teeth and nipped at his legs. In Heath's estimation animals were good judges of character, sensing things people couldn't.

Heath's gaze followed the man to the door. Like Jax, he didn't trust Zeb either. How would they know if that was the actual family Bible? Could easily be made up to support a story.

Maybe it was the way the man had appeared in the dead of night. No one did that unless they were desperate or hurt and he appeared neither.

Or maybe it was his shifty gaze that wouldn't quite meet Heath's.

And maybe it was the fact that Zeb had brought only what fit in his saddlebags. Kinda strange to come all the way from Tennessee with no supplies for cooking along the trail, extra clothes, and only one canteen of water.

The story that the man had had the presence of mind to throw in a Bible of all things when he'd set out was just a little too shady.

Questions swirled in Heath's mind. No matter how he looked at the situation, it just didn't add up.

Whatever the truth really was, Heath knew Zeb would bear watching. Closely.

Eden began to wail from the bedroom. Rachel set down the dishes she'd picked up. "Looks like duty calls."

"You go tend to the little princess and I'll clear the table." Heath stacked the dirty plates. It wouldn't be his first time to wash dishes and clean the kitchen. Sally never tolerated him not pulling his weight in every area. "You change her, and I'll get the bottle ready."

Rachel wiped her hands on her apron. "Thank you, Heath."

Heath had the table cleared and a bottle of goat's milk ready when she returned with the baby in her arms.

There was no sign of Zeb and his convenient Bible.

"Believe I'll go see what's keeping Thacker." He lifted his hat from a hook beside the door. Jax whined and scratched to go out. "Let's go, boy."

Heath stepped into the bright sunlight and didn't see Thacker anywhere. Deciding maybe the man was in the barn, he walked around the house to it. But the man wasn't in the loft where he'd slept.

Jax's bark alerted him. He emerged into the sunshine to see

Zeb rounding the corner of the barn. The man didn't have anything in his hands—much less the Bible he'd gone to fetch.

"Where you been, Thacker?"

"Nowhere in particular. Although I don't see it's any business of yours, I went for a walk around the property. Wanted to get a feel for the land."

Heath's eyes narrowed. Who scoped out property that didn't belong to him. If Zeb didn't produce proof he was Rachel's uncle, it didn't make any difference. The man wouldn't be around long enough to get a feel for anything.

"If I rightly recall, you went to get the proof of your claims for Rachel," Heath reminded him.

"Oh yes, that I was." Zeb ran a hand over his graying whiskers. "I near forgot. I'll just scoot up to the loft for that Bible."

An hour later, after Rachel had fed Eden and gotten the little darling back to sleep, she sat around the kitchen table with Heath and Zeb. Rachel held Zeb's Bible, reading the handwritten notations in it. Heath waited for the verdict.

Finally, she glanced up. "Ruth Thacker. I never knew what name my mother was born with. But then I didn't know a whole lot about her."

Heath tried to temper the misgivings he had about Zeb Thacker. Hope began to settle in Rachel's pale green eyes. She wanted to believe as desperately as she needed to breathe. How could he take that from her?

"So, what do you think?" Heath asked when he could stand it no longer.

"I need a private word with you, Heath?"

Zeb stood. "You two talk. I'll just take a walk down to the lake."

Once the man hurriedly closed the door behind him to put

distance between him and Jax, Rachel dragged in a ragged breath. "I don't know. I can't be certain if he's my uncle or not. He could've stolen this Bible."

"Exactly." Heath rose and put a hand on her shoulder. "I wish I could help you. You'll just have to trust your instincts."

"I used to but now I find it hard after all the death and facing the new changes by myself. I admit it's frightening."

The anger in her tone saddened Heath. He'd thought she was moving beyond that. "You're never alone, even on the darkest, coldest night."

"We've gnawed all the meat off that bone, Heath." She snapped Zeb's Bible closed. "You don't have to tell me what you think about Zeb because I can see it in your eyes. You don't trust the man. But the scribblings in this Bible appear to be genuine. To me at least. I want to believe Zeb Thacker is my uncle." Her voice dropped to a whisper. "I need family, someone to belong to. I have to give him a chance."

"Then, let him stay for a while until you figure it out, but you just need to be careful."

Rachel stood, giving him a shaky smile. "I will. I'm prepared that this may not work out and can always send him packing. Thacker may not look like much, but I yearn for family."

Heath also got to his feet. "I understand. But you have Eden."

"Yes, I have my Eden. My family is growing by the day." She bit her lip. "I don't know what I'd do if someone came to claim that sweet baby."

"Don't borrow trouble," he warned softly.

"It's the last thought before I go to sleep and the first thought when I wake up."

He smoothed back her hair. "Dwelling on it will solve

nothing. Now, tell me what I can do to help you before I head back to the ranch."

"That's another thing. With Uncle Zeb here now to help take care of the place, there's no need to worry about me. Uncle Zeb will help with the livestock and do some of the chores."

That remained to be seen. So far, the man hadn't shown much affinity toward work, leaving the egg-gathering and goat-milking to Heath. Thacker hadn't even seen fit to feed his own horse much less Rachel's.

No matter what Rachel said, Heath wasn't about to leave her to Thacker's care.

Not even if it made her mad enough to chew the hide right off a mangy buffalo.

"Uncle Zeb, do you want to ride with Tillie, Eden, and me to the trading post?" Rachel asked. Five days had passed since her uncle had shown up.

Zeb looked up from the shade of the cottonwood tree where he was stretched out with his hands behind his head. "I don't reckon so, my dear."

"Is there something I can pick up for you then?"

"As a matter of fact, I could sure use a bag of Bull Durham. I've been out for a few days and have a powerful need for a smoke."

"I'll see what I can do." Rachel handed the baby up to Tillie and climbed into the wagon box. "If you don't mind, do you think you could fix the hole in the chicken coop? I've seen coyote signs around the place."

"Sure thing, Rachel. As soon as I get my nap out."

Jax snarled at her uncle as if to say the man had better get the lead out of his britches. She grabbed hold of the dog before he jumped right into the middle of him.

"Come on, Jax," she called. The animal leaped into the bed of the wagon but put his paws on the side of it with his teeth bared.

"I don't think that animal likes me much," Uncle Zeb muttered.

As the wagon rolled toward the trading post Tillie laughed. "I don't think he does either. How long is your uncle planning on staying?"

"He hasn't really said. Somehow I get the feeling that he doesn't have anywhere to go."

"He's not much for work, is he?" Tillie remarked.

"So far, he hasn't done much," she admitted ruefully. "Are you sure it's safe to go to the trading post?"

"I'm positive. Quit worrying."

Zeb Thacker had been there a full week and to Rachel's despair he hadn't been much help around the place. Sure, he seemed to have good intentions, but those intentions never fully translated into doing chores or helping with the animals.

And then there was his habit of mysteriously disappearing.

She didn't know where he went or for what reason. When she asked him about it, he simply said he liked to explore and often lost track of the time.

Tillie lifted Eden to her shoulder. "What about Heath? Have you seen him or Sally lately?"

"No, not very often. I told Heath there was no need to worry about me since I have Uncle Zeb now." But she knew he was continuing to keep an eye on them because she'd spied him up on the canyon rim one morning when she'd risen early to milk the goats.

"You two didn't have a quarrel, did you?"

"Nope."

"That's good."

"Why do you say that?"

"I happen to think you and Heath Lassiter make a handsome couple."

"Tillie Gregory! There is no couple." But Rachel colored, remembering the kiss in the moonlight down by the lake. Thank goodness no one knew about that but her and Heath.

"I think you protest too much. He's sure a handsome man. So tall and strong. And all that dark hair." Tillie grinned, her eyes twinkling, and Rachel realized her friend was teasing, probably just to get a rise out of her.

Just like a sister.

Lord, she missed her brothers who loved nothing better than to josh with her.

The rest of the trip passed quietly, each woman engrossed in her own thoughts. They pulled up in front of Singer's Trading Post and Rachel set the brake. The store was busier than usual with several buckboards and horses tied to the hitching rail in front.

Rachel was about to climb down when Heath strolled out of the post. Shadowed by the brim of his hat, his grin stretched from ear to ear.

An unexpected stirring made her stomach dip and for a moment she felt as though she'd been thrown from a horse.

She didn't know why seeing him made her so happy.

"What an unexpected pleasure." He helped Rachel down then hurried around to take Eden from Tillie. "I've missed you. And the little princess here."

Watching him holding the baby again made the back of her throat burn.

Heath was so big but the gentle care he took of the tiny babe who'd brought untold joy to her life always made her heart swell. She realized just how much she'd missed seeing him.

She reached for the basket full of saleable items from the wagon.

"How have things been with your uncle?" He held the door for her and Tillie.

Like he didn't know. Really. She'd seen him spying on them from the ridge.

"He's just fine." She knew she should've been more honest, but she felt an odd loyalty to the man who appeared to be her only kin. "He's still settling in."

"Reckon it takes some longer than others."

She couldn't resist a jab. "I saw you up on the canyon ridge a few days ago."

A sheepish grin formed. It was good to let the man know she'd caught him. And if she'd seen him that once, chances were he'd spied on them other times as well.

But somehow that fact didn't rile her now. It was nice to be looked after, especially when it was this handsome rancher doing the looking.

Heath adjusted Eden's blanket. "I was searching for some strays that wandered off."

"Did you find them?"

"Yep. Say, do you mind if Sally and I pay you a visit soon?"

"I'd like that." She set the basket of bread and fresh churned butter on the counter noticing the black-veiled Cora Quinlin coming from a back shelf filled with hats.

Heath handed the baby to Rachel. "Guess I'd best head home. We'll call on you in the morning."

Her gaze followed him out the door. Tomorrow wouldn't come soon enough.

It was strange how upset she'd gotten with him constantly underfoot. Only now she wanted him to be. There was no figuring out her fickle heart.

Cora Quinlin's black dress of stiff taffeta swished with each step as she strode from the back. The strange neighbor set flour and sugar on the counter with hands that appeared young. She was a slight woman with a confident stride. Rachel tried not to stare yet she wanted to find out what kind of person and how old Cora was. Someone entered the trading post and a draft from the open door ruffled the veil, revealing a firm neck. Cora's skin was supple, not old and wrinkly.

Curiosity burned. Eden didn't move a muscle when Rachel suddenly thrust out her hand. "Hello, Miss Quinlin. I'm Rachel Malloy and I've been wanting to meet you."

Cora took her palm for a brief shake. "I'm sorry for your troubles. My place is at the end of the canyon, but I saw smoke from your burning house and was glad you survived."

The woman's voice was young-sounding. She was probably near her and Tillie's age.

"Thank you," Rachel said smiling. "I'm finding life on my own scary but I'm doing better, thanks to the Lassiters. I'd like to have tea with you one day."

"I stay too busy for socializing," Cora said abruptly, handing the clerk some money.

Rebuffed by her attitude, Rachel took a step back. Clearly, Cora had little interest in being friends. Whatever the mysterious woman's secret was, she didn't plan on ever revealing it.

Rachel's gaze followed Cora to the door. "If you ever change your mind, please stop by. We'll get acquainted."

"Maybe someday I'll surprise you," Cora answered without turning. Then she stepped out into the sunlight.

But Rachel had a few answers to her questions at least and that would have to suffice.

CHAPTER TWELVE

There were fresh holes in places Rachel had never seen them when she and Tillie returned from the trading post. Gophers? Prairie dogs? Zeb? Jax hadn't dug them.

Once again, the man was nowhere to be seen. This was getting mighty tiresome. She was all for giving him a chance, but her patience was wearing thin.

Jax leaped out of the back of the wagon before she even set the brake. The dog took off like a shot, snarling and barking fit to wake the dead. She got a glimpse of black fur disappearing around the corner of the barn. Now what?

She held the baby while Tillie climbed down then handed Eden to her. "I'll be right back, Tillie. I want to see what Jax's after."

Her curiosity piqued, she followed after the dog.

At the back side of the barn, she saw her uncle standing some distance away. Zeb Thacker was engaged in a serious conversation with three rough looking men on horseback while trying to keep Jax from biting him.

Rachel whistled for the dog. Zeb turned and saw her and the three men on horseback quickly rode away. Jax gave chase but was soon left in the dust kicked up by the horses. The dog trotted back and she grabbed hold of him.

She didn't know what all that was about but was determined to find out.

"Who were those men?" she asked when Zeb came closer.

"Strangers. Didn't give their names."

"What did they want?"

"Just asking directions."

That was a bit odd. To her it looked as though they were having a disagreement about something. And he wouldn't meet her gaze. A threatening growl rumbled in Jax's throat.

A bit leery, Uncle Zeb fell into step with her. "How were things at the trading post?"

"Fine." Her answer was curt. She wanted her displeasure known. "I saw Heath Lassiter. He wanted to know if he and his sister could come visit. They'll be here tomorrow."

"That man hangs around far too much if you ask me."

"He's a very dear friend. I don't know what I'd have done without him and Sally. They've been of immense help." Jax stood at Rachel's side, straining against her grip.

"Your dog has something against me," Zeb growled, rubbing his whiskers.

What gave him the first clue?

"I've found him to be an excellent judge of character." She gave Jax's head a pat.

"That's what I'm afraid of," her uncle mumbled and shifted his weight.

What a strange thing to say. Rachel made up her mind to set things straight.

"Did you remember about my tobacco?" Zeb asked.

She faced him, her voice stern. "I did but it's going to have to last you a while. Don't make a habit of asking me."

"Oh, I won't. I'm going to get some money soon."

Rachel moved a little closer and smelled liquor on his breath. "I'm fed up with you, Uncle Zeb. I fill your belly and give you a place to sleep but you don't lift a finger to help around here. Mend your ways or else you can move on. Understand? The choice is yours."

Zeb nodded. "I reckon so. I do appreciate you letting me stay and all."

"Reflect that in some work then," she snapped.

"I hear you." Giving no clue as to his choice, Zeb set off around the house.

Tillie watched it all and smiled. "I didn't know how long it would take you but I'm glad you finally laid the law down. It was time." Tillie handed her the baby and reached for her horse's bridle. "I've got to head home, Rachel. I'll come back in a few days."

"We'll see if my uncle mends his ways, but I meant it." Rachel took her child, hugging her friend. "Thank you as always for your company. Be safe."

Eden woke up then and let out a cry.

Tillie laughed, mounting her horse. "The princess needs something."

Waving goodbye, Rachel turned toward the house and Jax looked up at her. He was covered in dirt. "Good job, boy. But you're a fine mess." Rachel pointed to the lake. "Go take a bath."

The dog gave a pitiful whine and looked longingly toward the house then turned and ran down to the water's edge, diving in. Sometimes she swore he was part human.

Uncle Zeb hurried to hold the door for her.

"What did you do while I was gone?" Rachel asked.

"Well, you know. A little of this and a bit of that."

"It smells like you've been drinking."

"That's crazy. Must be the stuff I put on my face after I shaved."

Likely story. She stared at his full beard and snorted. "I don't know what you shaved but it wasn't your face."

Where had he gotten the liquor? The nearest place was a tent saloon her brothers had frequented. Riled by the Quakers of Estacado after they refused to let him open up a saloon, a defiant man had pitched a tent outside the small community and brought in a load of liquor. Her brothers said the cowboys on all the nearby ranches eagerly kept the man in business. Uncle Zeb must've sneaked off there while she was gone.

What else was she going to discover about her only self-proclaimed kin? Were they all rotten to the core?

HEATH AND SALLY arrived the following morning right after breakfast. They'd barely dismounted before they started arguing over who was going to hold Eden first. You'd think they'd never seen a little one before.

Rachel sat at the table just finishing up giving the babe a bottle and laughed at the way the brother and sister took on. What a sight.

Sipping on a cup of coffee, Uncle Zeb frowned. "You won't catch me making a fool of myself."

Heath gave him a curious stare. "Why's that?"

"Me and babies don't get along."

Heath just shrugged and took Eden from Rachel. "I might've figured you'd have something against little Princess here. She's such a beautiful baby with her big blue eyes and fair hair. A regular little angel." He pulled out a chair from the table and made himself comfortable.

Rachel didn't miss the loving care Heath took of the child and it stirred her heart. She jumped up and began clearing the breakfast dishes, hoping she could swallow the lump in her throat before she tried to talk.

Sally stalked to the apron hanging on a nail and tied it around her. "The least I can do is help clean up these dishes." She sent Zeb a pointed stare and released an irritated huff. "Heath, you need to see to Rachel's chores. That is if you can lay Eden down long enough. Zeb, off your lazy butt and go help."

Her booming voice scared the baby and made her pucker up to cry.

"I'll get to them. Quit fretting."

Rachel put her hands on her hips. "Now, I'll have none of that. You came to visit, not do my chores."

"Well, I think I'll take a fishing pole and mosey down to the lake and catch some fish for supper," Uncle Zeb declared, rising from the table. "That was a mighty fine breakfast, Rachel."

Heath's eyes met Rachel's as the door closed behind her uncle. "Is he always like this?"

"What do you mean?"

"Shiftless. Lazy. You need someone who'll work, and Zeb Thacker just doesn't seem to want to do much of that." His voice was quiet but thick with disapproval.

"We had a talk, Uncle Zeb and me, and I laid down the law. I'm fed up with him. If he doesn't change, I'll wash my hands of him."

Sally relieved Heath of the baby. "I'll just put her down for a nap. She's half asleep."

When his sister moved off, Heath lifted an eyebrow. "I was wondering when you would see your uncle for who he is."

"Why does everyone say that?" Her voice lowered to a whisper. "I need family but there's a limit with how much I'll tolerate."

"I have faith in you." He rose and covered the space between them and gently touched her cheek. "I'm proud of you."

"The last straw was when Tillie and I returned from the trading post and I smelled liquor on his breath. Made me mad that he had me buy tobacco yet had money for whiskey."

"You don't need that. I worry about you and Eden." He held the door for her and they went out.

The fall day was so lovely with barely a breeze off the lake as Rachel caught Heath alone when the two of them were caring for the goats. She told him about the three strangers she'd seen on her property the previous day and how Jax had reacted.

"You've never seen them before?"

"No. Hope I'm not being silly. Uncle Zeb said they were asking directions."

"Something's going on here and you need to keep your guard up." Heath pushed back his battered Stetson. "Promise you'll be careful."

She caught her bottom lip between her teeth. "I will."

"Don't be so quick to push your gut feelings aside. You can bet where there's smoke there's plenty of fire."

A chill swept through her. She prayed he was wrong, yet something told her he wasn't.

"I know. Believe me, I see plenty that doesn't sit right."

"I'm still not convinced he's your uncle. A few names jotted in a Bible don't make it the gospel. And are you sure your mother's maiden name was Thacker?"

"I never heard it spoken."

"Wanting it to be so doesn't mean it is."

"Maybe." Silence ensued. Rachel mulled that over as she checked one of her pregnant female goats while Heath hauled fresh water to the herd.

Fact is, the yearning for blood kin had blinded her to Zeb's shortcomings. It seemed he was simply too lazy to even take a deep breath. And how funny that he was digging holes all around the house and property. He could only be looking for the strongbox her father had kept.

Unless he'd ridden with her father, Zeb wouldn't know anything about that. The truth made her stomach knot tight. Heath seemed to be right.

Heath dropped a handkerchief he was using to mop the sweat from his brow. When he bent over to pick it up, one of the male goats spied a golden opportunity. Before Rachel could call out a warning, the buck lowered his head and rammed Heath's posterior. The impact sent him tumbling end over end like a rock rolling downhill.

Laughter erupted from Rachel's mouth.

"I'm glad someone sees the humor in this," he muttered.

"Are you all right?" She offered him a hand up.

Heath dusted off his clothes. "Nothing but my pride was hurt."

"I guess you'll live then."

She was grateful that something happened to break the strained silence. She didn't want to argue with him. And it seemed as though that's all they'd done since Uncle Zeb came to live with her.

As they walked toward the barn she cast a side glance at

Heath. "I hope you're not neglecting things at your place to help out here."

"I'm managing just fine. You worried about me?"

"A little I suppose. I can't help it." She met his gray eyes that seemed to see things others missed. "Is that wrong?"

The lopsided grin he flashed made her warm under the bright morning sun. "Rachel, nothing about you is wrong." They took a few more steps. "Say, there's supposed to be a circuit preacher coming through any day now according to George Singer. Would you go with me to hear him?" He snorted adding, "Might do your uncle some good too."

CHAPTER THIRTEEN

Unease flickered across her face and Heath already knew what her answer would be. His heart sank.

Rachel straightened. "I don't have time for such things."

Heath gave her a measured look. "For me or the circuit preacher?"

"Circuit preachers...mostly." She pushed back her hair impatiently.

"Because you still think God has forsaken you?" he pressed gently.

"I have plenty of evidence."

"What about his promise never to leave or forsake us?" He hoped to give her something to ponder. He wouldn't try to force his beliefs onto her. She had to make up her own mind.

"I only have to look at the graves under the cottonwood tree to get my answer." She increased the length of her stride, wanting to put some distance between them he guessed.

But she couldn't match his long gait and he quickly caught up. "Despite that you now have Eden?"

"Maybe someday I'll feel differently." She kept walking.

Heath put a hand on her arm. "I'm sorry you still hurt." He'd thought having Eden to care for would ease her heartbreak. She'd certainly seemed better of late. "I like spending time with you, Rachel, and I think you find it enjoyable too. If you won't go to the service, then think about saddling up the horses and going for a ride with me. We could go over to that Quaker community."

"Estacado?" Her eyes lit up and she chewed her bottom lip. "I can't leave Eden."

He could see excitement building. "Sally would be overjoyed to keep her for a few hours."

"Don't forget about Uncle Zeb. If I leave him, who knows what I'll come back to."

The strangers on horseback she'd seen with Zeb crossed Heath's mind. She was right to be worried. If he could only make her see the danger she was in without pricking her pride.

"True." He glanced at the shoreline of the lake and saw Zeb Thacker digging. What for he didn't know. "Let Sally come here to keep Eden. You better believe she'll keep an eye on your uncle."

A smile broke through and lit up her face. "You're a very persistent man."

"Then you'll go?"

"All right. Yes, I'll go."

"How about tomorrow?"

"You don't drag your feet much do you?"

"Nope." His hand dropped from her arm, and he reached for the pitchfork just inside the barn door. Happiness made his heart act funny that she'd agreed to spend the day in his company.

"Did anyone ever tell you how beautiful you are, Rachel?"

A flush colored her cheeks. "I look a fright."

He loved the way she instantly patted her silky blonde hair, trying to put it back in place. And those striking green eyes. Now that color had returned to her face, she was downright beautiful.

"I don't see a fright." His voice softened. "You're the prettiest thing I've seen in a long time."

"There's no else around except Tillie," she pointed out.

Her friend didn't interest him. On the other hand, Rachel's rosy lips and pink cheeks made him think of kissing. Shoot, everything about her made him want to be near her, touching her, kissing her, talking to her. He took a deep breath to calm the havoc inside and put himself out of temptation's reach before he did something stupid.

"Thank you, Heath." Rachel seemed flustered as well. She didn't appear to know what to do with her arms, first letting them hang at her side then crossing them at her waist. "Well, I suppose I'd best get inside and tend to Eden."

He stared after her, thanking God for bringing such a wonderful woman into his life.

RACHEL WOKE UP early the next morning, her thoughts on Heath. She was eagerly looking forward to their ride which surprised her a little.

What should she wear? Her best dress wasn't very pretty but it was a nice shade of gingerbread, and her orange and golden shawl would lighten it. She'd match the fall leaves. She quickly slipped into the dress then turned to her hair. No braid today. She brushed the light blonde strands to a sheen then twisted the mass, pinning it on top her head. Nice. She liked it.

As Rachel finished getting ready, Eden made adorable little baby sounds and waved her arms. She was such a pleasant baby. Unless wet or hungry she never cried. She reminded Rachel of sweet little Alice. Even as Alice lay in the grips of the fever she'd not often cried out.

Maybe she'd pick some wild sunflowers down by the lake and put them on her grave. With fall arriving within days, there wasn't a big variety other than sunflowers. But those were pretty.

A dark cloud settled over Rachel's heart. Heath thought her an angel but if he knew the ruined woman she was, he'd run. She snorted. He could never know the truth. Her worst fear was disappointing someone she loved.

If she hurried, she could pick the sunflowers before he arrived. She took Eden in her arms and kissed her sweet cheeks. "Good morning, sweetheart. I'd better get your bottle ready before you take a notion to let me hear about it."

Moments later, she moved to the kitchen and lit the lamps, then the stove. Uncle Zeb knew how to time it and came in looking for some hot brew.

"Good morning, Uncle. I'll have some coffee made in just a minute. Eden can't wait for a bottle. She's such a sweet baby but she wants to eat when she gets a hankering for it and not a minute later."

"Just do what you gotta do. I'll stoke us up a fire." But he stood watching her in no hurry to move.

Rachel fed the hungry baby then put Eden on her shoulder and patted her back. "Heath will be here in a little bit. We're going riding. Do you want to come with us?"

A strange light came in Uncle Zeb's eyes, piquing Rachel's curiosity. "No, you two go ahead," he said. "I'll be fine here by myself."

"Sally is going to keep Eden for me." She had lots to do before then and it didn't appear she'd get help feeding the animals or gathering eggs. "I'd appreciate if you could help with chores," she prodded.

"Oh sure. I'll get to that. Don't you worry." He shuffled on to the fireplace.

Whether he meant now or later she had no idea. She thought their talk had worked.

A loud burp filled the small kitchen. Satisfied that all was well, she carried the sleeping princess to her cradle and started cooking. She and Zeb had breakfast and she'd just finished the dishes when Heath and Sally arrived way ahead of schedule. "Would either of you like a cup of coffee?"

The corners of Heath's smoke-colored eyes crinkled when he smiled. She loved the way his hair curled around his collar. "No thanks. I'm all coffee-ed out. Must've drunk a whole pot this morning."

Sally declined also and peeked at little Eden who was fast asleep. "I hope you don't mind that I came here. I got to thinking it'd be best instead of dragging all her things to my house."

"I don't mind a bit. In fact, I agree it's easier this way." Rachel patted her hair and reached for a hat, an old one of Tillie's to replace hers that burned in the fire. "I just have to see to a few things outside with Heath. Sally, are you positive you don't mind keeping her?"

"Mind?" Sally grinned widely. "This is better than Christmas." She picked up paper and pencil and started writing.

Uncle Zeb with his feet propped on a stool, hands on his belly, spoke up, "Now you know Miss Sally wants to keep the baby. Don't be a worrywart, Rachel. It'll be fine and I've already fed the animals and gathered the eggs."

Heath sent Rachel a surprised look and shrugged.

Rachel gave her uncle a small even smile. "Thank you for that but I still need to see that everything is good and proper before I take off."

She didn't miss the quick hand over Heath's mouth to hide a grin as the old man frowned and stared at the floor.

Heath held the door for her and they made quick work of checking on the animals.

"Well, I'll be. He really did feed them," Heath said.

"Surprises me too. Well then, seems we're ready to leave." Back inside, Rachel turned to Sally. "Eden likes to have her back rubbed when she's falling asleep. And I give her a bottle every three hours. And she hates a wet diaper. The minute it gets wet she wants it off. And—"

Sally's raised eyebrows stopped Rachel cold. "You think I've never seen a young'un before? Granted, it might've been a while, but I do know how to care for one."

"I'm sorry. I apologize. Of course, you know how to tend to her. I was just trying to help." Rachel had no idea why she was being so overprotective. This wasn't like her. If she had any qualms, she wouldn't leave Eden. Not even on a bet. This baby meant more to her than anyone knew. If something happened to her...

Sally's face and her eyes softened. "It's okay to love a child more than life itself. I'll take good care of the little darling while you have a bit of fun. I packed you a picnic lunch."

"Thank you so much." Rachel hugged the woman and gave sleeping Eden a kiss.

Sally strode to Zeb and thrust a piece of paper at him. "I

made a list of chores for you to do, starting with chopping more firewood."

Zeb came off his chair. "Who made you boss?"

"Me. Now get to moving." Sally stood with her hands on her hips and Rachel had to hide a chortle of laughter. "I'll have a nice lunch made for you if you make it halfway through by noon. I'll have no shirking your duty on my watch."

"Zeb, looks like you have your work cut out for you," Heath said winking, a wide smile spreading. "Sally's a tough woman and it pays to stay on her good side."

"That's right." Sally patted Heath's arm as he went out. "I trained my brother and I know I can whip you into shape."

Zeb groaned and crossed his arms over his ample belly.

Rachel patted his shoulder. "It'll be nice having all the chores done for once."

Uncle Zeb pushed her toward the door. "Get along with you. Lassiter's waitin'."

A surprise greeted her when she stepped out into the bright sunlight. Neither horse even faintly resembled Blackie. One was the horse named Hondo that Heath always rode and the other a handsome appaloosa.

"Oh, Heath, he's beautiful."

Heath grinned. "I thought you'd see in him the things I do. Bought him from Skeet Slaughter. This horse and I are still in the get-acquainted stage, so you'll ride Hondo until I know his disposition."

"I'll be proud to ride whichever you want. Both are fine horses." She gave Jax a pat on the head along with stern orders. "You stay here and help Sally guard the place."

The dog gave a pitiful whine and sat on his haunches.

Heath helped Rachel mount and she didn't miss how his hands lingered on her waist. She loved his touch and started to tell him, but he stepped back and went to his mount. How easily he stepped into the stirrup and threw his leg over the saddle of the paint. Strong. Capable.

Just then, Zeb emerged from the little house, cussing and raising cane with Sally right behind swatting the air with the broom.

Rachel giggled as she turned her horse toward the lake.

"Where are you going?" Heath asked.

"I hope you don't mind a quick stop to pick some sunflowers for Alice's grave before we go."

With a nod, he headed that way and helped her pick them. Then they went to the family plot beneath the cottonwood. Rachel dismounted and laid the flowers on Alice's resting place.

Unbidden tears ran down her face and she whispered, "I hope you can forgive me one day, sweet girl. Just remember, it wasn't my decision. I still love you so much."

She rose and got back on Hondo. Once they rode out and Rachel left her sadness behind, the conversation turned to Sally and her uncle. "I think Sally will straighten Zeb out."

"His expression was priceless," Heath agreed. "Wonder if this won't make him pick up and move on."

"It might." Rachel let her horse pick the way up the path to the rim. The day was perfect. They rode in silence a ways then she asked, "Why are you so different when it comes to Eden? Most men want nothing to do with a child or their care."

Heath was silent a long moment before speaking. "Looking into the face of a little babe is a lot like I would imagine looking into the face of baby Jesus. There's such an innocence and purity that steals my heart. Eden is just starting out with her whole life ahead of her." His reverent voice held softness. "Just think you get to teach her about things, help her grow into a woman. I would think it to be the most rewarding experience any person may ever have."

"I never thought of it that way, but you're right. It's a lot more than keeping one fed and happy. Raising a child is a huge undertaking." She twisted in the saddle. "But what if I mess up?"

As she had in the past. Painful shards pierced her.

His eyes found hers. "You won't. You're already an excellent mother."

She held the reins loosely and glanced down the path to the house below. "Thanks for the vote of confidence."

They passed through a grove of cottonwoods, their leaves starting to turn a golden yellow. A slight breeze set them dancing on their branches as a sudden shower of gold fell around Rachel. She was so entranced she almost missed Heath's question.

"What are you going to let Eden call you? Will you be a mother? Or a sister?"

A cold chill passed over her. Shaken, Rachel stared. Had he guessed? But he wasn't even looking at her and wore an innocent expression. She relaxed. "I've never thought about it. What do you suggest?"

"This has to be your decision. Listen to your heart. I think you'll know when the time comes. One thing about it, you don't have to decide today."

Finally relaxing, Rachel glanced up at the bluest sky she'd ever seen and breathed deep. "I just love fall. Life is slowing and people aren't in as much hurry."

"I agree but my favorite season is spring when the earth is renewing."

"Spoken like a true rancher."

They rode for a bit in companionable silence, broken only

by the sound of the hooves striking the earth and the horses' snorts.

"How far is Estacado?" Rachel asked.

"Two hours thereabouts. Thought you might like to see what they have over there. And I want to see if those three strangers at your place might be there."

"I'll be anxious to see myself. I think I can recognize one or two."

"I want to know what they're up to."

Silence spun between them like a silvery web.

Excitement slowly spread through her, and it didn't have much to do with the destination. The fact she was going with Heath set a low hum under her skin.

She cast him a sideways glance. He sat tall in the saddle and rode with extreme ease, at one with the appaloosa. The worn Stetson pulled down low on his forehead shaded his eyes. And his broad shoulders seemed capable of carrying the world.

Or at least capable of comforting a woman who'd lost everyone she held dear.

She wondered what it would be like to marry such a man, bear his children and share his trials.

Maybe...

He turned and his gaze caressed her face. Unspoken promises filled the depths of his honest gray eyes.

She warmed under his stare and every sane thought left her head.

CHAPTER FOURTEEN

A good five miles outside of the Quaker town they passed the tent saloon sitting alone on the tall grass prairie. It wasn't much by anyone's standards. A banner shot full of holes declared the quiet place to be the Wildcat Saloon. Seemed kinda odd out by itself but from all accounts it did a fair business with the cowboys from nearby ranches frequenting it. It was no place for Heath.

He kept them moving past at a brisk pace. Rachel frowned and stared but was silent. He could almost see her thoughts turning, likely picturing her father striding into it. Or her so-called uncle.

They finally arrived in Estacado and as they rode slowly down the dirt street, Rachel's head swiveled from side to side, taking in the row of buildings in need of whitewash on both sides. Strolling people on the sidewalks were all dressed in somber black, and the women wore white caps on their heads while the bearded men opted for flat-topped, wide-brimmed hats. Everyone nodded to them.

"They're sure friendly here," Rachel murmured.

"I've always found them to be most welcoming." Heath tipped his hat at a group of Quakers. "Keep an eye out for those strangers, Rachel." He glanced at the horses tied to the hitching rails. A lot of good that did him since he hadn't seen the intruders.

"Do they have a telegraph office?" she asked.

"Everything but that. It would sure solve the dilemma about the strongbox though if they did. I'm sure a telegraph won't be far behind though."

They pulled up in front of the Stringfellow and Hume General Merchandise store and dismounted.

The town was built around the Llano House, a two-story hotel. There were two general merchandise stores, a two-room office occupied by Judge Swink, the county judge, and a half dugout that housed an attorney's office. At the end of the street stood a tall white church, its value evident by the flawless state of the building.

A public water fountain sat on the town square. And nestled around these six buildings were homes made from sod in addition to plenty of tents.

Rachel stood for a long minute taking it all in. Some bearded men in hats walked past with long hair curled on the ends. Heath wondered what she thought about everything.

He looped their horses' reins around the hitching rail, took her arm, and ushered her into the mercantile where she stood in shocked silence.

"What's the matter?" Heath asked.

"There's so many things I can't see it all. I've never seen such an assortment of goods."

A clerk approached. "Can I help thee?"

While Heath inquired about some colorful yarn for Sally,

Rachel wandered to the yard goods and ran her fingers across some soft, pink flannel. The price said ten cents a yard. He watched her count the coins from her pocket and her face fell. She put the cloth back and went to look at other things, carefully looking at the prices.

A woman clerk wandered over to him. "Your wife has a good eye for fabric."

"She's not my wife...yet. But soon if I have my way about it."

The woman's eyes twinkled, adding color to her drab clothing. "I see."

"Can you measure out two yards, ma'am?"

"Yes, I'll be happy to measure it for thee."

Heath leaned against the counter to watch Rachel staring wide-eyed at everything. He took advantage of the moment to speak quietly to the clerk again, handing her some bills before wandering to look at the bonnets.

Before he knew it, the heels of Rachel's boots struck the planked flooring like bullets from a rifle. Fire shot from her eyes eliciting a groan.

"Mr. Lassiter, the clerk said you paid for the fabric," Rachel whispered in clipped tones.

"I don't see the problem. It's my first installment for renting your bull." He kept his voice calm and even. Pleased with his handling of the situation, he smiled. "It's your money."

"Oh." She blinked, the wind leaving her sails. "In that case, I guess you're right."

"See? All it takes is logic." He took her arm and guided her to the knitting yarn. "Do you mind helping me select two or three skeins for Sally? I have no idea what colors to choose."

They ended up with some brown, blue, and dove gray.

Heath added new knitting needles, a box of cartridges, and some peppermint candy.

After telling the clerk he'd stop back for the purchases before he left town, he paid and turned to Rachel. "Do you want to check out the other mercantile?"

"Do they offer anything different?"

"I think it has mainly household and farm items."

At her nod, Heath offered his arm and, weaving around the horse-drawn wagons, they crossed the busy street, their boots bringing up little clouds of dust. It seemed everyone from the surrounding countryside was in Estacado.

Inside the other mercantile, Rachel removed her hand from the crook of his arm. She walked slowly around looking at everything. Heath loved the look of awe on her face and was happy to be able to give her this new experience. He'd give her the world if she'd let him. Problem was she drew the line more often than not on accepting things from him.

One thing for sure and certain Rachel was as stubborn and exasperating as an Arkansas mule. It was a frustrating thing really, this independence of hers.

But would he want her any different? Secretly, he was proud that she tried to make it on her own. She was whip-smart and could usually find a way to solve whatever arose. He just wished it extended to the man claiming to be her uncle, yet she seemed to be coming around.

Gazing out the window of the mercantile, he found the Quakers walking past all wore such a peaceful expression. Thoughts of Rachel as she'd paid a visit to Alice's little grave sprang to mind. She'd been awfully torn up. He said a silent prayer that he could help her regain her faith. If she could find peace inside for whatever was troubling her. It had something to do with those graves—Alice's in particular. Why that one?

Seemed rather odd behavior and he didn't like the direction of his thoughts.

He turned from the window. A searching glance found Rachel's lips pursed, peering intently at some sewing notions. Exasperation deepened the lines of her face.

He suddenly remembered that all her clothing had burned with her house. What she had on was what she'd been wearing the day she buried her little sister. Sally had given her a nightgown and a few essentials, and some of the rancher's wives had thrown in some dresses but she needed much more. Not that he ever heard her complain.

Making up his mind to do something about it, he strode to her side. "Will you be all right for a few minutes?"

"Yes. Why?"

"I remembered something I need to do. I'll be right back."

Taking his leave, he returned to the store they'd just left. He made his selections and asked the clerk to put them with his other purchases. He'd collect them in a bit.

Rachel was waiting outside the store. "I don't suppose you'd tell me what all that was about."

Heath grinned. "Nope. Are you hungry?"

"A little."

"Then we'll eat. There's a small creek behind the church that would make a nice place to have a picnic."

A few minutes later they spread a blanket on a patch of grass and unpacked the lunch. Sally had sent some ham, bread, pickles, and two pieces of raisin pie.

It was a secluded spot and a breeze gently ruffled Rachel's light blonde hair. Just perfect.

"Thank you for bringing me here, Heath. You don't know how much I've enjoyed this." Rachel lightly touched his hand.

"You're most welcome." He leaned toward her. He cleared

the huskiness from his voice before he tried to speak. "I want to kiss you in the worst way. Would you mind?"

"In broad daylight?" she answered in a whisper.

"We're shielded from view. No one will see."

"Then I think I should like it."

He lowered his head and slanted his lips across hers very gently. Then after tracing her lips with a finger, he slowly kissed her again and she returned it with surprising passion. This woman was making him crazy. Sure, she was beautiful, but it was far more. She'd become as much a part of him as breathing.

Heath pulled away. He was trying to be a patient man, but it was difficult being near her and not being able to tell her how very much he loved her.

A glance revealed flushed cheeks a becoming shade of pink. She lifted her fingertips to her smiling mouth, her breathing rapid but soft. The breeze lifted tawny tendrils of hair, laying it across her eyes, tracing delicate patterns on her face with the deft tips of a paintbrush. The sight mesmerized him and held him spellbound for a moment.

God, she was a stunning, gorgeous woman.

He swallowed hard and turned away. How could he ever measure up to that? They ate in silence then with a deep sigh he began putting the remains of their lunch back into the basket.

"I suppose we'd best gather our packages from the mercantile and head back."

Rachel stood, smoothing her worn dress. "I'm anxious to get back to Eden."

Their hands touched as they folded the blanket. Heath wondered if she felt the sparks or if it was just him.

"I hope we can do this again soon," he said.

"I'd love to. It's been a perfect day and I've had a wonderful time."

"Me too," he said drowning in her green gaze. "You don't know what this meant to me."

A flush rose to her cheeks and she turned to busy herself with Hondo. He helped her mount up then rode beside her to the first mercantile where he collected his purchases.

Rachel glanced back as they left Estacado. "Those people are quite friendly. I was a little afraid they'd treat us as outsiders. Do you come often?"

"About once a month or so. I can find more things here than the trading post."

Outside of town they again passed the Wildcat Saloon. Heath rode a little closer to Rachel. While the place seemed peaceful now, the quiet was known to erupt into violence from time to time.

When they were even with the opening, three men staggered out.

Rachel gasped. "Those are the strangers I saw Uncle Zeb talking to."

"Are you sure?"

"Absolutely. I'll never forget them."

The slow pace allowed Heath to commit the faces to memory. The trio had such a hard time mounting up, they never noticed his stare.

"I think Uncle Zeb comes here," Rachel said low. Her leg almost touched his when she moved her horse closer. "I don't like this place."

"Me either." He narrowed his gaze, glad he'd worn his gun.

"If Zeb had a lick of sense he'd ride on and leave you in peace to raise the little princess." Maybe he should talk to him. At least confront him about the three strangers.

"It's started to bother me of late. And I've caught him digging a lot of holes. He's looking for something."

"Promise you'll be on your guard until we figure this out. I can't stress that enough." Thank goodness they'd moved the strongbox to his barn. That helped.

"I will, Heath. I have more than myself to think about now. I won't take risks with Eden."

"Good." Once they'd passed the tent saloon, Heath breathed easier, glad the strangers turned their horses toward open country.

"Do you think Eden's missing me?"

He grinned. "Probably not as much as you are her."

Rachel shot him a sideways glance and a blush rose to her cheeks. "Am I that obvious?"

"A little. But I give you credit for trying to hide it."

"I'm being too protective of her, aren't I?"

"It's normal to want to love and protect your child considering your recent loss."

"I've given some thought about what I want Eden to call me."

"And?"

"I'm going to be her mother. I think of her as my child anyway and nothing would make me happier than for her to call me mama."

Heath cleared his throat of the emotion suddenly blocking it. "I think that's wonderful."

"I don't know what I'd do if anything happened to her. I don't know how I'd bear it." Pain clouded her green eyes.

"Nothing's going to happen." Not if he could help it. The child meant as much to him as she did to Rachel. He'd do whatever it took to keep the little darling from harm. "We'll make sure Little Princess stays healthy and loved." And her mama too, he added silently.

It was late afternoon by the time they returned. He stood back as Rachel ran into the house. Before he knew it, she'd snatched up Eden as though someone was about to plunge a dagger into Eden's heart.

"I've missed you, Eden. Your mama's home." Rachel left kisses all over her face.

Heath's attention went to the hurt filling Sally's eyes. His sister quickly turned away and began fiddling with Eden's things. He was glad he'd thought to get some skeins of yarn in Estacado for her. That would help smooth the wounded feelings.

"I guess you got Zeb all straightened out?" he asked.

"You better believe it. I kept that man busy all day." Sally laughed. "He didn't know what had gotten hold of him."

"Good."

"He's still outside working." Sally moved to the door. "He's coming this way."

When Zeb entered, Heath barely recognized him. His hair was standing on end, his eyes bulging.

"Keep that woman away from me! She tried to kill me!" Zeb yelled, scooting behind a chair.

"Stop whining, you big flea bag. I can work circles around you," Sally scoffed.

Zeb dropped into a chair and took his boots off. "I don't have the strength to lift a fork."

Rachel glanced up. "Then maybe we'll have a light supper."

Heath left Sally and Zeb bickering and got the yarn from his saddlebags. Returning, he handed Sally the brown paper wrapped gift. "Bought something for you, sister."

"For me?" she blared. "It's not my birthday."

"Just a little something for putting up with me."

Her eyes lit up when she saw the pretty colors. "Well, I declare. It's exactly what I've been wanting. Thank you, brother."

Rachel tucked a soft blanket around the baby. "That little town has amazing things."

Still smiling, Sally put the new yarn into a bag. "Yes indeed. Heath and I have gone a time or two."

"Thank you for the picnic lunch," Rachel said. "We found a stream behind the church, and everything was so delicious." She touched Sally's arm. "You're going to have to give me the recipe for your pickles. And that raisin pie was heavenly."

That perked Sally up to no end. "I'm glad. I'll bring the recipes next time I visit."

Heath watched the two women, his thoughts on the secret packages for Rachel. He didn't know how she'd take what he'd bought. Now to find an opening to bring them in. But he didn't have to work too hard. They all went outside and while Rachel was talking to Sally, he got them and hurried inside, putting them on the table.

He said a hurried prayer for a miracle and that she'd accept his gift.

CHAPTER FIFTEEN

Rachel stood with Heath next to the appaloosa, searching for words to tell him what the day had meant to her and how much she loved his company. Her hand hanging loosely at her side found his. "Thank you for such a fun time. I don't know when I've enjoyed anything more."

He brushed her cheek with a light fingertip. "I'm glad I could give that to you."

Heat rose to her face and she stumbled for a reply but found none so changed the subject. "I've been thinking about that strongbox. I'd like you to accompany me when I take it back but where would that be?"

He kept his voice low. "Clarendon is the closest with a stage office. It'll take ten days by wagon so you need to wait for Eden to get a little bigger."

"Most certainly." A second passed. "We really are isolated, aren't we? No wonder my father thought he was safe. He was." She sighed. "Guess it doesn't matter when I take it."

"Nope. It'll be a little while before you can rest easy, little mama."

Prickles of happiness swept through her when he called her that. She lightly squeezed his fingers. "Then I think it's safe enough for now and I won't worry about it. It would be so much easier if Estacado had a telegraph office."

"Yes, it would."

He looked as if he wanted to kiss her.

"You look a little tired," he said. "Try to rest a bit." He chuckled. "Thanks to Sally, Zeb did all the chores for probably the entire month."

A peal of laughter rose before Rachel could stop it. "Yes, Sally is a one-woman wonder. All I'll have to do from now on is threaten to send for her. I'm just going to slice off some ham, fry a pan of potatoes and onions, and call it good."

She bade him and Sally goodbye and went into the house, holding the door for Jax.

Uncle Zeb was asleep in the chair but jerked awake with a start. "Is she gone?"

"Yes, she left with Heath so you're safe." Rachel noticed a package on the table wrapped in brown paper and tied with string. It was just like the ones that Heath had toted from the mercantile in Estacado. She started to grab it up and run to catch him when she spied the note on top.

Dearest Rachel, don't make a fuss. I got these with your bull money. Picking them out gave me such pleasure. Thanks for spending the day with me.

It was signed Heath.

Bull money her foot! He'd use that explanation until he wore it out.

But how could she deny herself? She untied the string and pushed the paper aside. There was the length of flannel for Eden that she'd so admired, yards of calico that would make a pretty dress for her as well as buttons and lace, some fine white muslin for a nightgown and underthings, and a comb, brush, and mirror. They were all things she'd sorely needed.

Then she recalled what he said about it being just as important to accept as it was to give.

Heath wanted her to have these and gave them from the goodness of his heart.

She lifted the calico and buried her face in it, reveling in the soft cottony feel. Yes, just this once she'd keep them. Only because she truly had little choice, which Heath had known full well. Even though it was the reality of the situation, it rankled to have him know just how desperately she needed each item.

She put it all in the bedroom then grabbed a knife and started peeling potatoes. It wasn't long before she had a quick meal ready and called Uncle Zeb.

He ambled to the table. "I hope you don't plan to be gone again anytime soon."

"I don't have anywhere else to go right now. Why?"

"That Sally is a slavedriver." He filled his plate. "She nearly killed me. I haven't ever had a broom taken to my backside until today." He squinted, looking at her out of one eye. "I think she took pleasure in swatting me."

"Well, you have to admit you haven't done much to help out while you've been here." Rachel took a bite of ham. "I have a question and I want a straight answer. Why are you digging the holes around the house? What are you looking for?"

He stopped chewing and his Adam's apple bobbed up and down with his swallow. "I'm letting the ground breathe. I heard that you have to turn the soil over on occasion to help it grow things better."

"You're letting the ground breathe?" That was the most ridiculous thing she'd ever heard.

His nod resembled a cork on a fishing line. "That's right. My contribution to this plot of earth."

"Well, stop. We don't need any more holes."

"Sure thing. Consider it done."

"I saw your three friends today coming out of the tent saloon and they were mighty drunk."

"Friends?" He stared at her blankly.

"The strangers asking for directions. Remember?"

"No, you misunderstand. They're no friends of mine."

Without proof, it was best not to accuse. "Then, I don't want to see them around here again or I'll think you're in cahoots with them. I don't like their looks and I have Eden to protect."

"Oh sure." He resumed eating but kept looking at her when he thought she didn't notice.

THE FOLLOWING DAY, Rachel awoke full of energy. She fed Eden and put her back in her crib, then went out to do her chores and feed the animals. Uncle Zeb had already done most of it.

The minute Uncle Zeb Thacker swallowed his last bite he scooted back from the table and announced he was going fishing.

"I guess you've earned it. This place has never looked so good."

He rubbed his grizzled chin and squinted. "The fish bite best in early morning." Uncle Zeb avoided her gaze. "I thought I'd take a notion and ride over to Estacado way this afternoon."

"Stay clear of that saloon." Rachel gave him a stern look. "If you come back drunk, you'd best keep on riding because you won't be welcome here."

"I hear you." The man stumbled over his own feet in his haste to get out the door.

Once the breakfast dishes were washed and done up, she took out the new length of flannel and set about cutting out a gown for Eden. It was a beautiful fall day. Rachel carried Eden's crib outdoors and placed it beneath the cottonwood tree. Then she gathered her sewing notions and made herself comfortable. Jax lay at her feet.

It was a near to perfect day with the brilliant blue sky overhead, the gentle cooling breeze sighing through the large cottonwood tree, and contentment filling Rachel's heart.

She had much to be grateful for. Her gaze fell on the babe sleeping peacefully with not a care in the world. She loved this baby with every fiber of her being.

The infant was slowly filling the hole her family had left. Tears filled her eyes.

Just then Jax sprang to his feet. The hair on his neck bristled. His threatening growl made her glad that she was friend and not foe for it was fearsome. Before she could quiet him, he raced around the house toward the barn.

Rachel put down the little gown she was stitching and went to see what all the ruckus was about. By then Jax's bark was farther away, somewhere deep in the canyon. She called and whistled but the dog didn't come. Not wanting to leave Eden for long, she hurried back.

As she rounded the corner of the house, she spied a young woman bending over her daughter's crib. Alarm bells sounded.

"Hello," Rachel called. "Can I help you?"

The stranger jerked and quickly moved away from the crib. She was unkempt, her mousy brown hair tangled and dirty. She looked to be around fifteen or so. Tears ran down her face.

When the young woman didn't reply, Rachel asked again, "May I help you?"

Again, no reply, just a shake of her head.

"Do you live nearby? What is your name?"

"Becca," the girl mumbled, looking around like a cornered animal.

"Hello, Becca. It's nice to meet you. I don't get many visitors." Panic swept through Rachel. Her breath catching, she stayed where she was, afraid the girl would bolt if she moved closer. Or worse do something to Eden. "Can I get you something to eat or drink?"

"No."

The clopping sounds of a horse coming down the path into the canyon distracted Rachel. When she glanced back at the spot where Becca had been, the girl had vanished.

For a moment, Rachel wondered if she'd been nothing more than a figment of her imagination. Then she spied a blue ribbon in the crib next to Eden. The woman had been real all right.

The horse and rider she'd heard trotted into the yard and Heath reined to a stop beside Rachel and swung down.

"Hey, little mama." His wide grin stole her breath. "You look worried."

"Did you see a girl about fifteen years old when you rode in?" she asked.

"No, why?"

She told him about Becca and the strange way she'd acted. "Do you know her?"

"No. Sorry."

"What was so odd…Jax didn't bark at her."

"Which meant he must've known her. Becca, you said?"

"Yes, and she was crying. So disheveled. Hair uncombed." Tears filled her eyes and she gripped Heath's vest with trembling fingers. "I'm so scared she'll do something. You should've seen the way she stared at Eden, almost like she knew her or wanted to snatch her."

His arms folded around her, enclosing her in a protective circle. "I'm sure she meant nothing by it. You said she was very young?"

"About fifteen or so. Just a girl. I've been terrified someone will try to take Eden from me." She forced a laugh and loosened her hold on his vest. "I'm overreacting, aren't I?"

"It's understandable with all you've been through." He smoothed her hair. "I haven't seen anyone like that around." His gaze lit on the unfinished gown. "I see you're sewing. Mind some company?"

"I'll make a pot of coffee if you'll find Jax." As she told him how the dog just suddenly bolted his face grew as dark as a thundercloud.

"It's time I found out what's going on. I don't suppose Thacker is around?"

"I haven't seen him since morning."

Heath gave a short laugh. "No surprise there. Be back soon."

He mounted up and pointed the horse toward the thick wooded area to the right. Relief swept through Rachel. At least now they might get some answers.

The wind turned stronger and began to swirl down into the canyon in earnest. Taking Eden into the house, she gently laid her in the basket that she'd arrived in, setting it on the table. It might be crazy, but she didn't want the child out of her sight. Putting some coffee on, Rachel sat down at the kitchen table with her sewing.

Her thoughts turned to the girl named Becca. Why had she been crying? Was Becca Eden's mother?

Rachel sucked in a breath and her blood ran cold. She couldn't bear the thought of losing her precious baby. Not now. Not after she'd come to think of Eden as her own daughter.

Please, God, don't let anyone take her from me.

With a start, Rachel realized that this was the first time she'd prayed since burying her family. Why she couldn't say. Maybe her anger was lessening as her deep grief was beginning to become somewhat bearable.

Maybe Heath was right in saying that God promised never to leave or forsake her. And there was a reason why she was left behind. Didn't Eden prove that?

But why give only to take away? She sucked in a deep breath. Why take just like before?

Flinging the small gown aside, she put down the needle, too upset to sew. What was keeping Heath?

The wind battered against the front of the house, pushing on the door. Then over the roar of the wind she heard barking and hurried to the door. It was Heath with Jax lying across his lap.

"Thank goodness," she whispered and hurried out holding onto her skirt against the wind. "Where did you find him?"

Jax licked her face and whimpered as she lowered him to the ground.

Heath slid from the saddle. "Found him tuckered out about a mile from here. He was lathered up from running."

"What do you make of it?"

"Chasing someone is my guess." Heath put an arm around her shoulders. "Saw plenty of tracks, but no sign of anyone."

Rachel loved the weight of his arm around her and the scent of leather and wild sage on his clothes.

"Come on in and get out of this wind. I have the coffee ready."

"Sounds good."

But the minute they went through the door with Jax, he turned. "I'll give you my full attention in a minute after I see the little princess."

She hid the persistent smile. Sometimes she wondered if he only came to see the baby. Eden wasn't even a month old, and she already had the tall cowboy wrapped around her finger.

By the time Rachel took down two cups, he sat with Eden tucked in the crook of his arm.

"Heath, she was asleep," Rachel protested softly. "You can't come waltzing in and snatch her up whenever you take a notion."

Though she grumbled, the sight of Heath with the tiny baby created a warmth deep in her heart. But it wouldn't do to let him know that. Or how his nearness set her blood pumping.

"I swear I didn't wake her up. Her eyes were already open."

Yeah, and Rachel was a flying squirrel.

As soon as she set the coffee in front of him, he took a swig.

Jax lay on a rag rug she'd made and glanced up. She petted the dog and got back to the strange occurrences. "What do you think is happening?"

Heath's smokey gaze met hers. "I don't want to frighten you, but you have reason to be scared. You had trespassers. I'm almost sure Jax tried to bite them."

Shivers slid down her spine. "So you think there were more than one?"

"I found several different sets of tracks."

"What can I do?" she whispered.

"Stay close to the house and keep Jax nearby." He kissed Eden's cheek. "I'll tie him up before I leave if you want."

Rachel nodded. "If we don't, I'm afraid they'll kill him."

And whoever it was might not stop with the dog.

"I'll leave my rifle." He spoke as though he'd read her thoughts. "Do you know how to shoot?"

"My brother taught me. It was a way to pass the time since we weren't allowed to have friends. But it made my father mad enough to spit." The memory brought a tiny smile. Isaac Malloy had had certain ideas of how his daughter should while away her time and shooting weapons wasn't one of those.

"Aiming at targets is far different from putting a bullet in a man."

Her jaw clenched. "I can and will do whatever it takes to protect my daughter."

"I know you will, little mama. So will I."

"What about you? You'll need a rifle as well."

"Don't worry, I have more than one."

Eden whimpered. He murmured quietly to her and put her on his shoulder. "Now, let's talk about something pleasant. I noticed you're making Eden a gown from that flannel you so admired."

"I am." She leveled a frown at him. "Thank you for the gifts but you and I both know that wasn't bull-renting money."

He lifted an eyebrow. "You've gotten to be an expert on the worth of bulls now, is it?"

"No, but that's beside the point."

Heath set his jaw stubbornly. "The fact is you need a few things. I fail to see a problem."

"I need to learn how to be self-sufficient because you won't always be around." Her heart ached to consider that possibility. But she'd learned the hard way that people often left, not always by their own choosing. And if she didn't learn to fend for herself she'd be in dire straits.

His large hand supported the baby's head and back as he leaned forward to gently touch Rachel's cheek. "Who says?"

"Well...I mean..."

"I'm not going anywhere," he said softly. "Get that straight right now."

"But, you're bound to get tired of waiting for me."

"Rachel, I don't care how long I have to wait. One year, two, or fifty. I'm a patient man."

Sliding a hand behind her neck, he tugged her closer and gently kissed her.

"I'm not going away," he repeated firmly.

Her stomach fluttered. This man was a special breed. She would marry him in a heartbeat if only she didn't have so much standing between them.

The corded muscles in his arms spoke of his strength as he held the baby girl they both loved so much. But even greater than the power in his arms was his immense strength of spirit.

His love of God, the land, and the animals told her she could do far worse than plighting her troth with this man who had a heart bigger than the state of Texas.

Her stomach twisted and her mouth went dry. She yearned to trust him. But... Getting to her feet, she went to look out the window.

The chair scooted as he rose and followed. "Rachel, I feel there's something standing between us. Something that's keeping you from following your heart." He took her hand. "Tell me about Alice," he said softly.

The request from the blue sent her into a spiraling panic.

She licked her dry lips. "I've told you all about her. I don't..." She tried to swallow past the lie lodging in her throat. He knew. Despite her efforts to hide the truth, he'd figured it out. "I don't know what more I can add."

CHAPTER SIXTEEN

"*W*as she your sister? Or was she more?" Heath asked again, patting Eden's back when she let out a little cry.

"I...I don't know what you mean," Rachel stuttered. She was unprepared for this and thought she'd covered her secret well. When had she let it slip? "I loved her very much and buried her next to Jane."

"I don't want to upset you, but don't you think it's time to get this into the open?" His gentle brush of her cheek brought tears. "You're carrying a heavy weight. Let's talk about this. I think you'll feel better with the load lifted."

She stifled a sob and was barely aware when he moved her to a chair in front of the fireplace. The clock on the mantel ticked the minutes away. He moved the rocker close and sat.

Finally, she took a handkerchief Heath handed her and dried her tears. "You're right. I've carried this secret for five years." Her voice cracked but she went on. She had to get this out once and for all. "You see, Alice was my child, my baby."

"Let me guess whose idea it was to deny her—your father's."

Tears ran down her cheeks and her voice shook. "He said I didn't have any choice and that...that he was saving my reputation." She glared at the door angrily as the conversation thrust her back in time after working so hard to put the horrible incident behind her. "If I refused, he told me I would have to leave." Her gaze was one of confusion and hurt. "He knew I didn't have any place to go. He blamed me for this. Said it was all my fault."

"It's not. Don't think that." Heath squeezed her hand. "Who is the father?"

"That's the thing." She chewed her lip. "I don't know. When I was fifteen, I was abducted by some of my father's former gang who wanted to use me as leverage against him. Back then I hadn't a clue but now, I'm pretty sure he was holding all the money from their jobs. One man kept saying that they wanted their share and I was going to help them get it. Please don't make me tell the rest," she begged whimpering, holding a hand to her mouth. "I can't."

"No. That's enough to get the picture." The angry lines of Heath's face had deepened around his mouth and eyes. "How did you get away?"

"They held me for two weeks before I realized my father wasn't coming. When my abductors got drunk one night and passed out, I slipped my hands from the ropes and freed myself. I had lost weight from not eating so it was easy. I snuck from the hideout and walked home, hiding at the tiniest noise."

Heath leaned to touch her shoulder. "And when you got back?"

"My father called me a whore and only when Jane

threatened to slice his throat did he let me stay. But then…" Her voice cracked again with the horrible memories.

"Your body began to reveal what had happened," Heath added.

"Yes. And I…" She swallowed a sob. "I made a pact with the devil and promised I would never tell Alice. I denied my own child." Rachel rose and stalked to the door, her arms folded across her chest. Embarrassment and shame flooded over her that Heath now knew all the sordid details. "I denied her," she repeated helplessly.

Heath followed, standing beside her with the baby. "This wasn't your fault. You didn't cause any of it. If your father was alive, I'd horsewhip him within an inch of his life."

"It's over now." She turned and met his sorrowful gaze, taking Eden from him. "Now you know why I can't marry you. I'm ruined." She set her trembling lips in a firm line not sure she could get out what she must. "It's best if you stop coming around."

Several heartbeats passed in silence.

"Best for who?" He ran a hand through his hair. His voice took on a strange hoarseness. "You hold my heart, Rachel. I will marry you any time, any place you say. That hasn't changed."

"You're a stubborn man, Heath Lassiter."

A smile teased the corner of his mouth. "I just know what I want."

"Men expect—"

"What exactly do men expect?"

"They want a pure bride."

"Let me answer this way." Before she could stop him, he slanted a kiss across her lips and for a long moment, the ugly past melted away. She clung to his vest for all she was worth.

RACHEL GAVE EDEN a bottle then laid the darling in her cradle. She and Heath sat discussing Zeb and the girl Becca. "What will I do if Becca is Eden's mother?"

"Let's see how this plays out before we start worrying." Heath drew little circles on the back of her hand. "It could be nothing more than Eden reminding the girl of someone. You said she seemed a little slow."

"You're right." She let out a long breath.

"I have to head for home, but I'll tie Jax first. If Zeb shows up drunk, send him packing."

"Don't worry. I will."

They went outside. The dog's pitiful whine and pleading eyes tore at Rachel's heart.

Heath spoke softly. "Sorry to have to do this, boy, but it's for your own good. You keep chasing off after who knows what and you'll end up buzzard bait." He ruffled the dog's ears. "Besides, you need to keep watch over your mistress. Can't have anything happening to her, now, can we?"

Rachel's chest swelled as she watched Heath. Clearly, he loved her dog. It was also plain that it pained him to have to tie up an animal that had always roamed free.

The task accomplished, Heath put his arm around Rachel and drew her against his chest. "When things settle down, I'm taking you back to Estacado for more shopping."

She tilted her face for his kiss, very grateful he didn't hold the past against her.

"That's a date." Rachel petted her faithful dog. "Thank you for understanding."

"Of course. I'm glad you trusted me."

"I've missed Sally. Is she still upset over the way I acted the day we got back from Estacado? I really didn't mean to treat her like she couldn't watch Eden."

"No, she seems fine enough to me."

"Bring her with you next time you come."

"Will do." He put a foot in the stirrup and settled in the saddle, pulling his Winchester from the scabbard and handing it down to her. "Keep this handy and I'll bring more ammunition next time."

Taking the weapon, she carefully kept it pointed at the ground. "Thanks. I hope I don't need it."

Shading her eyes against the afternoon sun, she watched until he was out of sight. The wind had switched to the north and whipped her skirts about her ankles. The chill in the air promised that fall was getting serious.

She turned to go back inside when she spotted Tillie riding up the trail. Her friend hadn't been around much since her uncle had come and she'd missed her.

"Hi, Rachel. Expecting trouble?" Tillie pointed to the rifle. "And why is Jax tied up?"

"Come on in out of the wind and I'll tell you about it. But first let me untie Jax. I just don't have the heart to leave him out in this windstorm. He keeps running off chasing something."

Tillie dismounted and waited for Rachel to untie Jax then they all went into the house.

"Care for a cup of hot tea?" Rachel asked, watching Jax settle on his rug.

"That sounds wonderful."

Rachel put the teakettle on and they sat down at the table. Over the course of the next hour Rachel told her about the strange happenings with Jax. "Heath thinks Uncle Zeb might be responsible."

Tillie took a sip of her tea. "What do you think?"

"I don't know." Rachel gave a big sigh. "I confess that none of this went on until Uncle Zeb came." She told about Sally taking a broom to him and they both laughed. "Although he and Jax don't cotton to each other, I honestly can't see him harming my dog."

"My advice is to trust Jax's instincts. An animal senses things that humans miss because our hearts get in the way. I'm glad Heath left his rifle here. Don't be afraid to use it."

"Something else happened that I'm puzzling over."

Tillie laughed. "I've been away longer than I thought."

Rachel told her friend about young Becca and how the girl acted toward the baby. "She looked like she was going to cry. It broke my heart."

"You're thinking she may be Eden's mother?"

"I hate to say it, but yes, that's what I fear." Rachel's voice lowered to an agonized whisper. "I can't lose that baby."

"Tell me again what she looked like."

After obliging, she asked, "Do you know anyone who fits Becca's description?"

Tillie squeezed Rachel's hand. "Afraid not. If I find out, I'll let you know."

"I'd appreciate that. Want some more tea?"

"I've had enough, thank you." Tillie took her cup to the dishpan. "You want to hear my news now?"

"Oh, you poor dear. Here you've been busting to tell me something and I've spent the entire time prattling about my problems. Yes, please tell me your news."

Tillie grinned. "I have a job."

"That's wonderful." Rachel rushed to hug her friend. "What kind? Where?"

"Teaching school on Thorn Hill Ranch. At the trading post

one day I heard that several of the big ranches in the area had built their own schools and were hiring teachers for their ranch children."

"This is great."

"Now I'll be able to keep my head above water. Hopefully, anyway. The extra money will sure help relieve some of my parents' stress and let them focus on getting Mama well."

"How is your mother doing?"

Tillie's face fell. "The doctors are not very optimistic I'm afraid."

"Oh, Tillie, I'm so sorry." She knew how it was to wait and hope and worry when loved ones were sick. "Is there anything I can do to help?"

"Just continue to be my friend. It's nice to have someone to confide in. Yancy is all I've got and sadly the deaf man wears me out trying to talk to him."

Sally and her loud bellows popped into Rachel's mind. Yancy and Sally would surely make an exhausting pair. "I'll always be your friend and you can talk to me anytime you want."

Even in such a diminished capacity, it made Rachel feel good to be needed. Most of the time she felt like a burden to everyone around her.

"Papa is talking about bringing my mother home. If that Arizona air isn't making her better, she might as well be back at home in her own bed."

"I know how much you'd love to have her with you."

Outside the howling wind beat against the house. The door gave way and slammed back against the wall, scaring Jax. He jumped to his feet, barking at the ghostly intruder. It took both Tillie and her to get the door closed and fastened. Of course, the noise woke up Eden who burst into squalls. Tillie reached to pick her up, cuddling the sweet baby.

"I declare, this is awful." Rachel picked up a small branch that had blown inside. "I want you to stay here until this dies down a bit."

"I hate to be a bother."

"Don't even think that, not after what you've done to help me. I never could've gotten all that zucchini bread, goat cheese, and butter made."

"Speaking of that, we might as well make some more while we're waiting."

"Are you sure?"

"Absolutely."

"I picked the last of the zucchini this morning."

Eden had quietened so Tillie put her back in the basket. Over the next three hours the girls chopped zucchini, mixed the ingredients, and baked the succulent bread. They ended up with six loaves. A very good use of their time. Rachel didn't know how she'd make it through the winter. She had nothing else to sell except a few eggs, cheese, and butter. Thanks to Heath she wouldn't have to worry about feeding her papa's bull for a while.

And there was still money he was paying for renting out the huge animal. Yet somehow it seemed she was making money off something that wasn't hers—a beast she didn't even want. But he insisted on paying so she'd shut up and accept. It was a gift from heaven he would say.

Dusk had turned the sky vibrant shades of purple and gold by the time the wind finally died down. Tillie mounted her horse and headed for home.

Rachel went inside and lit the lamps. The house was quiet.

Eden had awakened so she changed and fed her then sat in the rocker. Wide-eyed, the infant cooed, watching Rachel.

"Hey, little one, I hope you're happy here. I'm so glad you came but I wish you could talk and tell me about your mother." Eden yawned then opened her mouth like she was going to speak. "Oh, do you have something to say? Well, let's hear it."

The baby smiled, only Jane would have said that it was not a smile but gas.

Jane would've loved Eden. Rachel looked around the small parlor remembering the way things used to be. If she closed her eyes, she could probably hear the voices of her family.

It occurred to her that a house was more than paint and walls. It carried a history of all the loved ones it had sheltered, their hopes and dreams, laughter and many sorrows.

It didn't matter that the original house had burned. It was the land that tied the old and the new together. The souls of her people were buried on Malloy land. That history belonged to her now and the house was continuing to shelter her and now Eden. Maybe one day it would shelter Eden's husband and children.

She fixed a quick meal of eggs and thick slices of sourdough bread with fresh butter and wild blackberry preserves.

Uncle Zeb still hadn't returned unless he'd hidden in the barn which was likely if he wanted to hide his condition. Tomorrow would be soon enough to deal with him.

Finally, she readied for bed and lowered the lamps. But thoughts of Becca kept sleep at bay. Her heart ached for that distraught girl, and she couldn't help but think of her own desperate plight years ago.

It had felt good to trust Heath and confess her secret. He was right. She was lighter without the wall between them.

His gentle understanding just proved how much her father wronged her with his horrible lies. He'd truly tried to destroy her at every turn. Not only her but Alice too.

Rachel rose and rested her palm lightly on her precious Eden, gratitude filling her.

CHAPTER SEVENTEEN

The first ribbons of light tiptoed through the bedroom window and pried open Rachel's eyes, seemingly with a hammer and chisel, just as she was getting comfortable. She groaned and turned over.

What a night. Eden had awakened with the colic, and she'd walked the floor with the baby jiggling and rocking her. The shrill cries had broken Rachel's heart. Panic had set in, and she'd automatically feared Eden had contracted the fever or another deadly disease.

The knots in her stomach hadn't loosened until she'd figured out the problem. Once she'd seen the tightly clenched belly muscles, she knew what to do. Putting Eden on her stomach across her knees, she'd rubbed her tiny back for what seemed like hours.

At last, the baby girl quieted and slept. Rising on her elbow, Rachel looked over into the cradle, relieved Eden was still snoozing.

Slowly Rachel got dressed, wondering what this day would

bring. She prayed it went better than yesterday as she hurried toward the milking shed to milk the goats. She had plenty to do before Eden awoke and she didn't like leaving her in the house alone. Jax followed her and quickly went to work rounding up the goats that roamed free.

At least the dog knew his job and did it without having to be told. More than she could say for one certain gentleman.

She sent the barn a scathing glance. Thus far, she'd seen neither hide nor hair of her uncle. It was just as well.

She'd barely finished milking the first two nanny goats when she heard Eden's cries. She lifted the pail of fresh milk and whistled for Jax. When he came, she strode toward the house.

Although it killed her to tie up her loyal companion, she knew it was best. She couldn't bear to think of the animal getting hurt—or worse. As she held the rope in her hand Jax looked up with pleading eyes and began to whine.

In the end, she called him into the house instead. She'd tie him up later.

Along about mid-morning Uncle Zeb came stomping inside. He poured some cold coffee and made a face on the first sip. "Morning."

"It's a little late, isn't it?" Scowling, Rachel glanced up from her sewing. "Almost noon."

"I reckon. I didn't want to disturb you last night so I went straight to the barn."

"How considerate." She gave him a stern stare. "Were you drunk?"

"No. I gave you my word."

Like that would stop him. But she wouldn't argue without knowing the facts.

"You'll have to do with cold biscuits and eggs. If you want a hot meal, you'll have to wake up before the day's half gone."

"I know. I know."

She moved to the table, giving Eden a bottle as Zeb wolfed down food that he'd had no part in bringing into the house. "How did you sleep?"

He turned bleary eyes on her, and she thought she detected a bit of shame. Maybe she simply wanted him to show some guilt and remorse for what he put her through.

"Reckon I slept fine," he mumbled. "Why all the questions? Can't a man drink his coffee in peace?"

Eden's soft suckling noises filled the long silence.

Finally, Rachel spoke. "We had trespassers yesterday. I don't suppose you know anything about that."

Zeb's head jerked around. "Did they do anything?"

"Jax scared them off before they could." She leaned forward and jabbed a finger in his chest. "If they're your friends, tell them I have a rifle now and I'll shoot to kill."

His Adam's apple bobbed up and down and he lost some color. "Rifle?"

"That's what I said. Think you can remember that?"

"Sure." He hurried to add, "That is if I see them again, which I doubt I will."

Rachel smoothed the contented babe's soft blanket. "I'm glad for family, but I won't tolerate any more of your disappearances and the drinking."

"If it's about last night…"

"That's only part of it." She raised her chin a notch. "When I took you in, I thought you'd help out around here. I'm used to hard work, but I can't do everything. Nor should I. You have to shoulder some of the load, and I need help putting in a winter garden."

"I'll get right on that soon as I finish my coffee."

"Thank you. I'd appreciate it." Rachel was relieved to have the talk over with even though it didn't go exactly as she'd planned.

HEATH STEPPED FROM his barn, his mind on a million different things. Anger and fury had kept him awake most of the night. Rachel had already seen the worst a young woman should. Now, it made sense why she'd turned down his offer of marriage. He pulled a stool over to milk the cow. He still had to repair a fence before he took Sally to call on Rachel and the baby. The cow munched contentedly on some hay and soon the full bucket held enough.

Outside, his pulse beat a little faster just thinking about spending time with Rachel. He never tired of her company. Soon. Wandering thoughts turned to Rachel's sweet lips. He certainly didn't get weary of kissing her.

Not the least. In fact, her kisses were like fresh rain after a drought. With her confession yesterday, he was making headway on the plan to wed her. He just needed to go slow and steady. Some things a man couldn't rush.

Movement in the sky made him glance up and his breath froze.

Circling in the sky were at least a dozen buzzards.

Something was dead. Had someone killed Jax? Or one of the goats? Or…

Surely something hadn't happened to Rachel. Please, no.

With a prayer on his lips, he set the milk down, stumbled back into the barn, and quickly saddled his horse. Barely taking a minute to put the milk in the house and let Sally know where he was headed, he gently slapped the reins on the animal's flank and sent it galloping toward the sight.

He had no idea what he'd find. But if someone had hurt Rachel or Eden, they'd best look over their shoulder because he'd come for them.

Heath raced into the Malloy yard and was off the horse before it stopped. He didn't bother with knocking. He barreled inside and drew up short when Rachel jumped to her feet. Jax went into a barking frenzy until he recognized Heath.

"What's wrong?" Rachel's green eyes widened with fear. "Tell me."

He covered the space between them in long strides and pulled her into his arms.

"Thank God you're all right," he breathed into her hair. "If anything had happened..."

"I'm fine. Maybe you'd best tell me why you thought I wouldn't be."

Heath released her and gave her a wry smile. "I noticed buzzards circling over this way and my mind jumped to conclusions I'm afraid."

"Buzzards? I wonder what could've happened now." Her brow wrinkled.

"No telling. Do you know where your uncle is?"

"I just had a heart to heart with him, told him how I stood with things. He's probably in the barn sulking."

Sounded about right. He turned to Rachel. "Do you mind if I take your dog?"

"Of course not." She chewed her bottom lip like she did when she was scared and trying not to show it. "I can't imagine what you'll find out there."

"Whatever or whoever it is hasn't been dead long or we'd

have seen the buzzards sooner." He patted Jax's head. "Come on. Let's go see what we can find."

She clutched his arm. "Be careful."

Just then Eden let out a squall. Rachel went to take care of her as Heath and Jax went out the door.

The dog appeared happy to be in the fresh air and took off with a bound. His sensitive nose picked up the dead scent long before Heath. Quickly mounting the horse, Heath set out behind.

They hadn't gone far when Jax gave an excited bark and left the trail, racing into the dense undergrowth. Heath slid from the saddle, jerked his rifle from the scabbard, and plunged after the dog. Thistle and cactus tore at his clothes, but he paid them no heed.

He could tell by the barking that Jax had stopped. He'd found whatever had died.

Gripping the rifle, he proceeded into a small clearing that was someone's campsite. Cold embers lay inside a circle of stones. A horse grazed on some tall buffalo grass, glancing up.

And lying on a bedroll was the form of a woman.

Jax sniffed at her then whined pitifully and sat on his haunches.

"It's okay, boy." He ruffled the dog's ears. "You did real good."

Heath laid his rifle down and got a closer look at the auburn-haired woman. From the amount of animal activity, she'd been dead probably a day or so. Her brown eyes were wide open, and her cheeks were sunken. He knelt to close them and mouthed a quiet prayer for the woman's soul, asking God to be merciful. This was an unforgiving country, and it took everything a person had to survive.

An empty bottle of laudanum rested next to her. Had she

killed herself? Aside from that, there were no obvious signs of death. She had no bullet holes or other wounds as far as he could tell. But flecks of blood showed around her mouth.

With a heavy heart he wrapped her in the bedroll then turned to get her horse. He'd have to get a shovel from Rachel to bury this woman.

How sad that she ended up dying here all alone. He wished he knew who her folks were so he could let them know. But it seemed she'd taken her identity with her to the grave.

Telling Jax to stay and guard, he got on his horse.

RACHEL WAS HANGING the wash on the clothesline when she spied Heath and she froze. He led a strange horse. What had happened? Her breath caught in her throat. Dear God.

So much for hoping the buzzards had been feasting on a dead animal.

She dropped a wet flour sack that served as a diaper she'd been about to hang.

"What was it?" she asked as she hurried to meet them.

Heath pulled up and dismounted. "A woman. Don't know who she is. We may never learn her name. I came back for a shovel to dig a grave."

Briefly, he described her campsite.

"What on earth she was doing out here all by herself?" Rachel pushed back tendrils of hair with a trembling hand.

"The horse wears the Thorn Hill brand. After I bury her, I'll ride over to their ranch and see if anyone knows her. Or at least say how their horse ended up with her."

Just then Uncle Zeb came from the barn. She told him about

the dead woman. "I don't suppose you'd know who she is would you?"

"Don't know anything about any woman," Zeb answered. He lifted a hand to his chin in thought. That's when she took notice that he'd shaved and put on clean clothes. She'd never seen him without his scraggly beard before. He looked years younger. Now that she could see him better, she'd put his age closer to early fifties.

"You've been all over this property and the surrounding area a lot lately, Thacker." Heath spoke up. "Did you happen to see smoke from a campsite?"

Zeb Thacker's gaze flicked from Rachel to Heath. "What are you implying?"

"Not implying anything. Simply asking a question."

A tense silence followed. Rachel stepped between them. "We don't have time for this. We have a woman to bury, and I suggest we get to it."

Heath sighed. "You're right."

"I'll get the shovel," Zeb said, taking off.

Rachel picked up the laundry basket. "I'll go back with you. I want to see what she looks like. Let me get Eden and my horse."

Before she reached the house, Sally drove up in the buckboard. "Got tired of twiddling my thumbs and waiting for Heath to come back for me," Sally explained, climbing down. "Decided to take matters into my own hands."

"I'm glad you came." Rachel told her what Heath had found. "Will you stay with Eden?"

"Honey, you don't even have to ask." Sally marched into the house and picked up the child. "My goodness, she's growing like a weed. I sure have missed her."

"We've missed you too, Sally. How have you been?"

"Fair to middling. Some days it's all I can do to keep from wringing Heath's neck. You know, I really suspect he's not deaf one bit. I think he just doesn't want to listen to me."

Rachel hid a grin behind her hand. "Don't get me in the middle of that." She kissed Eden and grabbed the comb and brush. A woman needed her hair brushed good and proper before being put in the ground. "I've got to go, Sally."

"Take your time. Me and this sweet darling will be just fine."

Rachel hurried out to find that Heath had already saddled her horse and Uncle Zeb was mounted on his.

After the men dug the hole, they all stood around the grave with reverence. Heath said some nice words and quoted a few scriptures. Then Rachel laid some pretty wildflowers she'd picked on top of the grave. Whoever the woman was she hoped someone somewhere remembered her.

Afterward Rachel rode back and with Sally's help made lunch for everyone. Then Heath left to return the horse to the Thorn Hill Ranch. It was mid-afternoon when Heath returned from Thorn Hill Ranch. She and Eden met him in the yard.

"Well, I have one piece to the puzzle," he said. "One of their ranch hands said the woman worked at the tent saloon over by Estacado. Her name was Alma. Didn't get her last name. When his back was turned, Alma lit out with his horse that was part of the ranch's remuda."

Rachel let her hand drift to Jax's dark fur. "Do you think my dog has been disappearing to her campsite?"

"Hard to say. Neither the dead nor Jax can speak. But I saw no tracks, either human or animal. But I did find the dog following those intruders, so I don't think he'd visited Alma."

Her thoughts whirling, she glanced down at her faithful

pet. "You're right. You've seen a lot out here and trust your gut. What do you think was wrong with the woman?"

"My gut says she was sickly. I saw signs of vomit." He knelt to give Jax some attention. "It would still be best to tie him up whenever you can't keep an eye on him. At least until we know the danger has passed." His gaze swung toward the house. "Where's Sally and Zeb?"

"I don't know. I was going to look for them after I hung the wash."

They rounded the side of the house and heard loud voices. Rachel stopped.

"Mr. Thacker, idle hands are the devil's workshop," Sally scolded. "You're gonna get the lead out of the seat of your pants or you'll answer to me. Rachel didn't have to take you in. But she did." Sally clucked. "Lord knows, that girl has a heart of gold. The poor thing is so desperate for family that she lets you get away with being a lazy good-for-nothing. But don't think for one minute that I'm going to."

"Are you finished, madam?" Uncle Zeb's voice sounded stiff and strained.

Rachel held Eden close and followed Heath. They peeked around the corner. Sally's hands were on her hips and smoke seemed to rise from the top of the woman's head.

"I'm just getting started. Not only what I think but what I know. Rachel has her hands full with taking care of that sweet baby and doing the washing and ironing and cooking and cleaning. She shouldn't have to do all the outside chores too."

Zeb squinted one eye. "How do you know what I do or don't do? Has Rachel complained to you?"

"Lord, no. She ain't a complainer. But I can see how tired she is and the circles under her eyes. I tell you it's got to change. One way or another."

Zeb drew himself up straight. "Or what, madam? You've been chewing on me since I came."

"Someone needed to." Sally paused to take a breath.

Before Rachel knew what her uncle was about to do, he grabbed Sally and kissed her. Heath stiffened and started to step forward.

She held him back whispering, "Wait, let's see what Sally does."

When Uncle Zeb let Sally up for air, she threw her shoulders back and bellowed, "Mr. Thacker! What are you doing? You're drunk!"

"Well, madam, if I have to explain it to you, I guess I didn't do it very well. Though you appeared to like it well enough while I was doing it."

"You're a sin and a disgrace." Sally wiped her mouth and spat.

"I figured I would give you something to think about." A light twinkled in Zeb's eyes as he pulled her close again. "You sure are a handsome woman if you don't mind me saying so."

"You wouldn't know a handsome woman if one bit you, you...you old codger!"

Rachel contained a giggle as Sally slapped Zeb's chest, her hands nothing but a blur.

"I know plenty." A perplexed frown creased his forehead as he sniffed.

Sally patted her hair that sported a few streaks of gray. "I thank you to remove your hand."

"Yessum. I reckon when I get ready." He squinted at her through half-closed lids.

Sally's face flushed. She was winding up to go after Zeb again when Heath broke free from Rachel's grip and stepped from the shadows of the house, his face a storm cloud. "Coming, Sally? We need to get back for evening chores."

Sally hollered, "Right behind you, Heath. Gladly."

Later, as Rachel held Eden, watching the buckboard roll out and head up the canyon trail Zeb appeared. "Rachel girl, I purely do admire a woman with gumption. I do for a fact, but that woman can sure pack a wallop."

"I think you've lost your mind. Sally didn't appreciate your attention."

"Aw, she's just playing hard to get." Zeb rubbed his chin. "I'll wear her down. A woman her age needs to be shook up once in a while."

"You've been eating locoweed. Best get Sally out of your mind because she isn't having it." Rachel stepped closer and caught the smell of liquor just as Sally had. "You are drinking!"

He waved her away. "Aw, it was just a snort. Don't get your bloomers in a wad."

Rachel pointed toward the path leading to the rim that the heavy dusk hadn't yet hidden. "That does it. Pack your things and get out of here. I gave you plenty of warning and I meant what I said about coming back drunk." Eden began to cry, and she jostled her.

"Fine with me. You'll regret this," he snarled, his eyes two angry slits.

"No, I only regret being taken in and believing you were kin to me. Heath tried to warn me. I wish Sally *had* beat you with that broom. Now get off my land."

She stayed where she was until he brought his horse from the barn and rode off, disappearing from sight. He was gone. With a heavy heart, she called Jax and went inside. Part of her seemed lighter. But another part held worry. Now except for Eden, she was truly alone.

CHAPTER EIGHTEEN

Still as mad as a sack full of snakes, Heath cast a sidelong glance at his sister who sat prim and proper on the wagon seat as they bumped along the trail rising to the rim. "Are you all right?"

Sally fidgeted with her worn skirt, keeping her eyes fixed on the horse's rump. "I don't know."

"Why was Thacker kissing you?"

"The old buzzard lost his mind and was drunk. I was laying down the law to him one minute and the next he just hauled off and kissed me. Out of the blue. With no warning. I told him exactly what he could do with his kisses." Fuming, she finally turned a miserable gaze on him. "I'm really worried about Rachel and Eden."

"Me too." His fear for them was much deeper than he let anyone know. Heath patted her hand. "Thacker rubbed me the wrong way from the start. There's something about the man I don't trust, and you'll do well to keep your distance."

"You needn't fret about that." Sally crossed her arms.

Noble Tucker, Yancy's son, crossed Heath's mind. Noble had lived and worked on Tillie's parents' ranch with his father. The man had asked for Sally's hand in marriage, and they'd even set the date. An hour before the ceremony, Noble disappeared along with Skeet Slaughter's daughter. It seemed Noble had gotten the young lady in the family way—while courting Sally. Heath and Yancy's friendship had been strained ever since.

"It took forever for the wound in your heart to heal after Noble," he reminded Sally.

"That was a long time ago, Heath. Sometimes I get so awfully lonely I can't stand it."

He reached to put an arm around her shoulder. "I'm sorry."

Sally sighed. "Sometimes it seems life has passed me by as if I'm no more consequence than a leaf blowing in the wind." Her voice sounded sad and much older than her thirty-eight years. "I just want to know that I matter to someone before I die, that my life hasn't been for naught."

The section of the trail they came to had fall trees on both sides decked out in reds and yellows so beautiful they took his breath. He loved this land and the changing seasons.

After a moment, he dragged his attention back to the conversation and softened his voice. "You're still a young woman, Sally. You matter to a lot of people. You matter to me. I don't often say it, but I love you and I know Rachel and Eden cherish you."

Sally straightened as though gearing for battle and inhaled. "I know."

"We all need someone special," Heath admitted softly, thinking of Rachel.

Sometimes the ache for her consumed him and he dreamed of the day he'd make her his.

Turning back to Sally, he said a silent prayer that God would protect his sister's heart. He didn't want to be the one picking up the pieces a second time.

A WEEK LATER, Rachel hitched up the wagon and drove to Singer's Trading Post to sell her eggs, butter, and goat cheese.

Enjoying the beautiful day, her mind flitted from one thing to another. Beside her on the seat was the wicker basket that held a sleeping Eden. She thought of Uncle Zeb and had caught glimpses of him down by the lake. So he hadn't left as she'd prayed he would.

What was he hanging around for? Would he hurt her? She didn't really know him.

Thoughts still circling like prancing horses, she pulled up to the post and set the brake. Climbing down, she tied the horse to the hitching rail and lifted the basket holding the baby. Movement drew her gaze.

Becca stepped through the open door and came to an abrupt stop at sight of her.

Sudden panic gripped Rachel. She instantly clutched the basket, drawing it closer. Then she noticed the pain filling the girl's brown eyes and forced a smile. "Hello, Becca, how nice to see you again."

The girl still wore the same tattered clothes and her hair unwashed. Rachel wondered about the girl's mother and why she didn't take better care of her daughter. Still, if Becca had gotten herself in the family way, maybe her mother had disowned her and kicked her out to fend for herself.

Becca kept her eyes down for the most part, glancing only briefly at the basket that held Rachel's heart.

"Do you like babies, Becca?" she asked softly.

The girl nodded shyly.

"I do too. It was awfully nice of you to give Eden the blue ribbon when you came visiting. Do you live around here?"

Before the girl could answer a group of rough-looking men rode up to the post making the hair on hair on her neck rise. An uneasy feeling washed over Rachel as well as memories of her abductors. One of the riders with an ugly scar across his face leaned an elbow on his saddle horn and boldly stared. He rode a beautiful piebald. Much too nice a horse for the likes of him.

They might be the same ones she'd found Zeb talking to but couldn't be sure.

When she turned back to Becca, the girl had vanished just like before.

Rachel clutched Eden and tried to shake off her jangled nerves. She wished for nothing more than to climb into the wagon, race for home, and hide in the safety of her house.

"I think you scared her staring like that, Billy," a rider with a red bandana said.

She wanted to bolt to her wagon, but chances were they'd only chase her. Ignoring them, she hurried inside in a flurry of skirts as they whirled around her ankles.

"Well, let me see that little darlin'," George Singer hollered when he saw her. He clucked over Eden declaring, "She's sure growing. Next thing I know she'll be walking and talking and giving me what-for."

Rachel took a deep breath to still her terror. "That she will, Mr. Singer."

"I hope you brought some eggs and such-like because I can sure sell 'em."

"Sure did. They're out in the wagon."

"I hope you have more zucchini bread. Folks from all around clamor for it."

"Sorry, sir. The crop is gone."

Footsteps sounded on the rough wooden floor. Rachel turned and her breath froze. The riders strolled inside like they owned it. Singer glanced up. "I'll be with you in a minute."

"We'd be obliged if you'd wait on us now," said the one with the scar they'd called Billy. All three of the men formed a circle around Rachel, Eden, and Singer. Rachel kept her gaze lowered.

Singer put himself in front of her. "You'll have to wait your turn I'm afraid."

Rachel laid a hand on Singer's arm. "Please, go ahead and take care of them. Eden and I are in no hurry."

George sighed and turned. "What will it be?"

"Ammunition, coffee, and tobacco," snapped Billy. "And don't dawdle. We ain't used to waiting."

While George set about filling their order, Rachel got the eggs, butter, and goat cheese from the wagon. Since she couldn't very well carry Eden and everything else, she left the baby on the counter in her basket with Singer guarding her. It killed her to leave Eden and she wished she hadn't left Jax tied up at home. Jax could intimidate people who didn't know him.

As much as she loathed Eden being out of her sight for a minute or two, she knew George would protect the child he doted on with his life. Trembling with fear, Rachel wasted no time in returning. Blood chilled in her veins to see the man wearing a red bandana bending over Eden's basket.

"Get away from her!" She set the basket of goods on the floor and quickly lifted Eden.

A plug of chewing tobacco bulged out one side of the man's cheeks and he aimed a stream of brown juice toward a spittoon on the floor. It didn't quite make it, leaving a big glob on the wooden floor. He wiped the back of his hand across his mouth and snarled, "That kid belong to you, girlie?"

Singer slid an arm around Rachel. "Gentlemen, I don't allow trouble."

"Now, ain't that just too bad?" Billy stuck a knife into a bag of sugar and watched it pour out.

Intent on escape, Rachel inched toward the open door.

Two riders blocked her way. "We didn't tell you to hightail it out of here, girlie."

Scarface snarled, "She ain't very hospitable. What's your name, girl?"

"Rachel," she said quietly, clutching Eden tight. Her legs shook, barely holding her up.

"Well, Rachel, how about we have us a little fun?" Billy lifted a tendril of her hair between his fingers and put it to his nose. "Whoo-ee! That smells right sweet."

Suddenly a tall shadow blocked the sunlight streaming through the open doorway. "Leave her be," a steely voice barked.

Rachel looked up at the tall commanding figure and breathed a sigh of relief.

Heath Lassiter.

"Who are you to give orders?" Scarface asked.

"I'm going to be your worst nightmare if you don't move aside and let the lady pass." He pointed his rifle at the trio. "Now."

"Maybe we best go," said another, casting a nervous glance at Heath.

"That would be a wise decision." Though Heath's voice was silky smooth, a deadly force lay beneath the surface. He took a few steps inside. "Rachel, are you all right?"

"I'm fine." She tried to keep the tremble from her voice but didn't quite succeed.

"Get behind me," he ordered quietly.

She squeezed around the man blocking her path and found safety behind Heath, praying the men would leave and he wouldn't get hurt. She didn't know what she'd do if the men turned the tables. The realization hit her that Heath had come to mean so much to her.

"Here's the way this is going to go, gentlemen," Heath said. "You're walking out of here and going to keep on riding. Don't know what rock you crawled out from under, but you'd best go back to it. And if I catch you near this trading post again, I'll give you reason to regret it."

The red bandana rider swallowed hard. "We was only funnin'. Didn't mean no harm."

"That's not what it looked like to me," Heath replied. "I oughta shoot you for being so darn ugly if for no other reason."

"Come on." Billy motioned to his companions. "Let's go."

"Excellent choice, gentlemen," Heath said keeping the rifle on them until they were out of the trading post. A minute later the sound of galloping horses reached them.

Heath turned to her. "You sure you're all right, Rachel?"

"I'm fine. I don't think I've ever been so glad to see anyone in my life though. Those men terrified me." She didn't object when he put down his rifle and tenderly took Eden from her. She had to find a place to sit down and fast.

George Singer obviously saw her need and rushed forward. After helping her to an upended barrel, he left to get her a drink of water from the well in front.

Heath stood beside her with his feet planted as tall and strong as an oak tree. "What were you doing coming here by yourself? Where's Thacker?"

Rachel took a cup of water from George and sipped on it. "I kicked him out and I had to get these things to Mr. Singer." She pointed to the basket of goods still sitting on the floor. "I forgot the rifle and I should've brought Jax. I'm going to have to do better."

"You will. I'm glad Thacker's gone but it sure throws you in a bind. Did you recognize any of those men from the riders you caught Zeb talking to?"

Rachel pushed her hair back with hands that still trembled. "Maybe but I'm not sure."

George took a deep breath. "Lassiter, I have to say you arrived in the nick of time I don't know what would've happened if you hadn't. I'm truly in your debt."

"Best keep a rifle handy, George."

"I have one behind the counter, 'cept I couldn't get to it." Mr. Singer wagged his head. "I've seldom had call to use it. Everyone trading here is a peaceable sort. Who do you think they were?"

Heath's jaw clenched. "Don't know. But they'd better pass on through." His deep voice vibrated the air.

Steel laced his words and Rachel was glad she wasn't on the receiving end of his anger. She'd never seen this side of Heath. One thing she'd learned and that was he'd defend her and Eden with his life if that was what it took to keep them safe.

She'd never felt so protected. Not once. Closing her eyes, she smiled.

CHAPTER NINETEEN

"Circuit preacher's ridin' through here on Sunday, Heath," George Singer announced. "An outrider brought the news this morning."

Heath's met Rachel's gaze. "I've missed church. Is it Reverend Holcomb?"

"Nope. This preacher's name is Anson Ledbetter. I hear Holcomb got himself shot last month up in Indian territory. It's sure dangerous up there. Yesiree."

Rachel's stomach knotted. Heath was going to ask her to go with him and she wasn't sure she was ready for any fire and brimstone. God was still a mystery. Sure, He'd given her Eden, but then sent Becca to take her. He seemingly gave with one hand and took away with the other.

Heath shifted Eden and the baby stared at him with big eyes. Then she gave him a goofy smile.

Heath chuckled. "Well, look at that! She's happy and content, Rachel."

"It does seem so." She couldn't help wonder if Eden would be as satisfied with Becca.

Singer bent and retrieved the basket of goods still on the floor. He tallied up what he owed her and handed her the small amount of change which she pocketed along with thanks.

"I'll see you home if you're ready." Heath carefully tucked the baby into her basket.

"I'm ready."

He put his arm around Rachel's waist and drew her to his side. The day was so perfect with a nip in the air. He offered a hand as she climbed into the buckboard then handed the basket to her that held Eden. Once he tied his horse onto the back, he settled beside her and lifted the reins.

"You don't have to do this, Heath. I'm sure those men are long gone by now." At least she hoped so. If she ever saw them again it would be too soon. The memory of Chewing Tobacco touching her hair made her shiver despite the sun's rays.

Heath's leg rested lightly against hers as they made the journey home and she found it a comfort. "Will you go with me Sunday to hear the circuit preacher?"

"I respect your right to worship and profess your faith. But I can't get excited over a God who strips a person of every last thing she has."

"Just promise me you'll think about it. That's all I ask."

"All right, but don't expect I'll change my mind."

They rode for a while in silence listening to the jangle of the rigging and an occasional snort from the horses.

They neared home when Heath spoke, "I've been thinking. Why not send a note to the stage office in Clarendon with the preacher? He travels around this area. That way they could send someone to pick up the strongbox and no one would have to go."

Relief raced through her. "That's a wonderful idea! It's perfect. Do you think he would?"

"We can ask."

"Then do." Curiosity got the best of her, and she couldn't help ask, "Heath, why did you happen to go to the trading post today of all days?"

His crooked smile took her breath. "Had a feeling in my gut that something wasn't right. I get those sometimes and I think it's God's way of saying that I need to listen. I also wanted to check the mail, which I plumb forgot."

"Whatever it was that made you go I'm extremely thankful. I don't know what those men planned but it wasn't good. And Mr. Singer was no match for them."

"I hope you've learned your lesson. No more traipsing off without company. And even on your land keep the rifle within reach. We may not have seen the last of those men."

"Maybe not. I've seen Zeb watching me from the trees and it makes me nervous."

"Rachel, think about coming to stay with me and Sally a few days." The somber quietness of Heath's tone sent chills creeping up her spine.

Whatever was going on, whoever those men were, it wasn't over. Danger followed her like a dark hulking shadow. She shivered. "If I do that, no telling what they'd do. Maybe burn the place down again." She shook her head. "No, I can't leave."

Heath suddenly began to hum and then burst out singing the old hymn *I Shall Not Be Moved*. He must really like it because she'd heard him croon it several times.

Or maybe it was his subtle way of making fun of her and her refusal to accept God's will.

"Just like the tree that's planted by the water, I shall not be moved," he sang in his beautiful baritone.

Yes, she did think he was poking fun.

Eden opened her pretty blue eyes and stared up at Rachel. Then she began to coo. Oh, no, not her too. The infant couldn't possibly know what the words meant, but she seemed to.

Rachel lifted her little darling from the basket and nuzzled her soft cheek. This baby had brought so much joy. The love she felt consumed every part of her.

That evening after putting the final stitches on the baby blanket made from the new flannel she set it aside. Jax dozed in front of a fire and Eden was asleep. Happiness wound around her heart.

She warmed her hands at the fire, listening for sounds of trouble outside. She couldn't afford to get too comfortable she reminded herself, reaching for the poker and turning the log.

Thoughts of the preacher filled her. She'd done a lot of things she wasn't proud of and didn't know if the congregation would accept her as the daughter of a hated outlaw. Word might've gotten out and they'd turn their back on her. Not everyone was as accepting as Heath.

Ugly gossip had a way of spreading.

ON SATURDAY MORNING after arming herself, Rachel loaded Eden in the wagon for a short ride to visit Tillie. She'd missed her friend since Tillie had taken the school teaching job.

Tillie rushed from the house when Rachel drove up. "How wonderful. I was just thinking about you. I have some news."

Rachel handed Eden to her friend and they went into the house, straight to the kitchen table. It seemed like all their problems had been hashed out at the table over hot tea. Tillie put hot water on.

"I have some things to tell you about also," Rachel said.

"Me first." Tillie grinned. "You'll want to hear this. The girl, Becca, whom you suspect is this baby's mother is in my class. Turns out her father is the new windmill man for Thorn Hill Ranch."

A vise tightened around Rachel's heart. She could barely squeeze out the words, "Tell me about her."

"She's sort of slow. Though she's fifteen, her father wants her to get an education. Becca has learning problems and can only read and write a little. I hope I can make a difference."

"Oh, Tillie, what should I do?" Rachel whispered. "How can I give Eden up now?"

Tillie rested a hand on Rachel's. "Even if Becca is Eden's mother, and I'm not saying she is, her father must've thought her incapable of raising a child. They might've given the baby up because they probably thought you could give her a much better life."

"I hope you're right."

"You should see them. It's just Becca and her father and they live out of an old sheepherder's wagon. They don't have anything to offer a child. I hear his wife died."

When the teapot whistled, Tillie handed Eden back and took the pot off the stove. She threw in a helping of tea leaves then took two cups from a shelf.

"How sad." And here Rachel had thought her circumstances were rough. Just showed there were people lots worse off than her. "But Becca and her father could always change their minds. Especially if their fortunes change." She would never relax, knowing they were close.

"I hoped this would ease your mind," Tillie murmured. "Now, what were you wanting to tell me?"

Over the next hour, Rachel told her friend about the dead woman Heath had found and the incident at the trading post.

"It was frightening." Rachel took a sip of her tea. "I don't know what would've happened had Heath not appeared in time."

"And you've never seen those men before?"

"Never. They were terrifying."

"Then I think you need to listen to Heath and take someone with you when you go back. In fact, just to be safe, you need to have someone along every time you leave your property. Your uncle or someone."

"Oh, I forgot to tell you—I kicked him out."

Tillie grinned and refilled their cups. "You certainly haven't been bored."

"Uncle Zeb got drunk and kissed Sally. She lit into him. I'd warned him about drinking."

They spent a few more hours discussing the turns their lives had taken. Finally, Rachel prepared to leave.

"I wish you didn't have to go so soon," Tillie said. "But I know you must." She kissed Eden and hugged Rachel. "Did you hear about the circuit preacher on Sunday?"

Rachel groaned. "Not you, too."

"What does that mean?"

"After telling Heath I won't go, I ended up promising to think about it."

A look of dejection crossed Tillie's face. "I really want to go. Please come with me."

Tears sparkling in Tillie's eyes broke Rachel's heart. She knew she couldn't say no. She'd do anything for Tillie. Even something she vowed not to do.

CHAPTER TWENTY

*S*unday morning, Heath put on the white shirt that he'd always saved for the Sabbath and saddled his new appaloosa. Anticipation built inside. He'd hated having to go so long between sermons.

If only Rachel was going with him the beautiful sunshine would be perfect.

Heath knew he had some things to talk over with the Man upstairs. One thing he sorely wanted help with was Rachel. It burdened his heart to see her continuing to be so conflicted and not know how to fix it.

Or even if it was his job to do so. He hadn't seen the white dove in quite a while, and he wondered what that meant. Had he mistaken the message? Maybe it hadn't been a sign of anything.

With his horse saddled, he hitched up the wagon for Sally. Wearing her best bonnet, Sally came from the soddy humming a tune and stepping smartly. His sister was in a good mood.

By the time they arrived at Singer's, about a dozen folks had already gathered.

"Reverend, we sure appreciate you coming. It's been a while since we've had an opportunity to worship." Heath shook Ledbetter's hand, happy to see he was younger than the previous one with a thatch of dark hair. Women would find him handsome and they'd be sure to notice the absence of a ring.

"The good Lord willing, it won't be long before I return," Ledbetter said, smoothing down his hair and beard. "There are sure a passel of lost souls on the Texas frontier. Working in the vineyard of the Lord keeps me busy from dawn to dusk."

Heath nodded and helped another man carry a bench and some barrels from the trading post for seating. Thankfully, women with large broods were spreading quilts on the ground.

He glanced around, hoping Rachel had changed her mind. Not seeing her greatly disappointed him.

The small congregation had just stood for a hymn when he felt the swish of skirts against his leg and someone jostled his elbow.

Surprise and joy spread to see Rachel, the babe, and Tillie Gregory sliding into place beside him.

His heart awash in happiness, he took Eden from Rachel's arms.

The words to *Amazing Grace* had never been sung with more fervor than the way he was singing them. His hand stole to Rachel's and lightly squeezed.

Preacher Ledbetter opened his Bible and a hush fell over the crowd. "Folks, it is happy I am to be here on this beautiful Lord's Day. Life is hard here on the prairie and we're forced to deal with many things. Death sometimes steals our loved ones and leaves our hearts grieving, our spirits raw."

Heath cast a sideways glance at Rachel. Tears swam in her pale green eyes. He mouthed a silent prayer that this preacher would say the words she needed to hear.

" 'To everything there is a season and a time to every purpose under the heaven,' " Ledbetter read from the Bible then went on. "We're not promised tomorrow. We're only promised God's grace to see us through. And folks, if you think you're the only one having trials and tribulations, you're sadly mistaken. Every person on this earth suffers tragedy at one time or another and sometimes it comes in twos and threes. We could learn from Job.

"In the deepest darkest night you're not alone," Ledbetter continued. "God hears your cries even when you think He's not listening. The Almighty God has a plan for each for us."

Heath sent Rachel a glance and found her biting her lip to stop its trembling.

"If we keep our faith and trust in the Lord Almighty, we can find a better day. Some folks have asked me what faith is." Ledbetter leaned forward. "I tell them this. Faith is the little bird that sings when the dawn is still dark. The bird can't see in the blackness, but it sings anyway, trusting that it'll get lighter soon."

Sally shouted, "Amen! Give us some fire and brimstone, Preacher. I want some good old fire and brimstone."

Heath hung his head and Ledbetter appeared taken aback.

Finally, the preacher found his voice. "Not today, sister. I always believed in laying a foundation before I start telling folks they're going to hell less'n they mend their ways."

"I see." Disgruntled, Sally adjusted her hat that had slipped.

The reverend delivered more words of encouragement then concluded with a prayer.

As soon as the service ended Heath turned to Rachel. "Thank you for changing your mind."

"It's all Tillie's doing."

His gaze followed Tillie as she went to talk to the reverend. The young lady must be a miracle worker. "I'm glad. What did you think of Reverend Ledbetter?"

"Let's say he's given me plenty to think about."

The remains of tears sparkled in her beautiful green eyes. Heath didn't think he'd ever seen a prettier angel. Sometimes in the dead of night he remembered her laughter and the sound of her voice and he knew he'd not be complete until she became his wife.

And if that day never came? He'd have to find contentment being in her life however she let him he supposed. But he knew in his heart that God would hear his prayers and grant him his fervent wish. He just had to be patient.

"Rachel, how would you and Tillie like to come eat with Sally and me? Not sure what we're having but I know Sally will whip up a dandy meal. She loves having someone to fuss over besides me." He lowered his mouth to her ear and spoke low. "And, I've caught the yearning in her eyes to get her hands on the little princess here."

"I'll have to ask Tillie. If she has no objection, then we'll do it."

IT TURNED OUT that they did indeed accept Sally and Heath's hospitality along with the preacher. Rachel looked around the table that day at the soddy and it hit her that they'd formed their own family of sorts. Formed by love and the desperate need to matter to someone.

She glanced at Heath and her heart swelled. He was a handsome man with his strong square jaw and broad shoulders. She'd always thought his eyes reminded her of smoke but lately several things made her decide they were more the color of gunmetal gray.

Heath Lassiter was a gentle soul who could still put the fear of God in a man in no uncertain terms. Something said he'd risk his life to protect her and Eden. Deep convictions drew her respect.

Though they'd not spoken of marriage of late she knew he'd not forgotten. She prayed that when she was ready, he'd still want her.

Heath had taken the preacher aside for a private word upon their arrival. Rachel gave it no thought since men liked to talk when they got a chance and had gone on inside with Tillie to help prepare the meal.

She sat across the table from the preacher and found him quite knowledgeable about farming.

"I once had a farm but fell on hard times and had to sell it," Ledbetter said. "But I love living off the land and growing things."

Rachel passed him the fresh bread. "Do you ever think you'll go back to it?" Rachel asked.

"I hope to one day."

Sally had done an excellent job putting together the meal of fried chicken, mashed potatoes, turnips and greens. There was even a delicious blackberry cobbler for dessert.

Ledbetter wore a wide smile. "Miss Sally, you sure set a fine table laden with wonderful food. I haven't had a better meal."

Sally beamed. "Thank you, reverend."

He leaned forward. "Can you call me Anson?"

"I suppose I can if you'd like."

"I do."

Rachel noticed the long glances Sally gave their traveling guest and wondered if she'd taken a liking to Anson Ledbetter. They seemed about the same age and Sally wasn't past the need for love. No woman was.

When the last bite was taken and the dishes cleared, Heath cleared his throat and asked Rachel if she cared to take a walk with him.

Her heart sped up. "I'd love to if Sally and Tillie won't mind watching Eden."

Heath's grin widened. "Surely you jest. They've been itching for the chance."

"You go on," Sally blustered, waving her arm. "Me and Tillie would like to listen to Anson's experiences on the trail."

"In that case, I will." Rachel threw her shawl over her shoulders. She loved the warmth of Heath's hand at her waist and the sound of her skirts swishing gently against his leg.

Alone at last, she asked, "Did you see how Sally seemed quite taken with the reverend?"

"I did and I'm happy for her. Like me, she needs someone." His arm slipped around her, drawing her closer. "I also spoke to him about delivering a note to the stage line office in Clarendon and he agreed. I already wrote it and gave it to him so that's settled."

"How soon until he reaches there?"

"A couple of weeks he thinks."

"I'm so relieved." A companionable moment of silence passed between them. "Where are we going?"

"Does it matter?" he mumbled against her ear, his warm breath stirring a tendril of hair.

"I reckon not."

"Thought we'd stroll down to the corral. I've named my new appaloosa Buttermilk."

His sudden grin caught her breath. "That's a good name."

When they reached the corral, she leaned against a post and watched the frisky horses. They made a good pair—Hondo with his black shiny coat and Buttermilk's all over gray with white spots on his hindquarters. She didn't think she'd seen happier, more contented animals. Beyond the corral was a pasture with probably two or three hundred grazing cows. The modest stone barn completed the picture. Nothing was in disrepair or in need of work.

"You have a beautiful ranch, Heath. It's really peaceful here, so neat and orderly. And you can go out of your house and not be afraid."

"This could be yours, you know." He lifted a tendril of her hair and rubbed it between his thumb and forefinger. "All you have to do is say the word."

She breathed deeply of the air and tried to calm her racing pulse. "If you keep asking, someday I might surprise you and say yes."

"I do hope so. Am I wearing you down any?" He seemed to study her. "We haven't spoken of love, but I've wanted to. My love for you goes beyond this world. What I feel is much deeper and it's an eternal, forever kind of love. Let me protect you and help raise Eden."

Rachel chewed on her bottom lip. If only she knew that she loved him and that she'd make him a good wife. She knew nothing about those things and had nothing to guide her. "Please don't ruin the day by pressuring me. I'm trying my best."

"I don't mean to press you. Forget what I said." He turned to walk away.

"Please wait." She reached for his arm. "I care deeply for you, Heath. More than I've ever felt for anyone. But love? I just know that if you were gone, I couldn't keep breathing. You give me strength and hope. You're a part of me that I need in order to rise each morning."

"I'm glad to know that I'm not just a casual friend."

"You're important to me in a way no one else is or ever was."

His gaze settled on her mouth and the day grew increasingly warm. Before she knew it, Heath leaned closer and kissed her.

"My darling Rachel, you certainly are something," he breathed into her hair.

"I could say the same about you, Mr. Lassiter."

"Now, stop with this mister business," he growled.

"All right, Heath. Just seeing if you were paying attention."

"I always am when I'm with you." He reached for her hand and lazily caressed her palm with his thumb.

She tried to contain the tingles but didn't succeed. When she spoke, the words came out breathless. "As bad as I hate to head home, I have animals to tend before dark."

He tucked an arm around her waist. "I'll be happy to go help."

"Stop." She laid a hand on his arm. "You have just as much to do here. I'll be fine."

"Check the house before you let Tillie leave."

Rachel balanced on tiptoes to kiss his cheek. "I will and I'll take the rifle when I go out."

"Good girl." He pulled her to his side and went back to the soddy.

Sunlight glistened on the pastureland with grazing cattle. It was beautiful. There was peace here and people who cared about her. Maybe she *should* consider coming to stay a few days. Only who would take care of things at home?

Tillie stood. "I have to be going, Rachel. Do you want to ride with me?"

"Yes, give me just a minute to gather Eden."

By the time Rachel got home the sun had begun its descent. She lit the lamps and fed Eden before she went out to tend to the animals.

She had the uneasy feeling of eyes watching her as she strolled out to gather the goats.

"It's simply your imagination," she scolded herself. "Get hold of yourself, you ninny."

Then Rachel heard a noise. For a moment she thought one of the goats had made the sound. But when it came again, she noticed it originated from some brush. Unbidden pictures of the chewing tobacco man at the trading post sprang into her head.

Glancing around for the rifle, she remembered she'd left it inside. Her heart sank as her mind raced.

Her gaze swept to the house. Eden was asleep in there. So innocent. The babe didn't know danger was on their doorstep. And Jax was nowhere to be seen. She'd failed to tie him.

Again. When would she learn?

She forced herself to walk casually toward the house as if she had no reason to be in a hurry. She didn't want to give whoever it was a reason to know that she'd heard him and come after her.

The house seemed a hundred miles away. Could she reach it in time?

MINDFUL OF THE approaching darkness, Rachel's legs trembled as she collected her rifle and returned to find the source of the noise. If someone was hiding, she had to get them out and off her land.

Jax bounded from the brush, his ears alert.

"Good boy. Stay with me." Hopefully, he'd obey.

Thoughts of her abductors and the recent run-in with the trio at the trading post brought fear so thick she could taste it. She swallowed hard. If only she'd taken Heath up on his offer.

When they reached the goat pen, it was only a few more steps to the brush.

She put some steel in her spine to keep the rifle steady. "Come out with your hands up."

The green tangle of vines, thistle, and leaves parted. A pair of glittering dark eyes peered at them.

"Come out!" she yelled again.

One of her goats emerged, chewing on some grass. Rachel lowered the rifle, laughing. "I could've shot you."

Jax got behind the animal and nudged it toward the pen, crisis averted. Slowly Rachel relaxed from the scare. But a sense of pride wound through her. She'd handled it on her own and had a new confidence that she could take care of whatever came.

EARLY THE NEXT morning Rachel awoke to the trill of a bird outside her window. The amazing thing was that it was still dark. The words of Preacher Ledbetter jumped into her head.

Faith is the little bird that sings when the dawn is still dark.

Though she continued to walk in grief for her family and

the child she'd had to deny, hope began to blossom inside her for the first time that she would see a better day.

Maybe she was wrong in thinking God had forgotten her. Maybe He still loved her. And maybe things would get better just as Heath and the preacher had vowed.

"We're not promised tomorrow. We're only promised God's grace to see us through whatever comes," the preacher had said.

She glanced over at Eden sleeping soundly and quickly dressed. Rachel wanted to see the sunrise, really see it in all its splendor.

And she wanted to glimpse the little bird that had sung so sweetly.

Not wanting to go far, she sat down on the stoop and for a good half hour watched the sky, marveling as it changed from black to pink and yellow. She listened to the sounds of an awakening world. The gentle coos of the mourning doves gave her such peace. The lake was serene with the lap of the water against the shore adding its own music. Just then, a gentle breeze feathered across her face.

A little sparrow flew down within a foot of her and chirped up a storm.

It all seemed a beautiful gift.

Before long, Eden's cries drifted from the house. Rachel got to her feet and went to take care of the sweet baby God had placed in her arms.

An hour later, Rachel found herself humming an old hymn as she went to milk the goats and feed the chickens.

She didn't even realize she was humming until Heath entered the milking shed wearing a big smile.

"This must truly be a first, Rachel."

"What?"

"You're humming and I sense a lightness in your spirit. It must be a very good day."

"For the first time in a long time I have happiness bubbling up in my heart."

"Did something happen?"

She told him about the little bird singing outside her window. "The bird had faith that the sun would rise. Heath, I've been thinking a lot about faith."

"Hallelujah!" He lifted her up and swung her around. "You don't know how much I've prayed for this."

"Put me down and let's go into the house. I have a hankering for breakfast. I suddenly have an appetite."

He picked up the bucket of milk and they strolled into the house arm in arm.

When they went through the door, Rachel abruptly stopped and turned in a circle. Something was very wrong. The hair on her neck rose.

"What's wrong?" Heath asked.

Rachel pointed at the bedroom. "The door is closed. I always leave it open because I want to be able to hear Eden."

She was barely aware that Heath set down the milk. With him beside her, she opened the door and gasped.

Eden was gone!

CHAPTER TWENTY-ONE

Heath caught Rachel as she collapsed in a heap. He swept her up in his arms and carried her to a chair with Jax whimpering and licking his owner.

"We've got to find her. What could've happened to her?" Panic and despair lodged in Rachel's voice.

He smoothed back her hair. "I'm darn sure going to find out, you can bet on that."

A feverish light came in Rachel's eyes as she jumped to her feet. "I've caught Zeb lurking about after I sent him off. Do you think he took her out of spite?"

"Maybe." Heath took a calming breath. "Let's not rush to conclusions." He covered the distance to the door in three strides.

"Where are you going?" Rachel asked.

"To pick up a trail."

"I'm coming too."

He turned and took her hands in his. "You might trample

on top of tracks. Give me a minute to see what's out there. I promise I'll let you know after I've scoured the ground. Why don't you look and see if anything besides Eden was taken—blankets, clothes and that sort of thing."

At least it gave her something to do, Heath thought. Lord knows she'd lose her mind if she sat around and worried. He couldn't imagine what was running through her head because his own was a jumble of different scenarios, none of them good.

The faces of the men that threatened Rachel that day in the trading post swam across his vision. He'd put his money on them. Or Zeb.

His jaw clenched and resolve filled his heart. If those men took Eden, they'd better ride fast and hard because he meant to find that baby no matter what he had to do.

And harm the child? He shook with anger. If they wanted to live, they'd best not.

Dropping to his knee under the cottonwood tree, he began to pray and ask God to guide them to the sweet little baby girl who filled their hearts with such joy. And as he prayed his favorite scripture came to him. "Ask and ye shall receive, seek and ye shall find, knock and the door shall be opened to you."

He didn't rightly know if it pertained to kidnapped babes or not, but he knew God's abundant grace would be with them.

"Please lead us to her. Eden has brightened our lives and given Rachel hope when she had none."

Over the next half hour, he combed every inch of ground around the house. He was about to give up in defeat when he spotted prints of someone barefoot. He tried to remember if Rachel might've walked barefoot out here. But he couldn't recall an instance since he'd known her that she had not worn shoes outdoors.

Excited, he went to get Rachel and tell her what he'd found.

A few minutes later, his fingers trembled as he saddled Blackie for her. It eased his mind some to hear that nothing but the baby's blanket was taken. He gave Rachel a flicker of a grin when he saw that she had packed a bag full of everything that Eden could possibly need in a month of Sundays. He just prayed they found her.

He grabbed the reins of their horses, and they struck out walking to keep an eye on the footprints. Jax ran ahead stopping to sniff every so often. The trail led east, up out of the canyon.

With every step Heath prayed they would find Eden.

An occasional glance at Rachel assured him she was doing as well as he could expect. As the trail rose steeply to the rim, he helped her on Blackie. She thanked him with a silent nod. Nothing would put a smile on her face until she had her baby daughter in her arms once more. Neither would he see any relief from this fist that had closed around his heart, squeezing the life from him, until he got Eden back safe and sound and set things to rights.

The trail led in the direction of Thorn Hill Ranch. That puzzled him. Who on that ranch walked around barefoot? No self-respecting cowboy would.

Overhead, the Texas sun beat down. Heath stopped several times to wipe the sweat from his eyes. For October it was an unusually humid day. A quick look at the sky showed storm clouds gathering in the west. They could sure use the rain. He just hoped it held off for a spell.

If it washed away the tracks...

He couldn't think about that. He closed his eyes for a second and murmured a prayer. When he opened his eyes, he saw that Rachel's lips were silently moving. Could she be praying? It seemed a lifetime ago that she told him about the little bird that sat by her window singing. Had it only been that morning?

Rounding a huge clump of prickly pear bearing ripe fruit, his breath caught in his throat.

Lying on the ground was a small blanket that had streaks of blood on it. Jax took it in his mouth and brought it to Heath.

Rachel gave a strangled cry. Dismounting, she ran to take it from his hand. Burying her face in it, she sobbed. "Oh God, oh God, oh God!"

Heath gently pulled her against his chest fighting tears of his own. "She's not dead. Get that out of your head right now."

She looked up into his eyes. He'd never seen such raw anguish before. "How do you know?"

"If she were dead, she'd be here with the blanket." He pulled her against his chest. "We're going to find her. We won't stop looking until we do. I'll turn over every rock. I promise you."

Distant thunder rumbled. The storm was getting closer.

"Let me help you back on your horse. We need to hurry."

She clutched the little blanket for all she was worth as he lifted her onto Blackie. Then, he struck off on foot, clutching the reins to his horse.

A short while later, they crossed the boundary line onto Thorn Hill Ranch. Luckily, they were still ahead of the storm, although he wasn't sure by how much.

The footprints were not visible on the rocky ground, but he kept that fact to himself. Rachel would lose what little control she had if she knew he was following a blind trail. He figured he'd pick up the prints again if he just kept going.

And sure enough he did. They led across the pasture and right up to the backdoor of an old sheepherder's wagon.

Fat raindrops fell as they reached the wagon. Heath removed his rifle from the scabbard and told Rachel to wait. He walked up to the door and knocked.

"Go away," a woman's voice ordered from inside.

"Ma'am, this is Heath Lassiter. I'm out here with Rachel Malloy and we're looking for a baby that someone took. I'd like to speak to you about it."

"I said go away."

Rachel's voice in his ear startled him. He hadn't heard her come up behind him. "I think this is where Becca lives. Tillie told me she lives with her father in a sheepherder's wagon. Let me try."

Heath moved aside, hoping they wouldn't have to storm the wagon. But he prepared to do that. He was getting Eden however he had to.

"Becca, this is Rachel Malloy. May we come in? It's starting to rain out here and we're getting wet."

"No, I'm busy. Go away."

"Did you take my baby, Becca? I need to get her back because she's probably hungry. Her name is Eden."

"I only have my brother in here. No one named Eden."

Rachel tried the door and found it unlocked. Heath didn't know what to expect, but he pressed close behind her as she swung the door out and cautiously stepped inside.

The only light came from the open door, but a young girl stood in the dim interior. The infant she cradled in her arms could only be Eden. Rachel gave a muffled cry. He knew everything in her wanted to rush forward but she held herself back. He sensed that scaring the girl would be the wrong thing to do so he eased his rifle to the floor.

"This is my baby brother," Becca said softly, brushing the top of the baby's head with her fingers. "His name is Samuel."

He laid a hand on Rachel's trembling shoulder to calm her. "Talk to her. Win her over," he whispered.

The bloody blanket they'd found was hard to get out of his mind. He strained to see in the shadowy wagon, but he didn't see any blood. Still, he knew Rachel wouldn't take a deep breath until she found Eden unharmed.

"He's a beautiful baby," Rachel said taking a step and then another. "Can I see him? I love little ones."

Becca turned her back to them. "He's asleep."

Rachel took two more steps. "I won't wake him. I promise. You're a good sister to him."

"I take good care of him."

"Yes, Becca, I can see that you don't let any harm come."

In the dim light, Heath held his breath as Rachel reached out to gently touch the girl. He prayed Rachel wouldn't spook her.

"Where is your mother, Becca?" he asked.

"She went away. Paw says she ain't ever coming back."

"You must miss her very much," Rachel said. "Can I hold Samuel? I'll be very gentle."

Becca scooted back, wildly shaking her head. "No, you'll take him."

Just then the door opened and a man's voice spoke. "Who are you?"

Heath turned. "I'm Heath Lassiter. You must be Becca's father."

Rain had soaked the newcomer. Deep sorrow colored his eyes. "I am." He sighed. "What has she done this time?"

"She took Miss Malloy's baby, and we came to get her back."

The man's shoulders slumped, and heavy sorrow filled the

man's eyes. "It's been hard on Becca since her maw and baby brother died. She doesn't understand the finality of death."

He moved past Heath and Rachel. "Becca, honey, let me have the baby."

"Please, Paw, don't take him away from me," the girl pleaded as big tears filled her eyes. A sob burst out. "Please. He won't be any trouble. I'll take care of him, you'll see."

"Becca, this baby isn't ours," he said gently. "It belongs to this fine lady here. Remember what I told you about your maw and little brother? They went up to heaven with Jesus. It's just you and me now."

"But when I close my eyes and go to sleep I can see them again?"

"Yes, honey. Now let me have these folks' baby."

Becca reluctantly passed the infant. He in turn handed Eden to Rachel who inspected the little babe for wounds before clutching her tightly to her.

"She's unhurt, Heath," Rachel said quietly.

For the first time in several hours Heath could take a deep breath without his chest feeling like it was ripped open.

"Becca, you can come see the baby anytime you want," Rachel promised.

"Samuel?"

A tender smile lit Rachel's face. "I suppose you can call her Samuel. Eden won't mind."

"Samuel Eden?" Becca asked.

"What a pretty name," Rachel said softly. "Yes."

Heath handed her his coat to wrap the baby in until they could get to the blankets in the saddlebags. He turned to Becca's father. "We found Eden's blanket in the pasture soaked with blood. What was bleeding?"

Becca raised her skirt to show her ankles. "I cut my foot. It hurt real bad."

"Yes, I'm sure it did. I'd be happy to doctor it for you," Rachel offered.

Becca's father spoke up, "I'll take care of it. I know you folks are anxious to get home. Looks like there's a break in the rain. With luck you can make the trip before it starts again. I apologize for my daughter. She didn't mean any harm. I hope you won't hold this against her. She doesn't know what she's doing."

"We understand." Heath laid a hand on the grieving man's shoulder.

"I'm at my wit's end trying to care for her." The man dug under a pile of things and pulled out a blanket. "Here, for the little one."

Rachel reached for it. "Thank you, sir. I'll return it."

"No need. It's...we don't need it." His voice was thick with sorrow.

"I'm so sorry." She laid a comforting hand on his arm. Going to Becca, Rachel gave her a warm hug and thanked her for taking sure good care of Eden. "I'll look for you to come calling."

Heath shook hands with Becca's father and thanked him.

Jax crawled out from under the wagon and nudged Heath's hand with his nose when they went outside. He ruffled the dog's ears. "Rachel, I think Jax wants to see for himself that Eden is okay."

Glad the rain had stopped at the moment, Rachel knelt down. Jax sniffed the baby up and down then licked Eden's cheek, evidently satisfied that she was all right.

Rachel's smile was a thing of beauty and made Heath's heart sing. Laughter sprang from him, thankful he had reason to. God had granted him and Rachel their prayers and delivered Eden safely to them.

The gloom of the cloudy day lifted. He looked up at the gray sky and took a deep, cleansing breath of the moist air, drawing it into his lungs.

Rachel took Heath's hand and squeezed. "Let's go home."

CHAPTER TWENTY-TWO

They left the sheepherder's wagon and began the trip home with glad hearts, the day half gone. Rachel held Eden in a warm cocoon of blankets. "Heath, I feel so sad for Becca. I wish I could do something to help. Running around the countryside like she does is dangerous."

"I agree. But I don't know what we can do." He maneuvered his horse around a large clump of cactus.

The bulk of the rain held off until they rode into the yard of her house. Then a deluge came down fast and furious with plenty of lightning and thunder. Rachel was drenched in a matter of minutes and so was poor Jax.

"Make a run for the house," Heath yelled to be heard. "I'll put the horses in a stall and join you."

Rachel made sure Eden was covered by the quilt and sprinted for the door.

The first order of business was stoking a fire and getting some heat into the house. Then she fed Eden and put coffee on.

Twenty minutes later, Heath came into the house. He looked a sight with his clothes plastered to him and water dripping off the brim of his hat like a small waterfall.

She realized she was staring and hurried forward with some towels with Eden anchored in the crook of her elbow. "I'd offer you a change of clothes except I don't have any."

Even as soaked as he was, Rachel's heart did a somersault and her mouth went dry like it did each time she was near him.

Whether he was calling her little mama, holding Eden with his big hands, or leading her across the prairie with a storm coming, he was the reason for the wild Texas storm inside her. She'd never known anyone like him before.

He removed his hat and toweled his hair and face. "I'll be fine. You just take care of Princess, little mama."

There he went again. Warm tingles danced up her spine like cavorting children.

Heath helped himself to a cup of coffee as she tucked Eden in her crib. He'd even poured one for her. She added some milk to hers and slid into a chair at the table opposite him.

"We got her back. I don't know what I'd have done if you hadn't been here."

"You'd have managed. You're strong." Heath reached for her hand and held it just as thunder shook the small house and rattled the windows.

For a moment she thought a bolt of jagged lightning had come through the window. She wondered if it felt that way to him too. Sometimes his touch was more like melted butter flowing over her and at other times like now it aroused every nerve ending.

She pulled her hand back and lifted her cup to her mouth. "I'm getting more confident."

"I know and I'm proud of you. But back to Eden. She's like my own flesh and blood." He chuckled. "At times I forget she's not." He became serious and his voice lowered. "If anything happened to that little girl, I don't know that I'd want to keep living. It'd be hard. I don't know how you did it after losing Alice."

"Finding Eden helped a lot. I had a lot to do, and it kept my mind occupied."

He squeezed her fingers. "You've managed very well."

She let her gaze wander over this strong man's features that spoke of pain and loss and happiness. It appeared Heath had a chink in his armor after all. He usually wore his faith around him like a shield, never wavering or allowing any hint of doubts. But this was a new side of him. Maybe that meant it was all right to be unsure at times.

"I learned something important today," she admitted.

Worry had left his gray eyes. "Yeah, what's that?"

"Becca is not Eden's mother. I've been so afraid."

"I'm glad you don't have to worry about that anymore."

"I'm not entirely worry-free. Eden's mother is out there somewhere. Who knows when she'll show up wanting her back."

"Just be thankful for what the good Lord gives and stop borrowing trouble."

Rachel rose and refilled their cups. "I did something that I haven't done in quite a while."

"I'd love to hear. If you want to tell me, that is."

She sat back down and idly played with her spoon. She wasn't exactly sure how to begin. Straight and to the point, she supposed. She took a deep breath. "I prayed today."

"I'm glad to hear it. If ever prayers are needed it's in times of trouble."

"I made a promise to God that I would put aside my anger if he'd just let me—let us—get Eden back."

"And He answered our prayers." Thick emotion put a quiver in his deep voice. "Are you at peace, Rachel?"

"Not totally, but more than I was." She met his questioning stare, grateful for the rain that kept him here longer. "How are your clothes? Still sopping wet?"

"They're fine. As soon as this storm passes, I'll head home."

"I'm sure Sally is worried about you."

"Can't be helped."

Rachel hoped the storm took its time. She wasn't ready for him to leave. She enjoyed his companionship, even if he did set a wild Texas storm raging inside her.

A PLEASANT THREE weeks passed, and they reached the end of October as Rachel busied herself with her sewing. The days and nights were colder. Using the fabric that Heath bought in the town of Estacado, she made herself a dress and some undergarments. She couldn't wait to wear the dress for Heath. He hadn't seen her in anything nice.

The weather was beautiful this time of year. The cottonwood trees by the lake and near the house had turned golden, taking her breath.

Rachel sighed. She loved the fall. It meant the sun-baked days of summer were over. It was a time of laying up for the long cold months. Not that she was particularly looking forward to winter. It could be pretty brutal in the canyon, sometimes keeping them homebound when ice and snow covered the steep trail.

Glancing around the small house that Heath and his fellow

ranchers had built, she was filled with gratitude. Also, the stack of wood outside her door would be nice when winter struck with force. Because of Heath's kindness she'd be safe and secure here.

She laid down her needle and happened to glance out the window to see four strange riders approaching.

The breath caught in her throat. Her mind went back to that day at Singer's Trading Post and the men who'd accosted her. She'd hoped and prayed that they'd moved on and taken their trouble with them.

While she couldn't be certain this far away, one horse looked awfully familiar. The man with a scarred face had ridden a black and white piebald.

A quick glance found the loaded rifle beside the fireplace. She grabbed it with hands that shook. If trouble came, she'd be ready. This was her home and she'd defend it. She knelt beside Jax who was napping on the braided rug. Thank goodness he was inside or he'd be running down to confront the interlopers.

She watched the group pull up by the lake. Maybe they wanted to water their horses. Then they got bolder and rode right up to the house. Jax bounded to his feet, snarling. She opened the door, turning the rifle on them. "Far enough. State your business."

Jax barked fiercely and tried to get past her but she blocked him.

"Howdy, ma'am." The speaker on the piebald was Billy, the man with the scar. "We're looking for work. We'll hire out to do most anything."

One of the riders snickered.

"I don't need any hired help. Keep riding, mister, or I'll turn my dog loose."

"We'd sure hate to have to shoot such a fine animal," the third rider drawled.

She put a measure of steel in her voice. "I'd hate to have to dig another grave. I'm mighty tired of burying people but I can definitely do it. Or maybe I'll let the buzzards eat you."

"Now that's not very hospitable," Billy drawled.

Rachel stayed silent, watching their every move. When one threw a leg over his saddle to dismount, she fired a warning beneath the horse. The animal reared, sending the rider tumbling.

Blistering curses rent the air.

Her voice rang out, "Anyone else foolish enough to test me? I shoot what I aim for. Now get off my land."

The rider on the ground ran after his horse then seeing he wouldn't catch it, he jumped onto the back of one of his friends and they took off, slinging mud in their wake.

They had no more ridden out than Heath arrived at a gallop and dismounted. She put the rifle down and ran to him, burying her face in his chest.

"Hold me, Heath. Hold me and don't ever let me go." She yearned for his lips on hers, for what he alone could make her feel.

"I've got you, little mama. That was some nice shooting." He tenderly lifted her face and kissed her then held her longer, his arms enfolding her in a safe cocoon. "I'm glad I was nearby hunting when I heard the shots. I want to always be close when you need me."

So did she. Memories rose of how he slept in front of her door when she'd first moved in. And how he came almost daily now to help with her animals. Heath took care of her and made it seem normal. How long would she keep him waiting?

"Do you think Billy and his partners will be back?"

"Yeah, they're hanging around for something. They don't scare that easily, Miss Annie Oakley."

"What could they possibly want?"

"The money and they won't leave without it."

An icy shiver raced through her. Her father brought them here and it was up to her to deal with them. She prayed she was strong enough.

CHAPTER TWENTY-THREE

On a gorgeous Thursday morning under a weak sun, Rachel bent over the rub board doing laundry. Nearby in her basket she'd about outgrown, Eden cooed happily, her alert blue eyes following every move Rachel made.

The beautiful baby girl grew by leaps and bounds and little resembled the newborn someone had left. She'd begun staying awake longer and babbled. The infant stuck her thumb in her mouth. She was such a good little thing, never crying unless she needed fed or changed.

Rachel realized she was going to have to make Eden some toys soon.

She put the diapers she'd washed over in the rinse tub and glanced around the yard for Jax. She hadn't seen him in a while.

Lifting a diaper from the tub, she wrung out the water and pinned it to the clothesline.

When she turned for another, Becca stood there in her bare feet. Rachel jumped, her heart beating wildly. The girl had an odd way of sneaking up on a person. Rachel glared at Jax who never barked at the girl. Some watchdog he was. Still, she knew he would when danger came.

"Hello, Becca," Rachel said, pretending Becca's sudden appearance hadn't startled her. "How are you today?"

The girl looked down, clutching a handful of her dress. "I want to see Samuel Eden. You said I could."

"Yes, I did. I'm glad to see you. Are you hungry, Becca? I made some gingerbread this morning. It would be awfully nice with a glass of milk, don't you think?"

Becca shrugged. "I guess. Can I carry Samuel to the house? Paw said I gotta ask and not just take him."

"Your father is right. And yes, you may carry Samuel to the house for me." Rachel hid the grin that persisted. It was touching how the girl insisted on calling the babe Samuel. Though she liked Becca, she didn't fully trust her. This time she'd watch the girl like a hawk and not leave her alone for a second with Eden. She didn't want a repeat of the abduction. The memory of that horrible anguish was still too fresh.

Becca gently took Eden in her arms and Rachel picked up the basket. Together they went into the house.

Minutes later, Becca set Eden in the basket with blankets around her. Rachel cut a big slice of gingerbread and put the plate in front of the girl. "Does your paw know you're here?"

The girl shook her head. "Nope. He thinks I'm at school."

"It's not a good thing to deceive your father. Why didn't you go to school today?"

Becca ducked her head. "They laugh at me."

"Who laughs?"

Becca mumbled, "Everyone."

Rachel handed the girl a glass of milk. "Honey, tell me why they laugh. Maybe we can do something about it."

"Don't got no shoes."

"You don't have *any* shoes," Rachel corrected.

"That's what I just said."

"I see." Although she had no quick solution in mind. Even if she had the money, she wouldn't know where to get them. She knew the trading post didn't carry anything like that. Maybe Estacado would have them. She'd ask Heath.

One thing she knew, Becca's feet would freeze without shoes.

In the meantime, she'd talk the situation over with Tillie. Maybe Tillie could put a stop to the ridiculing.

Rachel's heart twisted. The way the girl gobbled up the gingerbread she suspected it had been a while since Becca enjoyed such a treat. Probably hadn't had any since her mother died. The girl needed someone to take better care of her. She needed a real place to live. A sheepherder's wagon wasn't a fit place to raise a child. And although Rachel knew Becca's father was doing the best he could to provide, it wasn't enough. The girl desperately needed clean clothes and a bath.

Something had to be done. And today.

Becca played with Eden while Rachel finished the laundry then she said she'd take Becca home and hitched up the wagon.

She called to Jax and he leaped into the bed of the wagon.

Instead of taking Becca to her home on wheels, Rachel pulled to a stop in front of a sprawling ranch house.

Mrs. Thorn opened the door before Rachel had a chance to knock. "How absolutely delightful to have some company."

"Hello, Mrs. Thorn. I'm Rachel Malloy and I think you know Becca. Her father is the windmill man for your ranch. The baby Becca is holding is Eden, my daughter."

"Please come in. I'll put the tea on." The elegant lady with sparkling eyes ushered them into the parlor. "Have a seat."

"No tea for me, Mrs. Thorn. I'd like to discuss something if you might have a minute."

Mrs. Thorn nodded. "Of course."

Rachel told the woman of her concerns with Becca and her father. "That wagon is less than ideal for a young girl. I thought we might put our heads together and come up with a solution."

Mrs. Thorn pursed her lips. "I see what you mean. I'll have to speak to my husband about this, but I think I know of something that will suffice. There's a small dwelling not far from the bunkhouse. I believe Mr. Thorn is storing extra feed in there right now. If he can move that somewhere else, we could clean it out."

"A house? A real house?" Becca's eyes grew wide.

The rancher's wife patted Becca's arm. "Yes, dear."

Eden grew fussy but hushed when Rachel took her from Becca. "Another matter is shoes. I'd happily give Becca some if I had them, but you know a fire burned everything I owned."

"I can help with that too, my dear. My daughter who's away at a finishing school is about Becca's size." Mrs. Thorn stood. "I'll just be a minute. Make yourselves comfortable."

The woman returned shortly with her arms loaded down. By the time they left, Becca was wearing a pair of brown high-topped shoes and a new dress. The girl carried a box full of more dresses.

Rachel hugged Mrs. Thorn. "Thank you so much. You're truly a generous caring lady."

"I've enjoyed this, dear. It's more blessed to give than receive. Besides, I like to feel needed. Please come back again. I'd love to visit with you when you have time. And don't worry. I'll find Becca and her father a place to live."

"It means more than you know."

Rachel left Becca with her father after telling the man about her conversation with Mrs. Thorn.

"Thank you, Miss Malloy," he'd said with tears in his eyes.

Rachel was relieved that the man hadn't gotten angry for meddling in his affairs. A man's pride was often a ticklish thing. More often than not it got in the way of progress.

The next stop was at the little schoolhouse. Rachel found Tillie getting ready to leave for the day.

"I wondered where Becca was," Tillie said after Rachel told her the events of the day. "I figured it was something like that. Don't worry. I'll put a stop to the ridiculing. I'll not have that in my school."

"I knew you wouldn't."

"How nice of Mrs. Thorn to give Becca some shoes, clothes, and maybe a better place to live. You won't believe this, but..." Tillie pulled a pair of shoes from under her desk. "I brought these from home for Becca today only she didn't come to school."

Rachel hugged her friend. "Thank you."

"Let's get together soon. I've missed you."

"And I you. We will soon. In fact, ride home with me."

"Thank you for the offer, Rachel. I will."

Joy flooded Rachel's heart all the way back. As Mrs. Thorn so aptly put it, it felt wonderful to help someone in need.

She and Tillie turned into the yard and she pulled hard on the reins. "Whoa."

A nice-looking man stood on her porch knocking.

CHAPTER TWENTY-FOUR

With Tillie riding alongside, Rachel scrambled from the wagon and reached for Eden. "Come in for a moment, please. At least until I see who this is."

Of late, she never knew if someone was friend or foe.

With Tillie beside her, Rachel bravely strode toward the nicely dressed visitor, giving him the once over. He wore a dark suit with a gun belt with a pistol on his hip. "Howdy, mister. Can I help you?"

He removed his hat and spoke politely. "Austin Morgan, detective for the North Texas Stage Lines out of Clarendon, ma'am. Are you Miss Rachel Malloy?"

She relaxed and smiled. He'd finally come. "I am and this is my neighbor, Tillie Grant. Please come in."

Austin Morgan held the door. "After you and Miss Grant."

They entered the house and Rachel paused. "Have a seat and talk with Tillie for a moment. I need to change my daughter and fix her a bottle. We've been gone most of the afternoon."

"By all means, see to your daughter's needs."

As Rachel moved to the bedroom, Tillie asked Morgan about the long trip. After changing Eden and getting her bottle made, she sat down with them while the baby ate.

Tillie and Austin Morgan's conversation seemed relaxed and easy. He looked awfully young to be a stage lines detective. Couldn't be more than twenty-five or so.

Morgan turned to Rachel. "I believe you sent a note with the traveling preacher about something you need to return to the office."

Realizing Tillie knew nothing about her father or the stolen strongbox and Rachel didn't want to delve into that until they had some privacy, she played it casual. "Yes, it's something I discovered of my father's after someone burned this house down. We'll discuss it in a moment."

The shadows of the evening had lengthened. It would be dark soon. As though sensing her thoughts, Tillie rose. "I need to be going. It was nice meeting you, Mr. Morgan. I pray you have a safe return to Clarendon."

"Likewise, Miss Grant."

"Tillie."

"Yes, ma'am, Tillie." His eyes twinkling, he held her hand for what seemed long past the normal length. "I hope we meet again soon."

Tillie nodded. "Me too. Goodbye, Rachel. I'll work on what we discussed."

Once she'd left, Rachel laid sleeping Eden in her crib and made supper. Then over the meal, she and Morgan talked about the stolen loot in the strongbox.

"I knew nothing about my father's activities while he was alive. You have to believe me. He did leave mysteriously though and would be gone for weeks. I'll be glad to be rid of that money because strangers have come and I suspect they're searching for it. I'm in danger."

Morgan looked at her over his coffee cup. "It's a considerable sum and that makes men do stupid things."

"Another friend, Heath Lassiter, has taken it over to his place for safe keeping. We'll get it tomorrow. He worries for my safety. Will you stay the night in the barn? I'll make it comfortable."

"I'll appreciate the lodging since there's no town close by. Thank you."

They talked more about her father and the stages he'd robbed, and guilt washed over her. "I apologize on his behalf. I'm very ashamed of what my father did."

THE NEXT MORNING dawned bright and cheery. Rachel opened her eyes and smiled. Jax lay at the end of her bed. He opened his eyes and chuffed when she got up then jumped to the floor and stretched as she reached for her clothes.

She started to put on her worn dress and stopped. Heath might come calling today. She wanted to look her best in case he did. So she pulled on the new calico dress she'd made and smoothed the yellow and russet floral design over her hips.

Then she tied back her hair with a strip of the same fabric as her dress instead of wearing it in her usual long braid and picked up Eden.

She felt very pretty. With a light heart, she fed the baby then hummed around in the kitchen preparing breakfast.

The door opened and Austin Morgan came in. "Morning. I slept like a rock on that hay."

"I'm glad." She handed him coffee and as they sat down to

eat, Heath arrived looking especially handsome in a blue shirt and trousers. She didn't need a calendar to tell which day of the week it was. He'd once explained to her that he always wore the same color shirt on the same day of the week. A planner he called himself. Rachel introduced the two men and brought Heath some coffee.

Heath met her glance and nodded. "We're glad you've come, Morgan. Rachel and I will be happy to see that gone. The more it sits here, the more men will come looking for it."

Austin nodded. "Our feelings exactly. We never expected to get it back and were surprised when that preacher brought your note."

Rachel reached for her cup of hot tea. Coffee was fine for the men but she preferred something milder. "We trusted him."

Heath sat opposite her, a smile flirting with the corner of his mouth.

"What?" Rachel asked.

"You look very fetching today, Rachel. That's all. Is that a new dress?"

Heat rose to her face, especially since the exchange drew Austin Morgan's attention. The young man leaned back in his chair, staring. "Thank you, Heath. I made this from the fabric you bought that day in Estacado."

"It's most becoming." His eyes twinkled like stars as he filled his plate with eggs and buttered a thick slice of bread.

"I have to agree." Austin rose and looked out the window. "I'm curious about this valley. Besides Miss Grant, who else lives farther down?"

Eden began to fuss and Heath reached for her. Rachel answered the detective. "A woman named Cora Quinlan."

Austin turned. "Three women alone?"

"That's right. My father and brothers were the only males until they passed and Tillie's father took his wife to Arizona territory. Tillie still has a handyman but he's old. Why?"

"I'm only trying to get a picture of the area. You never know when I'll need it." He returned to the table. "I plan to leave as soon as I get the strongbox."

"I'll take you to it whenever you're ready," Heath said. "It's a long ways back to Clarendon."

"Yes, it is, and I'll move fast. I didn't bring help to keep from advertising it."

"I can understand that, but you should know we're being watched."

Austin's head jerked around. "How many?"

"One for sure and three others possible."

Rachel began clearing the table. "One man came posing as my uncle, but I had to send him on his way a few days ago."

"Helps to know these things." Austin pondered that a moment.

"Once my father died of a fever two months ago, men started showing up as well as a multitude of holes where they dug at night. And they burned my house looking for the loot."

"I'm really sorry, Miss Malloy. Thank goodness, Mr. Lassiter lives close by."

Rachel brushed Heath's shoulder reaching for his plate. He glanced up and her knees went weak. "Yes, I'm fortunate."

Once she cleared the table, Heath rose and handed Eden to her. The detective went out to saddle his horse.

"I'll be back. Don't go anywhere." Heath's fingers brushed her cheek.

A smile curved her lips. "I'll be right here."

When she tilted her head to look up at him, his mouth

lowered to hers, their breath mingling like a welcome breeze on a sultry summer's day.

Rachel's heart fluttered and her pulse raced. She reached up to touch his face and cup his jaw. The truth struck her like a bolt from the blue. She was falling in love with this man.

If only…

Just then Eden got restless in Rachel's arms. "You take her and I'll come out to see you off."

"I won't say no."

As soon as he took the child, Eden grabbed a fistful of his hair and Rachel was hard pressed to tell who was grinning the biggest, Eden or Heath. It was plain to see that the little girl who'd been left in their care worshipped the tall Texan.

That made two of them.

CHAPTER TWENTY-FIVE

*H*eath returned after getting Austin Morgan on his way. Rachel was outside, soaking up some sun with Eden. Change was coming, only she didn't know from what direction.

Eden put a hand in her mouth and sucked on it as she stared at Jax. The dog had jumped up on Rachel, wanting to be petted.

Heath dismounted with a chuckle. "Won't be long until Princess will be chasing after that dog. I swear, she's growing more every day. Hardly resembles the same babe you found."

Rachel kissed her soft cheek. "Sometimes I lie awake at night and wonder what she'll look like as a young woman."

"She'll be the prettiest thing around here. Uh...next to her mama of course."

"Why thank you, Heath. If you're thinking of turning my head, you just might succeed."

He pulled something from his pocket and handed it to

Rachel. "I made this for Eden. She's starting to hold onto things better."

The gift was a small dog carved from wood. The detail was excellent, and it was sanded as smooth as a piece of satin.

"Oh, Heath, this is lovely." She smiled as Eden's hand curled around it. "I was thinking just yesterday that I needed to get her some toys. You beat me to it."

"It occurred to me she's getting big enough." His grin faded and his voice lowered. "I think you can sleep easier now, Rachel?"

"I can't tell you how glad I am that the ill-gotten money is gone. But I've been wondering how those men will know, even if they're watching our every move."

Heath's eyes narrowed and grew hard. "I don't know. That's a problem."

Rachel watched him as he walked toward the barn, his long easy stride, loose and full of confidence. She admired a man who stood up to those who sought to destroy. He would never back down in the face of danger or hide when the going got rough.

The row of graves under the cottonwood tree drew her. She tucked Eden closer and strolled toward them. Her heart still ached for the family she'd lost, but the crushing pain was lessening. It seemed a lifetime ago that she buried Alice.

With tears clogging her throat, Rachel knelt to touch the cool earth. It was fitting that she'd found Eden here in this place of death and rebirth.

She brushed her eyes and gazed into the distance, reflecting on the fact that people lived, they died, and life went right on. The sun continued to rise and set and the seasons moved in harmony with the earth. Those were constants in a sea of constant change.

Suddenly a fluttering piece of paper that was caught on a prickly pear drew her attention. Curious, she moved closer and picked it up.

The penmanship was neat and though it had smudged in several places it was readable. Dried water spots on the paper indicated that it had been rained on. That told her it had been exposed to the elements for some time.

My darling Eden, My heart is breaking to leave you but I had no choice. I'm sick and fear the worst. I've watched Rachel Malloy and I think she'll be a good mother. I can see how much she loves you. Please rest in the assurance that I love you more than you could ever possibly know. Promise me you'll turn out better than what I did and stay away from saloons and men who frequent them. God, forgive me for stealing this horse. I was going back home to Walnut Creek but now I'll not make it. Something is dreadfully wrong. I'm so tired and sick. Your mother Alma.

Rachel stood, letting the words sink in. She had to have been the woman Heath found dead. She'd mentioned Rachel by name so had she watched her? But yet, she'd been a saloon girl. Deep sorrow washed over her. The woman had been up against a wall.

Heath came from the barn and looked toward the graves, the lines of his face relaxing when he spotted her. She noted that he wore a gun belt and pistol. It paid to these days.

Something saddened in her heart that other men had made this necessary. Heath had a gentle soul and didn't go looking for trouble. But she'd also witnessed the fierce protectiveness of his family and those he loved.

An odd quietness invaded her. Did he truly love her? Or did a sense of duty drive him? Was she nothing more than an obligation? She sighed, wishing for answers.

Rachel hurried, anxious to show him what she'd found.

"You know what this means," he said once he'd read it several times.

"That Eden's mother was the dead woman."

"Yes. I think you can give up the notion that Eden's mother will come to take her back." He put an arm around Rachel's shoulders and pulled her against him. "You are her mother. Sounds to me that this woman chose you to raise her little girl. She didn't leave her here on a whim, hoping that whoever found Eden would give her a good home."

"But how did she know I'd be the one to find her?"

"With her soiled background it's unlikely you two ever met. She had to have been watching and liking what she saw."

Eden dropped the carved dog Heath had given her. Her searching hand grabbed Rachel's dress and clung to it. When Rachel glanced down, Eden's grin stretched to cover her face.

"I don't think I've ever loved anyone except Alice as I love this babe. She's the light of my life."

"It's such joy to see God at work. Do you still doubt that He had a hand in all of this?"

Rachel shook her head. "My doubts have vanished."

"I'm glad."

She raised her head for a kiss that stole her breath and tilted her world on its axis. She wondered if Heath knew how much he'd come to mean to her. How adrift and lost she'd be without him.

"I intend to tell Eden about her mother when she gets old enough to understand. The woman had such an overwhelming unselfish love for her baby daughter."

"Like you." His breath ruffled the hair at her temple. "Right now I need to saddle up and scout the area, see if I can spot any sign of these men."

"There are a hundred places they could hide. Please be safe. I've gotten rather attached to you."

Heath flashed a crooked grin. "Sounds like I'm beginning to grow on you."

"I'll never tell."

The teasing banter made her heart light as she watched him mount up. He sat tall and straight in the saddle, his gaze already sweeping the unforgiving terrain of rocky ravines, thick brush, and steep sides of the canyon.

The truth was the more she got to know Heath Lassiter and saw the deep spiritual strength he wore like a cloak around him the stronger she was and the more this thing between them grew.

He'd managed to wiggle into her heart when she wasn't looking and now she couldn't imagine life without him.

DAYS PASSED WITH no sign of the riders or watchers. Heath began to relax as did Rachel.

He'd spent the night in her barn because today he'd split the daylight hours between her place and his. He'd hired a cowboy off one of the ranches to see to his place and helped out as he could. Preparing for winter included rounding up the herd and moving them to a closer pasture to make it easier to see to them when it was cold and icy.

Pausing just inside the door, he stood watching the woman who had stolen his heart. His chest tightened as it always did when he was near her.

Rachel hummed, moving about the small kitchen like the rhythm of a cool clear stream, slow and easy, teasing the banks, smoothing the rough rocks as it tumbled past on the way to its destination. Yes, Rachel Malloy was a woman of purpose, even though she had yet to realize it.

She constantly surprised him. Just when he thought he had her figured out he had to rethink things. One thing he'd learned was that Rachel had grit and toughness. She couldn't have endured all she had without plenty of backbone. And in his book that made her a woman to admire.

Thanks rose for this and every moment alone with Rachel. He shut the door and cleared his throat to announce his presence. "Good morning."

Rachel turned, a bright smile lighting her face. "Morning, Heath. I trust you slept well?"

She took down a cup from the shelf. "I guess you have a busy day planned."

He accepted the coffee and found a place at the table. "I need to go to the ranch for a bit. Check things out there and see about the herd. Fall roundup is upon me."

Joining him at the table, she added milk to her hot tea. "I'm sorry to add to your load."

He'd do anything to erase the worry clouding her beautiful green eyes. "You're not."

Her gaze met his. "I dreamed those men were back and they'd shot you."

He pulled her close and smoothed her hair. "It wasn't real. I think they must've figured out Morgan took the strongbox with him."

"I hope so. I can't live like this."

Jax rose from the rug in front of the hearth, stretched big, and padded to Heath's side.

Heath leaned down to smooth the animal's brown and gray coat. "If they've left, we'll know it soon. Try not to worry. That's what I'm here for."

Though he hated to give Rachel false hope, he told himself it was for her own good. His gut said that the men were merely lying low, waiting for an opportunity. And one thing he was sure of. When they made their move, it would be under the cover of darkness.

The weight of his pistol in the gun belt reassured him that if trouble found them, he'd be ready. He just prayed he wouldn't have to use it.

Lord knew, Rachel asked for pitiful little, just peace and freedom to walk her own land whenever she took a notion. It made him mad enough to fight a mountain lion that those men had stolen her sense of security.

"I ran into Skeet Slaughter at the trading post last week and he told me Estacado is growing by leaps and bounds. They have a doctor now, even built themselves a jail. It'll only be a matter of time before they'll have a sheriff and no telling what all. It's shaping up to be a real town."

"That's fast. We were only there a month ago. They must really be working hard."

"Yep. But their progress has brought riffraff and people who try to ruin what they have. I hear they're having trouble with some of the cowboys in the area. Seems they get drunk at the tent saloon then ride through the middle of town whooping and hollering and shooting their guns, daring the Quakers to do anything."

"That's sad. The Quakers are such a peaceful people."

"They are. They don't hold with violence, not any sort. I don't know why others can't leave them be."

"Do you think it could be the same men?"

"I honestly don't know." He'd already given some thought to that possibility.

A BIG FULL moon came out that night and that suited Heath just fine. After supper he and Rachel took a walk down by the lake. The moon reflecting on the water was a beautiful sight.

He didn't know what was more breathtaking, the moon or Rachel. The light surrounded her, creating a halo of sorts about her golden hair. He inhaled the special scents of the night and the lady by his side.

Rachel's hand curled around his arm. "Thank you for asking me to walk with you. I wouldn't have missed this."

"I think we both needed this moment of peace and calm to help us relax after our busy day."

"Serenity is hard to come by these days." She stepped back from the circle of his arms.

"One of my favorite verses is Psalm 4:8. 'I will lie down and sleep in peace, for you alone, O Lord, make me dwell in safety.' That's what I want for you, Rachel."

"I'd like that. You have a lot of favorite verses. I guess you've read the Bible all your life."

"And memorized a good deal of it."

"I'm not that familiar with it."

"He's with us through every trial. One verse says, 'Be still and know that I am God.' Sometimes a body simply has to stand in one place and reflect on all they have."

A fish leaped out of the water then slid gracefully back in, creating a few ripples. And nearby a frog added his voice to the sounds of the night.

He put his arms around her and drew her close. The fragrance of her hair teased his nose. He could feel her heart beating against his chest. Closing his eyes, he let her presence wash over him like a gentle wave upon a seashore, lapping against the rough edges of his fear that she'd never offer him more than friendship.

However, if friendship was all he'd ever get, he'd cherish it as a rare, sweet treasure.

Overcome with emotion, he gently took her hand and raised it to his lips. The kiss he pressed on the back of it came from his deep feelings for this woman.

She tilted her head to look up at him, her green eyes enchanting. Kissing her was as natural as drawing air into his lungs. Cupping his hands around her face, he kissed her long and deep, much as a drowning man clutched a passing tree branch floating by.

Later, he left her at her door with the advice to get some rest. He saddled Hondo and rode to the bluff overlooking the canyon. Here he had a good view in all directions. If anyone moved or a campfire burned, he could see it. The brilliant moon illuminated everything.

The saddle creaked when he dismounted. He made himself comfortable on the ground and waited. It was time to see if those strangers, and Zeb, lurked about.

With no stolen money around, would they just kill Rachel out of anger?

That's what he had to find out.

CHAPTER TWENTY-SIX

Heath sat there on the ridge for a long while, watching every night movement and reflecting on his many faults. The beautiful woman down below was everything he wanted. She and Eden and would make his life complete.

How long would he have to wait for her? And what if she never decided to become his wife?

God had sent the sign he'd asked for—the white dove. But then nothing.

Was he only seeing what he wanted to happen and it had all been in his mind? He rubbed his face. Doubts troubled him.

The door of Rachel's little house opened, and she emerged holding a lantern. She clutched a shawl she'd thrown over her nightgown.

Where was she going at this time of night? He leaned forward watching as she went to the row of graves under the cottonwood tree. Though the distance blocked sound, he knew she was probably sobbing. She still missed her little daughter.

He started for his horse but froze at a campfire below that was hidden from the house by the trees.

Mounting up, he made little noise as he rode down the steep trail from the rim to the canyon floor. There he swung off Buttermilk and commenced on foot. Parting the branches of a sapling, the campsite sprang into view.

Four men sat around a low fire. He made out Zeb's face and recognized one of the others as the scarred ringleader in Singer's store.

Well, well. Rachel was right about Thacker not riding off. It was no surprise to Heath that the charlatan uncle was involved with these other men. He crept closer.

"I tell you, that strongbox ain't on this property," Zeb said. "I've looked everywhere and it's gone."

"So where did it go?" Billy snapped, the scar more frightening in the flickering light.

"I think Lassiter took it and either buried it or hid it at his place. That's what I think."

"Then we need to search his barn," one of the other men said.

The fourth man spoke up, "We already did, Joe. Where is your mind? Of course, we had to do it awful quick because of that sister. I'd rather face a den of snakes than tangle with her." Chuckles swept the circle. "I have a theory if you want to listen to it."

Zeb chuckled. "Go ahead, Charlie. Might as well speak your piece."

"I think we should follow that stranger that rode up and spent the night. What if he was working for the North Texas Stage Lines? He collected it, and now he's gone. That's exactly what I think."

Zeb snorted and uncorked a bottle, taking a drink. "That's

dumb. How would they have gotten word to the stage lines that Rachel has our money? In case you haven't noticed, there's no telegraph anywhere around."

"Beats me." Charlie licked his lips, watching the bottle eagerly.

Quiet until now and staring into the flames, Billy laid back on his saddle. "Well, there's that girl Tillie. Maybe she either passed a note or the money to one of the ranchers."

The more Heath heard, the more his fear grew. Someone had to warn Tillie. She could be in danger. The talk ceased and the drinking got serious. He quietly returned to his horse.

The house was dark. Rachel was probably asleep. He could tell her what he'd learned at daylight so went on to the barn to grab a few hours of sleep before he rode back to the campsite to check on the lawless group.

MORNING ARRIVED FAR too soon but Rachel was dressed and at the stove. Eden was happily sucking on a bottle Rachel had propped up using a folded blanket.

At the sound of the door, Rachel turned. "Good morning. I noticed you riding toward the ridge last night and it made me curious. Did you see anything?"

His lazy smile made her heart flip. "Learned a few things for sure." He turned to the baby. "Good morning, little beauty."

Eden's face lit up in a goofy smile, losing the bottle. The man had that effect on young and old.

He picked her up and put the bottle back in her mouth. "I hope you got some rest, Rachel."

She set a cup of coffee in front of him and pushed back her hair. "Enough. Probably as much as you did. Heath, I feel a black storm coming and it's not the weather. When will this end? I thought I'd be at peace with Austin Morgan's arrival and the money gone but I'm not."

"I don't know when it'll end or how." He reached for her hand and pulled her into the chair beside him. "I found the outlaws' campsite last night and they aren't giving up."

Rachel listened to what he'd overheard and fear rolled over her. "I have to warn Tillie."

"The sooner the better."

Rachel searched Heath's eyes. "She knows nothing about my father's criminal enterprise, and I had hoped I'd never have to speak of it."

He squeezed her fingers. "You have no choice. She'll be at school today, but we have to go over there when she gets home."

A troubled sigh filled the kitchen. "I never thought the outlaws would turn their focus on her."

He nodded and put Eden on his shoulder to burp her, patting her tenderly.

Rachel rose and moved to put breakfast on. She blinked back tears and her voice cracked. "I don't know what's going to happen at any given moment. This swing keeps me off balance."

"They want it this way." He got to his feet and came to her. "Don't let it rattle you."

"You've been very patient with me, and I appreciate that as I sort through things. I do want to make a life with you, but this isn't the time."

He gently cupped her jaw. "Don't worry. Like I told you before, I'm not going away. Take all the time you need. But, I won't ask you to marry me again. You know where I am when and if you make up your mind."

CHAPTER TWENTY-SEVEN

Heath's words rolled around inside Rachel's head all that day. She didn't want him to give up on her and it seemed the case. After breakfast, he disappeared saying he was going to scout around.

She missed the way his fingers brushed across her cheek and the way his breath softly disturbed the hair at her temples right before he got ready to kiss her. An ache for his presence filled her. She wished she could talk it over with her stepmother, Jane Shining Star, like she'd always done with anything that troubled her.

But she couldn't. Wanting to feel close to the woman who'd raised her, she moved aside the door in the floor and went below with Eden in her basket. Removing the white buffalo robe from a trunk that had been returned from the barn, she buried her face in its softness then wrapped it around her.

That's where Sally found her a little later. "Rachel dear, is everything all right?"

Rachel wiped her eyes and swallowed the lump in her throat. "As well as it can be."

"Oh, honey, it's plain to see that your heart is breaking." Sally knelt beside her and put her arms around Rachel's shoulders. "Tell me what I can do to help?"

"If you could bring back my stepmother…"

"I would if it were possible." Sally smoothed back Rachel's hair. "What's wrong?"

"Just feeling blue I suppose and missing my stepmother."

"I didn't think you had anything left after the fire and all." Sally fingered the soft folds of the robe. "What is this if you don't mind me being nosy?"

For a second panic set in then Rachel remembered that Jane Shining Star was far beyond the reach of hurt and prejudice. She no longer had reason to hide the beautiful robe.

"It's a treasured wedding gift given to my Comanche stepmother by her father when she came to live with my father. We kept it hidden all these years for fear of reprisal. I kept it in a trunk, and it escaped the flames."

"Well, honey, you don't have to keep it hidden now. It came from a magnificent animal. It's also a source of comfort to you and as such you should bring it out in the light of day where you can look at it and remember the good times you shared with your stepmother."

A sob escaped Rachel's mouth. "She loved me so much and I loved her. I didn't care that she was Comanche."

"Of course not. I wish I could've met her. She sounds like a wonderful woman."

"You'd have liked her."

Sally felt around in her pocket and pulled out a handkerchief. "Dry your eyes and let me get you up these stairs. I think we could both use a cup of tea."

As though hot tea could make trouble leave and keep friends safe.

Blowing her nose, Rachel picked up Eden and took Sally's extended hand. It wasn't until they were back in the kitchen that she noticed Sally carried the robe. The woman laid the beautiful white hide on the table and got the water on to boil.

"It'll be ready in a flash." Sally turned. "Now, while we wait for the water, tell me where you want to put the robe. But if it were mine, I'd put it on my bed so I could reach out and touch it when these spells come."

"Yes, that makes perfect sense."

In her take charge way, Sally carried it into Rachel's bedroom and returned. A short while later they sat at the table sipping a nice cup of dandelion root tea.

"I don't think you're telling me the whole of it," Sally said, her eyes piercing Rachel's. "It's true that you miss your family, more at times than at others, and it's true that sometimes such a longing for loved ones washes over us like a black wave. But, that's not all that's got you blue."

Rachel set down her cup and sighed. She couldn't keep anything from this woman. She might as well tell her. She knew Sally well enough to know she'd pester her until she did.

"The outlaw gang still wants to kill us and if you must know, Heath has given up on me." She tried to still her trembling chin.

"Oh posh! I don't know where you got your information, but I'll tell you one thing. My brother, even if he is deaf as a post, thinks you hung the moon. And the stars. And anything else that's up in the sky." Sally gave a short laugh. "He doesn't just like you, he adores you. He hasn't been the same since he brought you home so I could nurse you back to health."

"Then why did he tell me he wasn't going to ask me to

marry him again? Just tell me that. He's tired of waiting and cutting his losses."

Sally sprang to her feet. "You just wait until I get through with him."

"No." Rachel grabbed Sally's arm. "Leave him be. He knows his own mind. You'll only make things worse. This is between Heath and me and I'll thank you to stay out of it."

"If that's the way you feel about it." Sally sat back down.

"It is."

"Well, I don't have to like it." Sally refilled their cups. "What happened to that sweet Tillie? I haven't seen her in a coon's age."

"She's teaching school on the Thorn Hill Ranch. I don't see her much either."

"When this is all over and we're not under siege anymore, I think we oughta throw a party and invite all our neighbors."

Rachel brightened. "That's a wonderful idea."

They could have tables full of food and lots of music and dancing. She wondered if Heath danced. She could just imagine him holding her close and twirling her around until she lost her breath. And then she remembered the distance he'd placed between them, and she sucked in a tremulous breath.

I won't ask you to marry me again. You know where I am when you make up your mind.

She was going to surprise him.

Just as soon as she figured out how to say the words.

Mid-afternoon, Heath rode up and came inside. He wasn't surprised to see Sally. That was good. She could keep Eden while he and Rachel rode over to Tillie's.

He'd spent the day thinking about things while trying to figure out Zeb's next move but it sure appeared they had focused on Tillie.

Both women looked up when he strolled into the house. Rachel's gaze met his. "I was worried about you."

"Sorry. I was keeping an eye on Zeb and time got away from me. I'll have some coffee then we need to ride to the Grant place."

"Sure. I'll have it ready soon." Rachel hurried to the stove.

"Wherever you're going, I'll keep the little darling," Sally offered.

Rachel took down a cup. "I'd like that. Thank you, Sally."

The woman gave them a pointed stare. "I'm curious why you're going to Tillie's. You both act like you're hiding something."

"Well, it's—" Rachel didn't know how to finish.

Heath laid a hand on Rachel's arm. "I overheard something the outlaw gang said that suggested they were going to focus their efforts on Tillie."

"And Zeb is in cahoots with them?" Sally asked.

"I think he might be the leader."

Sally's face darkened. "I should've whacked his rear end good with that broom when I had the chance! Those types never do a speck of honest work."

Rachel laughed. "I don't think one whack would've made much of a difference."

After Heath had his coffee and some meat and bread Rachel forced on him, they set off with Jax beside them. Tillie was just riding into the yard when they arrived. Jax immediately engaged in a game of chase with Tillie's dog Boomer.

"Get down and come in," she said dismounting.

They did and went inside.

Rachel took her hands. "Tillie, I've kept something from you, but I can't any longer. Your life is in danger."

With Heath at her side adding bits and pieces, Rachel told Tillie everything. "And that's why Zeb Thacker came posing as my uncle."

Tillie put a hand to her heart. "I always found it odd that your father kept you from making any friends. Now I understand. Also about that nice Austin Morgan. A detective for the stage lines, huh?"

"That's right." Heath rose from his chair in the parlor to look out the window. Night would fall in a couple of hours. "The circuit preacher carried a note to the stage lines for us."

"But how does this concern me?" Tillie asked.

Heath turned. "I overheard the outlaws talking last night and they think you're hiding the stolen loot here."

"Oh dear! I'll have to warn Yancy to be on the lookout."

"And keep a rifle handy," Rachel added.

"I absolutely will."

"How are things with Becca?" Rachel asked. "I haven't seen her in a few days.

"I think her father's keeping a closer eye on her and she's coming to school. Such a sad case. Becca grieves for her mother so badly. She needs a woman's guidance."

Heath went out to find Yancy, leaving the women to talk about the ranch school. He felt a little better about things. At least Tillie was aware of the danger. That's all he could do.

He took in the shabby appearance of the Grant place. The corral fence was broken, everything needed a coat of paint, and weeds were taking over. He'd have to see about coming to help.

CHAPTER TWENTY-EIGHT

Sunday morning's golden dawn bounced off the walls of the canyon in a magnificent display. Heath didn't think he'd ever seen a more glorious sight. He rose and went about his chores. His mood had lightened considerably. This was the Lord's Day, and nothing could put a damper on it. He had much to give thanks for.

He knew the distance he'd put between himself and Rachel had caused her confusion but it seemed the best course to take. She'd gotten too accustomed to his presence. He wanted her to realize that she shouldn't take him for granted. Hopefully, this would jar her into making a decision about marriage as well as send a message.

She'd either want him or they'd go their separate ways.

But who was he kidding? With each passing day the possibility of her agreeing to spend the rest of her life with him grew more remote. He was fast losing hope and he hadn't seen even a glimmer of the white dove.

After breakfast, Heath got out his Bible and announced that they were going to have a small service down by the lake.

Sally beamed. "I think it's a wonderful idea, brother."

"I'll get Eden ready just as soon as we finish in the kitchen." Rachel began clearing the table.

In a short time everyone had made their way to the lake. Heath was glad to see that Rachel hadn't raised any objections. In fact, she seemed delighted about the prospect of celebrating the Lord's Day to the best of their abilities.

He led them in *Rock of Ages* then opened his Bible. He chuckled at Jax sitting straight, his attention on Heath. Before he could read the scripture he'd selected, Becca joined them. She found a seat on a tree stump near Rachel and listened intently to the story of Joseph and his coat of many colors. The girl's coughing interrupted Heath several times. It was moist and came from deep inside her chest. He wondered if she was ill. But surely she wouldn't have walked all this way if she was. It bothered him just the same.

Jax spied a squirrel and raced off chasing the varmint that dared enter his domain.

"I came to see Samuel Eden," Becca announced when the last amen was said.

Rachel put a hand to the girl's forehead. "Are you sick?"

"Just a little puny. Ain't nothing."

"You're warm. Does your papa know?"

Becca shook her head. "Nope."

"Why didn't you tell him you weren't feeling well?"

"On account of he was gone."

"Where on earth would he be on a Sunday?"

"Fixin' a windmill that got itself broke."

Heath listened to the exchange. Becca's father still seemed

overwhelmed with his responsibilities and his daughter paid the price.

"Come to the house," Rachel told her. "I'll see what I can do for your fever and that cough."

Sally put her arm around the girl. "We can fix some nice willow bark tea."

Rachel nodded, shifting Eden to her side.

"Can I carry Samuel?" Becca asked.

Indecision was evident by the way Rachel chewed her bottom lip. Heath searched for a good reason to deny the girl but couldn't come up with anything Becca would understand.

"Well..." Rachel hedged.

"I won't drop him," Becca begged. "I'll be real careful. Please?"

"Let's wrap her in a blanket. And if you need to cough, turn your head away from the baby. All right?"

Becca held out her arms and took Eden. "Hello, Samuel. It's me. Becca. I came to see you on account of I'm your big sister. I've missed you."

Heath grinned at the girl's simple ways and took Rachel's arm. There was no getting through to Becca that Eden was not her brother. But then, did it really matter? The important thing in the end was the love shining in Becca's eyes. Love was truly all that really made a difference after everything was said and done.

His eyes met Rachel's and he leaned to whisper in her ear. "Just relax. It'll be okay."

"I wish I could be sure. What if Becca makes Eden sick? What if she—"

"I'm sure Eden will be all right."

Rachel knew she was being overcautious. Still, she'd seen firsthand how fast an illness could sweep through a family. She lengthened her stride to catch up to Becca and panic struck her when she noticed that the breeze had lifted the blanket from over Eden's face. It took all the strength Rachel had not to cry out in panic and yank the child from Becca's arms. But she didn't want to frighten the girl.

As soon as they got inside the house, Rachel reached for her baby daughter. "I'll take her. Eden needs to go to sleep now."

Sudden tears filled Becca's eyes. Rachel could only watch in alarm as the girl pressed her lips to the little forehead. Rachel took Eden and hurried into the bedroom.

"She was asleep as soon as I laid her down," Rachel announced, entering the room.

"I noticed those droopy eyes. I'll take Becca home after lunch." Heath went to make a fire to take the chill from the room.

When Eden didn't get sick within the next two days, Rachel began to relax. It seemed she'd worried for nothing. She went about her chores, breathing easier.

Becca hadn't returned and that sparked some worry. Rachel wondered if the girl lay sick in bed. If it wasn't so dangerous for her to leave the protection of the house, she'd hitch up the wagon and go check on the girl who set such store by Samuel Eden.

A heavy sigh left Rachel's mouth. She wanted all this to be over with and soon. She yearned for a normal life, to be free to come and go when she wanted and to raise her daughter in peace.

But did that include Heath?

Her searching gaze quickly found the man who had given

her so much. She touched her lips with her fingertips remembering his kisses. A life without him in it was difficult to imagine. Yet, despite his vow that he wasn't going anywhere he'd become withdrawn and detached. She missed his warmth and the way his smile crinkled the corners of his eyes. And she'd give anything to have him gaze into her eyes and call her Little Mama in that deep voice of his that made tingles race along just under her skin.

The way he'd distanced himself from her could only mean one thing. She'd waited too long. Heath Lassiter had given up on her. Not that she blamed him. Lord knows the man had the patience of a saint but he'd reached his limit.

Eden's insistent cries interrupted her thoughts. Rachel picked up a basket of clothes she'd just taken off the clothesline and hurried toward the house.

She might not know what to do about Heath Lassiter but at least she knew how to satisfy her daughter's needs.

CHAPTER TWENTY-NINE

Something was dreadfully wrong. No matter what Rachel did she couldn't quieten Eden's screams.

And when fever set in, Rachel's heart twisted in panic.

Surely her land must be cursed. It had taken her family and now it threatened to take Eden too. Was it possible that yellow fever was in the very soil, contaminating everything? Or could Becca be to blame?

She held the sweet body and rocked, hoping the motion might ease the babe's pain and allow her to sleep at least for a little bit.

The door opened and Heath entered. He removed his hat, laid it on the floor, and knelt beside the rocking chair. "I heard the cries. What seems to be the matter?"

Rachel's lip quivered. "I wish I knew. It's bad though whatever it is. I just don't know what to do."

Heath gently touched her cheek and that simple act caused the tears to flow that she'd held firmly in check.

"I'm sorry. I don't mean to cry. I'm just so worried. Heath, what if she has the fever? What if she dies? I don't think I could go on."

"She's not going to die," he said sternly. "Get that out of your head right now."

"But—"

"No buts. Princess just has a cold. She'll be fine."

She met the strength in his gray eyes and hope filled her heart. "You're right. I shouldn't jump to conclusions. I'll fix some willow bark tea and maybe that will help her fever. I don't see how a few drops would hurt."

Her Indian stepmother had cautioned on giving the tea to infants and children. "Only give little bit," she'd said.

Despite the risks, Rachel felt she had nothing to lose.

Heath held out his hands. "Let me hold her while you get it fixed."

Transferring Eden to his arms, she put water in the teapot and added some ground willow tree bark. Her attention was on Heath and Eden. He walked the floor, crooning a soft tune. The babe slowly began to respond to him, her shrieking cries becoming painful whimpers instead. It seemed the water would never boil. When it finally did, Rachel removed the concoction from the fire to steep.

After letting it cool a bit, she dipped her finger in the tea several times and put it in Eden's mouth while Heath held her. Rachel breathed a sigh of relief when the blue eyes drifted closed at last. Heath carried the sleeping babe into the bedroom and tucked her in her crib.

"Thank you, Heath."

"I think she's feeling better," he whispered, touching Eden's forehead. "You get some rest while you can."

"Want some coffee?"

A crooked grin curved his lips. "You know better than to offer. I can always use some stout brew."

He settled at the kitchen table while she put the coffee on. "Have you seen my sister?" he asked. "I figured she'd be hovering over the baby, and I was surprised when she wasn't."

"I haven't seen her since we ate lunch. I was wondering where she'd gotten off to myself." It wasn't like Sally to miss having her hand in every pie and being underfoot with her endless array of suggestions, if not downright orders. The bossy woman did like to tell a body how the cow ate the cabbage, how often, and in what amounts.

"She'll turn up. She probably went to the ranch for something."

Rachel took in the tired lines in his familiar face. "I suspect you've been standing watch at night and then working all day."

"You won't hear me complain."

Didn't the man ever get tired of being perfect? "You can't be and do every single thing," she said softly. "Everyone has their limit and I think you reached yours a while back."

His eyes pierced hers. "Does that mean you're worried about me?"

"I'm only saying that everyone is human. It's okay to let yourself get some sleep."

He ran a hand wearily over his eyes. "And who will keep you safe if I don't?"

"Let the rest of us share the burden. We're more than willing and able." Honestly, it irked her that he thought himself the only one capable of standing watch and taking part in the defense of her property. As if he alone stood between them and the men who sought to harm them.

"It's my duty."

"Heath, you've wondered why I won't marry you. One reason is that I don't want to be merely a duty or a responsibility. If I marry it'll be because I feel I have true value and can share equally the ups and downs, highs and lows of such a relationship. I want to work side by side with my husband and know at the end of the day that I helped to make our lives richer. I need to know that I contributed something, that I made a difference. I want to matter."

He looked stunned but the words had needed saying. He set her on a pedestal to be looked at but not seen as being vital.

"I'm sorry. I didn't realize but you're right."

"I'm glad you see. You've done fit as though my opinions and wants weren't worth listening to," she said gently.

"That's not the whole of it. I always wanted to make your path easier. That was always the goal." He pulled her closer, mindful of the baby, and gave her a tender kiss. "I love you, Rachel Malloy. God help me, I love you."

She gazed up at him in shocked silence.

Before she could think of a reply, he dropped his hold and stepped away. "I need to see if I can find Sally."

SALLY WAS OUT by the goat pens when she heard men arguing nearby. Her curiosity aroused, she crept through the thick brush for a look.

Peeking around a boulder, she spied four men. One was Zeb, the other three strangers.

What in the devil were they planning? She glanced around for something to use as a weapon and picked up a short piece of wood to use for a club if needed. She'd just listen and go to get Heath.

"Thacker, you ain't upheld your end of the bargain and

we're gettin' tired of it." A scarred man jumped up and jabbed his finger into Zeb's chest. "What's the holdup?"

Zeb licked his lips. "I didn't agree to killin' anybody, Billy. I want no part of it."

Who were they talking about?

Quickly putting her hands over to mouth to keep from making a sound, she sucked in her breath.

A shorter man spat a stream of chewing tobacco and jabbed Zeb in the chest with a finger. "You said you could run the Malloy girl off. Said it would be easy as skinnin' a rabbit. Then you said taking her would fix everything."

Giving the man a big shove, Zeb yelled, "Well, I done changed my mind, Charlie. Didn't see the need in runnin' Rachel off. I've been looking harder than any of you and it's plain that holding her for ransom in exchange for it will get better results. Lassiter will do anything to get her back."

Charlie squinted through one eye, standing nose to nose with Zeb. "How do we know you didn't already find the money an' decide to keep it for yourself?"

"That's a bunch of hogwash," Zeb shouted.

Charlie drew his pistol and pointed it at Zeb's chest. "If you're holdin' out, thinkin' to keep the money for yourself I'll put a hole clear through you right now and drop you where you stand."

"If I could find where Malloy hid it, I'd gladly give every last cent to you so I could be shed of the lot of you once and for all. The whole mess is your doin's anyway for lettin' him take off alone with that strongbox. Weren't my fault he got hisself dead before he could tell us where he buried it."

"I tell you what," said Billy quietly. "You got until tomorrow to bring the money to us. After that, we'll go in with guns blazing an' wipe out everyone. Their blood will be on your hands."

"If you think I'll sit by and let you harm Rachel, you don't know me very well."

"You crazy old coot. Rachel Malloy is no kin to you. She's not your niece. She's not your family. She's nothin' to you. Nothin' except trouble standing between us and our money."

Sally threw caution to the wind and scrambled toward the house as fast as she could. The noise brought the men on her heels. The scar-faced Billy lunged and brought her to the ground in a bone-jarring tackle.

"Let me go." She twisted and delivered a hard kick to Billy's midsection. He grunted and doubled over. When she clambered to her feet, he grabbed her leg and yanked her down then sat on top of her.

"Gotcha. You're that Lassiter woman that's always givin' orders. I figure Lassiter will as easily do anything to get you back as he would the Malloy girl."

"So what?" Sally blew the hair out of her eyes. She just needed a small opening. Zeb stood apart from the others and wouldn't meet her gaze. His goose was cooked but good and she'd tell him so in no uncertain terms the first chance she got.

Billy hauled her to her feet. Of the men, Billy scared her the most. The icy coldness in his eyes and hardness in his face said he wouldn't mind snuffing out a life if it suited him. In fact, he'd most likely take pleasure from killing. She'd heard of men like him with no respect for anyone or anything. Yet she wasn't about to cower and beg. It wasn't in her nature.

"You don't have to be so rough." She jerked against his punishing hold but couldn't get free. "Let me go for five minutes and I'll make you rue the day you were born."

"What're you gonna do with her, Billy?" Zeb asked.

"Hide an' watch." Billy twisted her arms behind her back and tied them with a length of rope.

"She won't cause any trouble. I'll see to that."

"Thacker, get outta my way." Billy shoved Zeb aside and dragged Sally through the thick brush.

Despite the pain of the rope and Billy's grip of steel, Sally kept silent, refusing to cry out. A steep narrow trail led up to a cave in the canyon wall. Reaching it, he thrust her inside.

She pulled herself to a sitting position against a wall and glanced around. The cave completely shielded her from view. Despair washed over her. It would be up to her to get out of the pickle she was in. No one would be able to find her unless they knew exactly where to look.

But she had one small advantage. These men didn't know Sally Lassiter. They didn't know that she would fight and claw and never give up until she was free.

CHAPTER THIRTY

Eden woke up screaming her head off as the sun sank below the purple and tangerine horizon. The fever had come back with a vengeance. Rachel gave her a few more drops of the tea, but this time it did nothing. She pumped some water into a shallow pan and removed Eden's clothes. She put her baby daughter into the coolness and sponged water over her hot skin. That's how Heath found them when he entered with Jax.

He hung his hat on a nail beside the door. "How is she?"

"The fever is back. I frankly don't know what we're going to do."

Heath covered the space in three long strides. "Tell me what you want. If you want me to go for the doctor in Estacado, I'll saddle up and ride."

That he asked for her opinion instead of taking over and doing what he wanted wasn't lost on her. Maybe their talk had opened his eyes. She wished it had been under different, less dire circumstances.

"I'm so scared, Heath," she whispered.

"I know." He slipped his hands underneath the long braid she wore and cupped her neck. "I am too. If anything happens to our baby girl I don't know I'll do."

His voice cracked. Rachel turned and discovered tears in his eyes. The love he had for this child equaled hers.

She took a deep breath and found strength. "Shhhh. She's going to be okay. We have to believe that. Will you say a prayer?"

Heath bowed his head, his deep voice filling the room as he prayed for mercy and healing. Rachel silently mouthed her own prayer and felt a little better after the amens.

"Thank you, Heath." She removed Eden from the water and dried her off. "If you'll go for the doctor, I'd be ever so grateful. He may be unable to do anything to help, but he can tell us what's wrong and what we're dealing with."

"I agree. I'll go saddle up."

The house would be so empty once he left. She longed for someone to keep her company until Heath got back.

"I don't suppose you located Sally?"

"Nope. I don't know what to make of it." He kissed Eden's cheek. "I'll be back in to say goodbye before I mount up. I hate to leave you and I wouldn't if it wasn't necessary. You'll be unprotected except for Jax."

"We'll be fine. I have a rifle and I know how to shoot."

A wry smile flickered on his lips before he turned. He lifted his hat from the nail and walked into the fading light.

Rachel focused on Eden. She spooned a few drops of the willow bark tea into the tiny mouth. At least Eden had stopped screaming. She laid the babe in her crib to rest and listened for Heath's footsteps.

When she heard them, she hurried to meet him.

"When I leave, bolt this door. Don't let anyone in unless it's Sally." He pulled her against him and she could feel the pounding of his heart. "I'll be back as soon as I can. With any luck by first light. I won't return without a doctor."

"Just be careful." She wanted to reach up and smooth the worried lines from his face but knew if she did she wouldn't be able to let him go.

"We need to talk when I get back," he murmured against her temple.

Curiosity picked at the frayed edges of her mind like fingers plucking lint from a dress. She had no idea what was on his mind.

"Just hurry please."

Rachel's pulse quickened when he lowered his head and slanted a long kiss across her mouth. In that moment she knew she wanted to spend the rest of her life with this man if it were possible.

I won't ask you to marry me again. You know where I am when you make up your mind.

Heath's words replayed in her head. She wouldn't know if they could have a future until she put the black shadows of the past to rest once and for all. It was time to start anew.

She'd inform him of her decision.

CHAPTER THIRTY-ONE

Sally lay beside a small dying fire in the cave but her eyes had yet to close. Her mind whirled in desperation. She needed to escape. She wondered about Heath and Rachel and knew they must be worried sick.

The rumble of thunder came from beyond the cave and lightning occasionally lit up the interior. A storm was brewing. That was just dandy.

Her captors had gotten drunk on whiskey and were snoring fit to beat the band. She doubted much would wake them. If she was ever going to do something now was the time.

She again tried the rope that bound her arms and feet but it held fast. Glancing around, she spied a slender piece of wood that had fallen from the fire. The smoldering end of it would work if she didn't burn herself in the bargain. She turned around and backed up to the fire, carefully feeling her way toward the burning ember.

At last she located the cool end of it and scooted back to her place against the wall. Holding the ember between her bound hands, she managed to get it angled just so. She kept it pressed to the rope and in minutes it had burned through releasing her hands. But not without burning her wrists. Small price to pay for freedom she decided.

She'd just started to work on the binding at her feet when a noise alerted her. She strained to see in the dim light.

A dark figure edged into the cave and inched toward her.

Was it another of the outlaws? She knew there was one more besides Charlie and Billy. They'd called him Frank. Yes, that was it.

The man was less than a foot away from her. She wielded the piece of wood like a club and struck his shoulder using all her weight.

"Ow!" He grabbed her hand. "Sally, it's me."

"Zeb?" She jerked her hand free.

"In the flesh."

Billy snorted and turned over in his sleep.

"You have a lot of nerve showing up here," she whispered furiously.

"I came to rescue you."

"I don't want anything to do with you or your kind. And for your information I don't need rescuing. I've already gotten myself free."

"I don't blame you for being mad."

"You've disappointed me at every turn," she whispered back.

Charlie Ford mumbled something and sat up. Prickles ran up her spine. She quickly put her hands behind her and pretended they were still bound and held her breath. The man wiped his mouth with the back of his hand and lay back down.

Sally turned her attention back to the bindings on her feet. She pulled at the knots but couldn't loosen them. Zeb silently reached into his boot. Drawing out a knife, he cut through the rope.

If she was in a forgiving mood, she'd thank him. But he could drop dead for all she cared.

He stood and helped her to her feet. "Come on."

Shaking her head, she picked up a length of wood that had yet to be put on the flames. Drawing back, she whopped Charlie and Billy on the head as hard as she could.

"Does that make you feel better?" Zeb asked.

"It darn sure does."

Zeb took her arm. "Come on. Let's get out of here."

Wrenching her arm from his grasp, she led the way from the cave. A short distance away, she stopped.

"You conniver, you may think freeing me from those outlaws' clutches will win favors. In fact, I'll never give you the time of day."

Zeb hung his head. "Reckon I got that coming. You cain't say anything that I ain't already said to myself. But don't the Good Book say that everyone deserves mercy if he just sees the errors of his ways and sets things to rights? Yours is a loving God, ain't He?" He squinted up at her. "Leastways that's what you always said."

"What are you up to now?"

She was suspicious of anything that came from Zeb Thacker's mouth. He was a master at saying what he knew people wanted to hear. She trusted him about as far as she could throw one of Heath's bulls in a driving rain with one hand.

"I'm sayin' I've changed. I took account of my life after Billy drug you off to the cave. I ain't never done much I've been proud of. But being here with Rachel I realized I finally had a family. Never had one before and I finally knew what it was like to have someone care about my old hide." He paused, meeting her stare.

"I swear, Zeb Thacker. What are you trying to pull?"

"I wouldn't fault you for not believing."

The bushes nearby rustled. The outlaws must've come to and found her gone. Sally whirled and took off running. In the darkness she didn't see the hole until she stepped in it and went down. Searing pain shot up her leg.

Zeb knelt down beside her. "How bad is it? Can you stand?"

"I'll try."

He took her hand and gently pulled her to her feet. The minute she put her weight on it, she collapsed to the ground.

"It's either broken or sprained bad."

Zeb removed her high-topped shoe and tenderly felt her ankle. "I cain't tell. I'd best get you somewhere so you can rest until daylight."

"I thought I heard the outlaws coming."

"It must've been a wild animal. Come on."

Jagged lightning lit up the sky and the thunder rumbled.

"Thanks, Zeb. We need to find some shelter before this storm breaks. How far are we from Rachel's?"

"Too far to make it in the dark. And unless I miss my guess we'll soon be in the middle of a gullywasher."

"Any ideas?"

He didn't reply. He scanned their surroundings. Finally, he turned to her. "I think I know of something that might work. It's an old trick we used once to hide from the posse."

"Then I'm sure it's a humdinger." Sally hated the heavy dose of sarcasm that came from her mouth but she couldn't help it. She wasn't ready yet to make amends with him. For one thing she still wasn't sure about this new leaf.

She watched as he cleared away some brush from an

indentation in the rocky canyon wall. It was just large enough for two people to sit in it.

"Let me help you into this space. Once you're in it, I'll put the brush back over it and no one will be able to see you."

Just then big fat raindrops fell splattering the ground.

"Where are you going to be?"

"I'll find somewhere nearby."

"There's room enough for you in there with me."

His face lit up. "Sure. I reckon if you want me that close to you."

"Wouldn't say it if I didn't," she grouched.

After all, the man had rescued her from the cave. It was the least she could do. Technically, she'd already gotten loose from her ropes. But it felt rather nice to have someone save her for a change, even if he really hadn't.

Zeb helped her into the hiding place and crawled in beside her. Then he pulled the brush over them.

Sally patted his hand. "This is real nice, Zeb."

"I'll get you home tomorrow."

She couldn't see his face in the darkness but it felt nice to have him for company.

Outside Rachel's door, the sky opened up and a deluge of rain pounded the roof.

Her thoughts turned to Heath and the doctor he'd gone to get. Eden was getting worse by the minute. Every time the fever returned Rachel bathed the babe in the tepid water. She didn't rest. This was a life and death battle and this time she meant to win.

It must've been close to midnight when Jax leaped to his

feet with the hackles on his neck bristling. He padded to the door and sniffed then began barking ferociously. Rachel's heart jumped into her throat. She grabbed the rifle and pointed it at the door.

If someone was out there she wouldn't hesitate to pull the trigger.

But it could be Sally.

"Who's there?" she called.

The only answer was rumbling thunder like a wagon rolling over cobblestones.

Rachel licked her dry lips and tried to control her trembling. "Whoever is out there had better speak up," she yelled. "I have a rifle and will shoot."

Still no answer. Maybe it was the wind or an animal trying to escape the storm. Though Jax stopped barking, he didn't return to the rug by the fire. Instead, he lay in front of the door with his ears raised, alert to any strange noise.

She wondered if Heath had reached Estacado and found the doctor. It would be miserable riding back in the pouring rain.

Eden seemed unusually quiet. Rachel put down the rifle and went to check on her.

Fear clutched her heart when she saw the infant.

Her mouth gaped open and she didn't appear to be breathing.

"No! No!" Rachel lifted the limp body in her arms and held her to her chest.

Pray, she told herself. If ever she needed to it was now.

"Dear Heavenly Father, I'm a little rusty at this, but I hope you won't hold that against me. Please reach down and hold this little baby in your hands. She hasn't done anything to deserve this. She's pure and innocent. You took her mother from her so she has no one but me. I need her. I have so much love to give her. Just give me a chance and let me pour out all the love I have. I beg you not to make her suffer for my faults."

Rachel wiped away tears with the back of her hand. "It's true I've been angry with you, Lord, and felt so forgotten and lost. But I understand things better now. If you'll please let Eden live I'll do my best to walk in the way you'd have me go. I'll praise your name." Then she added, "And God, if I'm allowed extra, please watch over Heath."

CHAPTER THIRTY-TWO

*H*eath arrived at Estacado around midnight in a driving downpour. His clothes were plastered to his body and he had doubts he'd ever be able to get warm again. But that was the least of his worries. His thoughts were on his beloved Eden.

If he didn't make it back in time...

Stop it. He pushed that possibility from his mind. He'd find the doctor and ride like a crazed man back to the Malloy farm. He didn't believe God would take that sweet babe from them. Rachel was technically Eden's mother and Heath felt every bit like the babe's father. His heart overflowed with love for both of his ladies.

A rivulet of rain spilled from the brim of his hat into his lap. He shivered against the cold. But he kept riding.

As expected Estacado was dark, not a light burning anywhere. He paused in the main street, looking for the doctor's shingle. When lightning split the sky, he finally saw a sign that read *Dr. William Hunt* and urged Buttermilk in that direction.

Springing from the saddle, he pounded on the door. Several minutes passed before a woman opened it and peered out at him.

"I apologize for waking you, ma'am. I need the doctor."

"I'm sorry, sir, he's over at the Jessop's place."

"It's extremely urgent. If you can tell me how to find the Jessop's, I'll ride on over there."

Mrs. Hunt provided the directions and closed the door. Heath mounted up and took the path she said. He must've ridden two miles before he came to the house. A flickering candle burned in the window of a soddy.

Mrs. Jessop handed him a hot cup of coffee while he explained the situation to Dr. Hunt.

"Sounds like the same thing this youngster here has," Dr. Hunt said. "We'd best be riding. An infant that young won't last long."

The doctor went to gather his bag and supplies. Heath took advantage of the few minutes to hurriedly finish his coffee. By the last gulp he felt a tad warmer and his spirits bolstered.

Everything was going to be all right now.

Dr. Hunt returned with his black bag. "Let's go."

RAIN BEAT AGAINST the side of house like an angry beast clawing to get inside.

Rachel barely heard it. Her attention was on the limp babe in her arms. "No! I won't let you have her!"

She couldn't, no she wouldn't bury another person she loved. No more.

A rag doll Sally had made for the babe out of scraps of material drew her gaze. Eden might never play with it.

Her heart broke into a million jagged pieces. It was too much. Too much grief. Too much pain. The unforgiving land had taken everything and everyone and left her broken and alone. She had no more strength. She was finished.

Then Eden coughed.

What a blessed sound. It didn't matter that the cough came from deep inside the babe. She wasn't dead. Not yet. And Rachel would do everything she could to keep it that way.

Chills wracked Eden's fragile body. Rachel wrapped her tightly in a blanket and held Eden to her chest. She prayed and rocked and sang through the long night. Memories of another time not long ago with her sister Alice came unbidden to her mind. She wouldn't let herself think about that fateful night. She refused to let the ghosts determine this outcome.

When she paused in her singing, she realized the rain had stopped. "Thank you, God."

Hopefully, Heath would arrive soon with the doctor. She got up and walked to the window to stare out at the breaking dawn.

Suddenly she heard an amazing sound. It was the white dove cooing by the window. She remembered what the circuit preacher had said. *Faith is the bird that sings when the dawn is still dark.*

Their omen.

For the first time since Eden had taken ill hope rose that everything would be all right. A gentle quiet peace filled her.

Horses galloped into the yard. She placed the baby in her crib and grabbed the rifle.

"Rachel, open the door," Heath yelled. "I have the doctor."

Her knees shook as she put down the rifle and threw back

the bolt and rushed into Heath's arms. "I'm so glad to see you." Then, she caught sight of the weary man behind Heath and stepped back. "Thank you for coming, Doctor. This way."

She showed him to the crib and stood by anxiously. She didn't realize Heath was near until his arm slipped around her shoulders. His warmth filled all the cold frightened spots.

The doctor turned. "Get some water boiling fast. We don't have a second to waste."

Rachel whirled and raced to the small kitchen area. She added some wood and got a fire going while Heath pumped water into a large pot. Once that was done they returned to the bedroom.

The doctor had kindly eyes that appeared larger than normal because of the wire-rimmed spectacles he wore. His wrinkled face told of many nights like this one too numerous to count. He'd removed his black coat and rolled up the sleeves of his shirt as though preparing for battle against some unknown foe.

"What are we dealing with, Dr. Hunt?" Heath asked quietly.

"Influenza," he answered grimly. "I don't wish to alarm you but it's almost always fatal in one so young."

Rachel sucked in a breath. That meant Eden contracted it from Becca. She'd known better than to let Becca anywhere near Eden that day. It was all Rachel's fault. She was to blame for her baby daughter lying near death's door.

Tears blurring her vision, Rachel stumbled out into the damp dawn that was just breaking. She didn't know that Heath had followed her until he drew her against his broad chest.

"It's all my fault," she sobbed. "I never should've let Becca hold her. If Eden dies it'll be on my hands."

"Shhhh!" He tenderly smoothed back her hair and drew a finger across her cheek. "I share equally in the blame. I assured you it would be fine. We didn't know Becca would make Eden sick. Besides, Eden isn't going to die. Dr. Hunt will fix her up."

"What if he can't? Doctors aren't miracle workers. Sometimes they can't fix things. Sometimes people die despite everything." A sob broke free.

"I know because I had a long talk with the Lord as I rode for help. I know He's looking down and seeing our every need."

Rachel clutched the sleeve of his shirt and for the first time realized that his clothes were soaked through. He hadn't given a thought to his own discomfort. His only thought was on Eden and what she'd needed.

"You best find some dry clothes and tend the horses." The poor drenched things were still standing by the front door where Heath and the doc had left them.

He put his arm around her waist. "Let's see if that water's boiling first. Don't know about you but I'm kinda curious what the doctor wants with it. And I'm sure he's wondering where we disappeared to."

"Heath, you're my rock. If you weren't around, I think I'd fly off to the far corners of the world. You ground me."

"Any time, pretty lady. Can't have you flying off."

Kissing her nose, he opened the door for her. She paused for a minute, her gaze scanning the lake and trees and sky that had turned from indigo to pink and lavender. She seemed to be waiting for something but she didn't know what.

Just then the sun's glorious golden rays spilled into the canyon, reflecting on the rock walls and banishing the chill in the damp air. Amid the newborn rays, a dove took wing.

It was God's promise to her.

Hope sprang into her heart as a calm peace drifted over her crowding out the fear and utter despair.

Drawing a deep breath into her lungs, Rachel turned to do what she could to help.

CHAPTER THIRTY-THREE

*H*eath turned. "Coming?"

"Just looking at the beauty of this land. I think God has sent us a sign."

"I think so too." He squeezed her hand.

"Sally didn't come home last night. I'm worried, Heath."

"I am too. But we can only deal with one problem at a time and Eden needs us right now. As soon as I can I'll go look for her."

"Not until I get some coffee and food into you and dry clothes on your back."

A grin curved his lips. "Yes, ma'am. I love when you're bossy."

They soon discovered what the doctor wanted with the hot water. He set the pot on the table and threw some peppermint leaves into the water to create a vapor. He then made a tent over the pot with a blanket and stuck Eden's head under it.

"This will help the baby breathe better and loosen the tightness in her chest," Dr. Hunt explained. "We have to get the mucus out of her lungs. If not, she won't make it. When the water gets cool, you'll have to boil it again. This isn't going to be something quick. You'll have to do this for days. There'll be many sleepless nights ahead I'm afraid. I'll leave you plenty of peppermint leaves."

"I was so afraid it was the fever," Rachel said. "It wiped out my entire family."

The lines in the doctor's face deepened. "My sympathies, ma'am. You seem to have borne a great deal of pain. With any luck we'll get this little one well soon. Hold off giving her any milk until the fever is gone."

Heath took Eden from the doctor and followed his instructions while Rachel fixed them all some breakfast.

A short while later, Rachel watched as the doctor and Heath wolfed down big plates of food. It was the least she could do to repay them for their long trip. When Heath finished eating, he fed and watered the horses and brushed them down good.

Dr. Hunt promised to return in a day or two to check on their progress.

While Heath saw the doctor off, Rachel sat with Eden's head under the tent. She prayed with all her heart that God would spare the babe.

Heath opened the door and stepped back inside. "Things are going to be all right. I feel it in my bones."

"No, things will never be all right. Not for me."

"Rachel, why are you crying? Is it the baby?" He crossed the floor to her side.

"Eden is no worse. It's me." She stared up at him through her tears. "I've decided something."

"Mind telling me?"

"If Eden lives I'm going to give her to you and Sally."

"Why? You love this baby. She's your whole life."

"It's the best for her. Just accept my decision."

"I don't know what brought all this on, but you love her. You're her mother, not Sally. Eden couldn't be more your flesh and blood than if she'd been born to you. God chose you."

Rachel shook her head furiously. "I'm the worst kind of mother. I'm not fit to raise a child. I don't deserve her."

He pulled out a chair and sat down next to her. "You're the most loving, caring mother I've ever seen. There's nothing you wouldn't do for Eden. You'd move heaven and earth to make sure she grows up strong and healthy."

"I knew in my heart Becca shouldn't get close to Eden but I let her anyway." She pushed his hand away that was caressing her hair.

Heath grabbed her shoulders and turned her to face him. "Listen to me. You've taken care of Eden the best anyone could. And you didn't want to hurt Becca by telling her no."

"If only I'd made some excuse."

"Hush now." He placed a finger on her lips. "Let it go. You can't accomplish anything by looking back. It's time to move forward. The important thing now is that Eden needs you. She's fighting for her life and depending on you."

Rachel was so very weary. "The part that haunts me most about my Alice is not knowing if she cried out for me. If she reached for me. Or if she needed comforting. She was only four years old. She had to be frightened and I wasn't there to offer solace, not even a sip of water to ease her parched throat. I failed."

"You have to forgive yourself. God knows your heart and He loves you no matter what. He's watching over Alice now. You are Eden's mother and she belongs with you."

She drew in a ragged breath. "Heath, if you still want me..."

"I want you." His statement came out husky and bruised as

if it was forced through a narrowing in his throat. "I love you, Rachel. I've loved you since I first saw you lying unconscious on the ground."

Rachel tenderly caressed his strong jaw. "I love you, too, Heath. I have for a while. I just didn't know how to find the words. I want to be your wife if you're sure you'll still have me. I want to have more children for Eden to play with."

"I'll have you. Don't you worry your pretty head about that."

Overcome with emotion, Heath took Rachel's face tenderly between his hands. He kissed her eyes, her cheek, the curve of her jaw, before lowering to her mouth. He opened up his heart and poured all his love into that kiss.

Difficult times would come but she'd face them with Heath.

Heath rose. "Well, I need to scout around and see if I can find Sally."

"You haven't changed your clothes yet."

"No use changing now. They're already dry."

"All right. Just please be careful. You don't know what you'll run across out there."

"I won't go too far just in case you need me."

"Find her, Heath, and bring her back."

He bent to kiss her and then grabbing his hat, he was out the door. Buttermilk deserved a good long rest after the long grueling night ride but that would have to wait.

Climbing into the saddle, he paused to look around. The rain had washed away any footprints. He really had nothing telling him which way Sally had gone. So he plunged ahead toward the campsite he'd found.

He soon reached a small clearing that had broken branches strewn about and the remains of a cold campfire. Dismounting, he reached for his rifle.

A flurry of activity in the brush alerted him. He cocked his rifle.

Sally's voice came as a surprise. "Don't shoot, Heath. It's me and Zeb." Then the brush parted and Sally, supported by Zeb, hobbled out.

"I'm glad to see you," Heath said, lowering the rifle. "What happened to your ankle?"

"Stepped in a rabbit hole and sprained it. We spent a wretched night in the rain, hiding from the outlaws." She glanced at Zeb. "I have lots to tell you."

"It can wait," Zeb spoke up. "Right now, we really need to get to safety before they find us."

Heath raised an eyebrow. "Who are they?"

"Desperados," Sally said.

Heath helped his sister onto the horse.

A short while later, Sally sat in a chair in Rachel's kitchen with her swollen foot propped on a stool. Rachel thought they'd have to tie her down because she kept trying to get up every few minutes to check on the baby in Heath's arms.

"Heath, you're not doing that right," Sally erupted after watching him with Eden. "Let me up from here and I'll show how you're supposed to hold that little thing under there."

"You budge from that chair and I'll tie you to it," Heath growled. "I'm not just whistling Dixie either."

Sally huffed and crossed her arms over her ample chest.

Rachel had cooked Sally and Uncle Zeb a big breakfast while Heath held the baby under the tent like Dr. Hunt had shown them.

The loud wheezing noises coming from Eden as she struggled to breathe created a pall over the group. Each one kept their attention riveted on the blanket hiding Eden's face.

Taking a seat near Heath, Rachel gazed from one face to the

other. "You don't know how happy I am to have you safe." She reached for Heath's free hand and held it. "We have some big news. I've agreed to marry Heath and become his wife."

"That's the best news I've heard in a coon's age," Sally boomed. "When?"

"Eden will have to get well first then we have to find a preacher." Rachel rose to refill Uncle Zeb's coffee mug. "I don't want to hear any excuses for your behavior. Thank you for helping Sally. For that, I can forgive you for lying."

"I appreciate that, Rachel. I'm sorry for everything."

"I think it's high time you tell us where you and Sally were after you disappeared," Heath said quietly.

Tension crackled in the air, like a giant storm brewing on the horizon from which there would be no escaping. She sensed a violent whirlwind that would forever change her life and she didn't have the power to stop it.

CHAPTER THIRTY-FOUR

Uncle Zeb took a sip and set his cup down. He met Rachel's eyes. "I...you're...this is gonna be right painful for you to hear. Don't exactly know where to start."

"The beginning would be a good place." Heath shifted the baby to the other arm when she coughed from deep inside her tiny chest.

The rattle of that cough filled the room and struck fear in Rachel. She tried to focus on what Uncle Zeb was saying but all she wanted to do was put Eden to her shoulder and hold her as tight as she could and fight death tooth and nail.

"Years ago, when I was young and foolish, I got mixed up with Malloy and his outlaw gang," Zeb began. "We roamed around the country, robbing stagecoaches, trains, you name it.

"I thought I was happy. You see, I'd never had a family so I didn't know how special that was until I came here. Rachel, you showed me the kind of love and acceptance that I'd always longed for. I knew for the first time what a real family was. When you hear what I gotta say, I 'spect you'll ask me to leave."

"Why did you lie about being my uncle?"

"To be able to poke around for the loot Malloy kept from us." He hung his head.

"I think deep down I always knew it. I needed you to be my uncle very badly."

"The lie was a sight better than Billy's first plan."

"Which was to kill Rachel?" Heath's mouth was in a thin line.

"Yep. They tried that. Remember the storm that came up while you were diggin' your sister's grave?"

Rachel thought back to that day. The push to her back. "Someone shoved me and I caught my foot on a large root, losing my balance. I remember."

"It was Billy. Then when that didn't put you in a grave, they burned your house."

"So I wouldn't come back. That gave them free rein on the property to search all they wanted."

Zeb nodded. " 'Ceptin' they still couldn't find the money. And Heath built you this house and you moved in. That's when they said I had to make you believe I was your long-lost uncle. Billy said I didn't have a choice. And I figured if I went along with it they'd at least leave you alone. But then Jax kept trying to bite them. At first they kept catching him and tying him up." He turned his attention to Heath.

"I knew you suspected me of doin' it. I wanted to tell you about the outlaws then, but they told me if I did they'd kill me and Rachel and the baby too. I couldn't let any harm come to you and Eden. I'd have done and said most anything to keep that from happening."

About to bust to a gut, Sally took up the tale. "I stumbled on them talking and they took me captive. They told Zeb if he didn't find the loot and bring it to them today they'd kill me."

"Only I wasn't going to let them do that," Zeb said firmly. "I'm not much fit for crow bait but I do have a few principles."

Sally went on. "Zeb rescued me but I turned my ankle. We found a place to ride out the storm. And here we are."

Eden took a coughing, wheezing fit and struggled to catch her breath.

Heath lifted the blanket that formed a tent over Eden. "Rachel, you'd better come."

Rachel's heart stopped. "Oh, God! What is it?"

"Come and look." He grinned. "Her fever broke. She's cool to the touch."

She stumbled in her haste to see for herself. "That means I can give her some milk now. The doctor said I couldn't as long as she had fever."

She tenderly smoothed the pretty blonde curls. Her thoughts returned to the early morning when the dove appeared outside her window before the sun rose. God had heard her cries. He'd returned Eden to them. She felt as though she'd been given a fortune in gold.

"Hallelujah." Sally wiped a tear from her eyes.

Grabbing a pail, Uncle Zeb hurried out for fresh goat's milk. Rachel watched him go. She knew what it had taken for him to admit he'd buffaloed them. He was clearly ashamed for the role he'd played and for the lies he'd told. She wasn't quite sure what she was going to do about it yet. He'd taken her trust and used it against her.

But everyone deserved a second chance. Didn't they? Wasn't the Bible littered with people who messed up bad but got another opportunity to do the right thing?

A short while later, she sat in the rocker feeding Eden. It took a long time to get the milk into her because Rachel had to stop every few minutes to let Eden catch her breath. The child was still in a terrible way but Rachel knew the fever breaking signaled reason for renewed hope.

"She'd do better if you'd hold the bottle a little straighter," Sally said. "I can feed her if you want me to. I can't do anything but sit anyway."

"Thanks, Sally, but I want to do it this time." Rachel gently wiped the dribble from Eden's mouth. "I'm glad you're back."

"Me too. You know, I've been thinking about Becca. I'd like to take her in and provide a home. I'm going to be lonely once Heath is gone."

"That's a wonderful idea but you'll have to see what Becca's father says about it. Maybe he'll welcome your help. I do hope so."

"I suppose we'll see." Sally paused and smoothed back a lock of hair that came loose from the bun on the back of her neck. "I think that circuit preacher might've taken a fancy to me. Maybe he'd want to settle down and take care of the land."

"You know, that sounds like a good idea."

Things seemed to be working out for everyone. Rachel kissed Eden's soft cheek, grateful for God's mercy.

DARKNESS HAD JUST fallen that night when the outlaws struck. They galloped in on horseback, peppering the house in a hail of gunfire. Windows shattered, sending shards of glass in all directions. It seemed to be a lot more than the initial three. Where did they get more?

Jax barked and clawed at the door, trying to get out.

Rachel screamed and ducked under the kitchen table with Eden. She called Jax under there with her, praying to survive the onslaught.

"Can you douse the lamps, Rachel?" Sally yelled, crawling beside her.

Rachel laid Eden down on the floor and crawled from under the table. Jax took up guard duty in front of Eden. The look in his gentle eyes said he'd protect the baby with his life.

Making herself as small a target as possible, she went from one lamp to another until the house was pitch black.

Sally was mad enough to lay into a grizzly with a switch. She let loose a stream of dire warnings concerning the outlaws' fate and hobbled toward the rifle. She yanked it up and parked herself at a broken window where she released a volley of bullets. With each shot she spoke a prayer that it would find its mark.

"Let this one turn these heathen outlaws from their ways and deliver us from their evil clutches," Sally prayed over the noise of the gunshots. "Especially that heathen scoundrel Billy," she added.

"And let this one strike fear into their hearts." Sally fired again. "And please send help, Lord! I don't want to die."

Outside, Heath and Zeb found shelter behind a wagon loaded with bales of hay and returned fire.

Heath squeezed off shot after shot, Rachel praying they'd hit the mark. When one of the riders gave a loud yelp, she knew he'd struck him in the shoulder as he raced by on his horse.

"You okay, Zeb?" Heath yelled.

Rachel smiled, glad he was alive.

"Yep," Zeb answered. "The devils ain't got me yet."

"Cover me. I'm going to run to the house and see if the women folk are all right."

Rachel opened the door a crack. "We're fine in here."

"Good. Keep your heads down. I'm coming in."

With Zeb keeping his backside covered, Heath zigzagged

his way to the house and burst through the front door and hurried to the window in the bedroom. Rachel was at his elbow. Side by side, they fought. She took aim at a rider. The bullet hit the man's leg. Screaming in pain, the ruffian clung to the reins and galloped out of range.

Finally the riders backed off to the edge of the lake and waited.

THE MOON REFLECTED on the riders' faces. Heath stood in the doorway of the house staring. When Rachel stole to his side, he put his arm around her.

"Do you think they've given up?" she asked.

"Not a chance. They're just trying to figure out something and come up with another plan. I figure they'll hit us hard again as soon as they lick their wounds."

"What's going to get them to leave? Our deaths?" she whispered, afraid to say the thought too loud.

"Don't think that, Rachel. We're going to win. We have God on our side."

"What if we send someone to the Thorn or Steele ranches for help?"

"Who? It would take too long, and we need every hand that can hold a weapon."

"Surely if we talk to them—"

"No use. Probably liquored up. They're after blood." He kissed Rachel's forehead. "When they come again, I want you to lift the trapdoor in the floor. Take Eden and get down there where you'll be safe. Promise me."

"What about you?" Her voice trembled. "I can't bear to

think that you might be hurt. Or worse. I won't lose you. I refuse."

He pulled her against him and buried his face in her hair. The rapid beat of her heart told of her paralyzing fear. He inhaled deeply. She smelled of honeysuckle. It was a scent that connected him with this unsettled land. Right now it created an unbreakable bond between them. He had to make her believe that everything would be all right.

"Now you listen to me. Nothing is going to happen to me, to any of us. God isn't going to let these outlaws win. It isn't how He does things. We have right on our side and right always wins."

She pulled back and looked up at him. She kissed her fingers and pressed them to his lips. "Have I ever told you how much I love you?"

"As a matter of fact, you did but I don't mind hearing it again. When we get married, I may put it in your vows to tell me at least a dozen times a day."

A grin curved her lips. "And I may add a line to yours about being so bossy."

He glanced at Sally. "I had a good teacher."

"You sure did."

"I can't wait to be married to you, lady. Do you have a date in mind?" he asked.

"I won't wait long. I'm afraid something might happen to delay it more. You just get a preacher here and that's the day we'll do it."

"Yes, ma'am." He gave her a tired grin.

Uncle Zeb gave a cry and got to his feet. "They're coming again!"

CHAPTER THIRTY-FIVE

"*D*on't forget what I told you about the trapdoor." Heath gave her a quick kiss and sprinted out into the night with Zeb.

Trembling, Rachel picked up Eden and took a few steps. Then she stopped. She couldn't. She wouldn't hide like a scared child while they risked their lives for her.

This was her life, her land, and the people she loved. She'd fight with everything she had to protect it and them.

We need every hand that can hold a weapon, Heath had said.

That meant her too.

She put Eden inside her crib and picked it up. She threw aside the rug over the trapdoor and carried the baby down to safety. If something happened to Rachel and she didn't survive this onslaught Heath would know where to look for Eden. Then she went up for Jax and carried him down as a volley of bullets rent the air.

"You look over Eden. Don't let anyone get her." She patted

the faithful dog on the head and climbed the stairs, replacing the rug over the trapdoor.

Knowing Eden was safe from flying messengers of death, she could focus on making every shot count. Sally was already hard at work and laying down a stream of dire threats.

Locating her rifle in the dark, Rachel took up a position at the window. She aimed at the men on horseback. When she ran out of ammunition, she reloaded. She didn't know if she made a difference, but it felt good to be helping.

The outlaws kept coming over and over again. Then suddenly they rode down to the lake and stopped.

"What do you think they're doing, Sally?"

"Don't know."

"How long can they keep this up?"

"'Til either they run out of bullets or we do I reckon."

That possibility was very real. Rachel only had about a dozen left in the box and she figured the others were running low also.

Rachel kept her gaze on the shadowy figures. Torches suddenly lit up the darkness. She clutched her hand to her chest, her breath freezing in her throat. "They're going to burn us out. Oh, God, they're going to burn us alive."

"They just think they are," Sally bellowed. "A bullet in the right place will stop that nonsense."

Rachel wished she could be as confident as Sally. If the woman was afraid, she sure hid it well. Rachel readied the rifle. This was a fight she didn't intend to lose. Eden needed someone to protect her. Rachel would shoot any man who came near the house.

But the gang had other plans it seemed. They focused on the wagonload of hay. One of the men drew Heath's and Zeb's fire while the others threw their torches on anything that would burn. They didn't bother the house though and that puzzled Rachel.

She watched Heath and Uncle Zeb desperately trying to put out the blazes. With her attention on that, she realized she'd lost track of where the lawless bunch had gone.

A deafening crash sounded just then as two of them broke down the door and rushed inside.

Rachel screamed as one of the men tackled her to the floor. Her rifle flew across the floor. Her breath came in gasps as she stared up into the man's hideous scarred face.

"Well, girlie, looks like you and me are finally gonna have ourselves some fun."

"Get off me," she ordered coldly through clenched teeth, struggling against his steely grip.

"Naw, I ain't ready." His leering grin struck fear in her heart. "Gonna show you a good time first. Your man is too busy to come save you this time. We made sure of that."

"You seem awfully confident." She twisted and landed a solid kick that drew a grunt from the man.

"Whoo-ee! I knew you'd be a little spitfire. Just the way I like my women. You just go ahead and work up a good sweat and then you and me will get down to business."

Flames from the bonfires lit up the dimness inside the house. Rachel could see that Sally had her hands full with the second outlaw. First Sally was on top and then the outlaw. The two rolled and wrestled and tried to outmaneuver the other.

"Ow! You gouged my eye," the outlaw yelled.

"I'll gouge worse than that, you good for nothing, low down polecat!" Sally yelled.

If one of them could get free she could help the other. Heath crossed her mind. She knew for a fact that if he could, he'd help her and Sally. But he had his hands full outside.

No, she couldn't count on help. She would have to use her brains and save herself this time.

Rachel eyed her rifle. It lay just beyond reach of her fingertips. She gathered her strength and prayed for an opening.

Eden, in the room under the floor, let out a sudden yowl. The poor little thing was hungry most likely.

Scar Face raised his head and snarled, "Where's the baby?"

"She's safe where the likes of you can't get her."

He grabbed her hair and brutally yanked her head back. "Tell me where or I'll strangle you right here."

"In the kitchen." She hated to lie but she'd be no use to Eden if she was dead. "Under the table. What are you going to do?"

"I'll kill you if you're lyin' to me."

The man lifted himself off her and jerked her to her feet. Pulling her behind him, he made his way to the small kitchen. Rachel knew she had one chance. He'd have to release his hold on her and kneel down to look into the darkness under the table. She was too far from her rifle, but her thoughts turned to any assortment of weapons that might be available.

Sure enough, Scar Face turned loose of her to peer into the blackness.

Rachel raced around the table and lunged for a knife on the sideboard.

The man realized her intent and dove, catching her ankle in a punishing grip.

She stretched, her hand searching for the handle of the knife.

"You're gonna regret this," Scar Face bellowed. "I'll kill your baby as sure as I'm standin' here. If you want to keep it alive, you'll do as I say."

Anger washed over Rachel. This man would not win. It didn't matter what she had to do or how painful it was for her, she would not let him have Eden.

At last the handle of the long butcher knife slid into her palm. She gripped it tightly and drew it to her, keeping it from Scar Face's view. She slowly took three steps back. "Looks like you win, Billy. But be careful what you ask for."

"You're one crazy woman."

He rose from his position on the floor and stood straight.

With a sudden whirling move, she slashed at his arm and chest. The knife became slick with blood, but she kept stabbing and slashing until Sally caught her arm.

"I think you won the fight, Rachel."

The knife fell from Rachel's fingers. "He was going to hurt Eden. I couldn't let him do that."

"Of course not. I've never seen you so mad." Sally whistled through her teeth. "Remind me never to do anything to get on your bad side."

"Is he dead?"

"Nope, but he might wish he was after I douse a fair amount of alcohol on his wounds."

Eden's screams filled the small house. Rachel raced down the steps to the secret room and picked her up from her crib. She cradled the babe to her, and the baby's sweet scent calmed her. Jax scampered up the stairs ahead of her.

When she emerged into the kitchen she turned to Sally. "What happened to the one who had you?"

"Let's just say I don't think Charlie's going anywhere." Sally lit the lamp and light spilled on the two outlaws.

One was bleeding like a stuck pig and Charlie was sitting by the fireplace with his pants over his head. Sally had tied him up with strips of what looked like a bed sheet and then wrapped his complete body with blue, gray, and red knitting yarn. Rachel could even see the knitting needle poking out from all that mess.

Rachel laughed. "Why take his pants off?"

"It's my observation that once you remove a man's pants the fight goes out of him quicker'n a buzzard can smell his dinner."

Heath and Uncle Zeb came running in. Heath didn't stop until he was standing close enough to tenderly finger Eden's blonde curls.

"Are you all right, Rachel?" His voice was husky.

She met his steady gray gaze. "Yes. Yes, I couldn't be better. How about you?"

"Not a scratch on us."

"Is it over?"

"It is. I think we won the war. Guess who came to help."

"Who?"

"Apparently, Austin Morgan didn't get far on his journey back to Clarendon. The more he thought about it, the more convinced he was that we needed help. He rounded up all the ranchers and they rode to our rescue."

"Thank you, Jesus!"

Heath helped Rachel to a chair where she gratefully collapsed. Now that the fear and worry was over, her knees had gotten wobbly. She felt good though. She'd done what she needed to do, and God had seen her through.

By the time daylight turned the lake from near black to a brilliant blue and awakened the world, they'd managed to get the outlaws bandaged and fixed up and the house put back to rights. As much as they could anyway. They would have to buy new windows for the ones the outlaws had shot out and do a little patching and painting.

Heath had kept watch over the outlaws while Rachel and the others caught a little sleep. He grinned when he thought of what a ferocious mother lion Rachel had turned into.

He should've known she wouldn't hide as he asked her to. She was far too independent. He was so very proud of her.

Rachel Malloy was a woman to reckon with.

And she'd soon be his bride.

He'd just have to remember not to boss her around, recalling that long butcher knife she'd used on Billy and what he'd looked like afterward. Not that the man hadn't deserved it. Anyone who threatened Eden was going to pay dearly.

And if Rachel wasn't around, Heath would be glad to fill in.

CHAPTER THIRTY-SIX

Come morning, Heath was repairing a fence around the sheep pen when a wagon pulled into Rachel's yard. It had come! His gift to his soon-to-be bride.

"Is this the Malloy place?" the driver asked.

"Yes, sir, it is." He hurried to the wagon and threw back a tarp covering the load in back then nodded. "It's perfect. I'll show you where to put it and there's extra for you just like I promised."

"Thank you, sir. Climb in and show me where to go."

They drove to the spot and Heath helped unload it then stood back. A lump settled in his throat. Rachel stepped from the house then came toward them with curiosity in her eyes.

He went to meet her and put an arm around her shoulders. "A gift to you, honey."

The little hitch in her breath told of expectation. "What is it?"

"Come see." He led her to the burial plot. "This needed to be done so I arranged it."

The granite tombstone sparkled under the sun. Rachel's fingertips touched the little lamb on top and read the words, "Here Lies Alice, The Beloved Daughter of Rachel Malloy."

Tears streamed down her face as she swiveled in the circle of his arms. "This is very precious to me, and whatever led you to do it, thank you. I love your big heart, Heath Lassiter."

His reply had a huskiness he couldn't smooth out. "You needed this to show the world how much you loved your daughter and to claim her as your child."

"Yes." Overcome with emotion, Rachel nodded and smiled through her tears. "You know me so well. I can't wait to be your wife."

"Soon, sweetheart."

The white dove flew down and perched on the cool stone.

"Our talisman, a sign from God that everything is right and good." Heath squeezed her tighter.

"I've never seen a dove do this," the driver said. "I'll tell my boss." The man climbed into the wagon and set off for the rim.

Bathed in the early morning sun, they stood arm-in-arm, watching him go.

"I've got to check on Eden." Rachel glanced toward the house, wiping her eyes. "Jax is babysitting."

"That's one smart dog. I'd swear he's almost human."

"I love the tombstone, Heath. It's better and more meaningful than a sparkly diamond."

The dove cooed and lifted its white wings in flight.

"It doesn't rival your shimmering eyes though." He kissed her there in a shaft of golden light, his heart bursting with love and God's goodness.

All their bright tomorrows were waiting. They only had to claim them.

TWO WEEKS LATER, Heath looked over the yard of Rachel's house that was packed with wagons, buggies, and horses. It seemed folks had come from all over the county for the big celebration.

Their friends and neighbors stood all around the yard talking and laughing. Food weighed down long tables and a group of fiddlers were warming up for the dance.

Birds sang and the water gently lapped along the shoreline of the lake. It was a slice of heaven.

He drew in a calming breath. In just a few short minutes he'd stand with Rachel and they'd say their vows.

God had answered his prayers. It was more than luck that the circuit preacher just happened to be in the area. God had had a hand in that too.

Anson Ledbetter was courting Sally and they were making plans for their wedding. They would live in the soddy until Ledbetter got a house built. He'd split profits from the herd with Heath until Ledbetter got his own herd established.

Heath and Rachel would live here on her land. He had big plans on how to make it turn a profit. The soil was rich and water plentiful. It should be perfect for growing things.

He'd had a busy two weeks. After the gunfight, they'd built a strap-iron jail for the outlaws and kept them in the open in front of Singer's Trading Post. Finally, a column of army soldiers had taken possession and marched them on foot all the way to Clarendon. It had taken some doing to keep Zeb from going to jail but in the end the marshal decided that Zeb's good deeds far outweighed the bad. The marshal had dropped the charges against him in return for his testimony against the others.

Then, Heath rode over to the tent saloon and found out the

name of Eden's mother. He looked toward the graves under the cottonwood tree where they'd reburied her. Alma Montgomery would be pleased with the marker he erected marking her time on earth. It had put a big smile on Rachel's face. He learned a long while ago that putting the kind of smile that lit up Rachel's eyes made him the happiest man in Texas.

A whine drew his attention. Heath bent his tall frame to stroke Jax's silky fur. The dog wore a pink bandana around his neck. "How you doing, boy? We finally did it, didn't we?"

The dog looked up at him with complete adoration as he licked Heath's hand.

The door opened. The vision in wedding finery stood in the shaft of light and his breath left him in a big whoosh. He'd never seen anything so beautiful.

"There you are, cowboy." Rachel's new rose-colored dress rustled as she strode to his side. She slipped her hand in the crook of his elbow. "I was afraid you'd changed your mind and hightailed it out of here."

"Not a chance. I've waited too long for this moment." He kissed the tip of her nose. "Besides, I'd be too worried you'd come after me with that butcher knife. I've seen the results of your work."

"Just don't forget it. Seriously, what are you doing out here?"

"Waiting. Taking stock. Counting my blessings."

"You have a lot of those, do you?"

"Too many to count, ma'am," he said softly.

"That's the way I feel too. I never dreamed I'd find this kind of joy and contentment. I can't think of a thing more that I need."

"You're awfully pretty today. Don't exactly know how I

managed to find a woman who's prettier than a golden sunrise and smart in the bargain."

A rosy blush colored her cheeks. "You sure know how to sweet talk a lady."

"Expect a lot more because I'm just getting started."

Sally stood holding Eden under the arbor she and Anson erected for the ceremony and shouted, "Get a move on. We're waiting for you. This preacher don't have all day."

Heath ground his teeth and groaned. His sister sure cornered the market on bossiness. He was glad that she'd soon be Ledbetter's problem. It hadn't surprised him that they'd decided to get *hitched*. But hitched was an accurate word for it. It was two old mules yoked together to pull a wagon...or a plow. Heath didn't know which one was the most contrary.

The sound of Rachel's laughter was music to his ears.

"Are you ready, Mr. Lassiter?" she asked.

"Born that way." His pulse beat wildly. This was God's plan for him, for them both, and he was happy to fulfill it. "You're my angel, Rachel. And I promise that you'll never be forgotten. Not by God or me. This is our day, our life, our future. For as long as we both draw breath and even beyond that when we're taken to Glory. You're mine forever."

Rachel's skirt swished against Heath's pant leg as they walked. He loved the sound and his bride's closeness.

"Heath, I wish my family was here. My stepmother Jane would love this. And Alice could meet her baby sister."

"Sweetheart, they're watching and smiling down upon us. They know what you've been through and how rocky the road has been."

"I hope you're right." She chewed her bottom lip.

"What else are you fretting about?"

"I don't know how to dance. I'm afraid I'll look like a dunce."

"You're in good company because I don't know how either. I reckon we'll be just fine." He kissed her cheek.

They took their place in front of the preacher. Just then the white dove flew down to roost on the preacher's shoulder. The bird's coos provided the music.

"Dearly beloved, we're gathered here to join Heath and Rachel in holy matrimony," the reverend began.

Rachel met Heath's gaze, her pale green eyes shimmering with tears. She was his beloved and that would never change. He had lots of plans for his bride. First he intended to build her a big house with plenty of room for all the children he knew would one day fill it.

From the corner of his eye, he noticed Becca whispering something to Sally then reaching for Samuel Eden. Becca was a loving big sister, and it didn't make a hill of beans what the girl called the baby that had stolen all their hearts. Becca's father had given his blessing and the girl moved in with Sally. Becca wouldn't want for anything, that was for sure.

"Do you, Heath Lassiter, take Rachel as your lawfully wedded wife?" the preacher asked.

Heath gazed into her face and saw honesty, truth, and a love for God shining. "I do. For now and for always. To eternity and beyond."

He squeezed Rachel's hand and murmured low so that she was the only one who heard. "You give my life color and noise. I love you, little mama."

ACKNOWLEDGMENTS

Deepest thanks to my sister, Jan Sikes, for reading and critiquing for me and whose comments I treasure. Also Dee Burks, Bruce Edwards, and Charles Curfman who offer valuable critique and insight on this and all my books. Special thanks to Jodi Thomas for her unending friendship and pearls of wisdom on writing and life.

I also wish to acknowledge Dr. Keith Souter and his book that I refer to often regarding medical issues, The Doctor's Bag, Medicine & Surgery of Yesteryear.

I meticulously researched the Quaker Community of Estacado which is also near where I live. The library in Ralls, TX had several wonderful accounts of this community from settlers in the area. It's a ghost town now and not much left of it. I found it very unusual for Quakers to come so far from the East where most live. They were looking for opportunity but weren't prepared for the harshness of West Texas.

ABOUT LINDA BRODAY

At a young age, **Linda Broday** discovered a love for storytelling, history, and anything pertaining to the Old West. After years of writing romance, it's still tall, rugged cowboys that spark her imagination. A New York Times and USA Today bestselling author, Linda has won many awards, including the prestigious National Readers' Choice Award and the Texas Gold. She resides on the high West Texas plains where she's inspired every day.

TV westerns, books, and movies fed her imagination and regular trips to museums and libraries sealed it. At times she's felt that she once lived during the 1800s because it seems so familiar. Perhaps she did.

She's the mother of three grown children, five grandchildren, and two great grandsons. Linda always looks forward to family get togethers that are noisy affairs filled with laughter. She has six grand dogs that liven up things.

Linda collects rocks, coins, and books as well as surrounds herself with pieces of the past. Give her something old and she's in hog heaven.

**Thank You for reading this.
If you enjoyed the story, I
hope you'll consider
leaving a review.**

9 781732 319998